Captive

Captive

BRIGHTON WALSH

ST. MARTIN'S GRIFFIN ☙ NEW YORK

CAPTIVE. Copyright © 2015 by Brighton Walsh. All rights reserved. Printed in the United States of America. For information, address St. Martin's Press, 175 Fifth Avenue, New York, N.Y. 10010.

www.stmartins.com

Designed by Omar Chapa

Library of Congress Cataloging-in-Publication Data

Walsh, Brighton.
 Captive / Brighton Walsh. — First edition.
  pages ; cm
 ISBN 978-1-250-05963-5 (trade paperback)
 ISBN 978-1-4668-6501-3 (e-book)
 I. Title.
 PS3623.A4454C37 2015
 813'.6—dc23

2014040248

St. Martin's Griffin books may be purchased for educational, business, or promotional use. For information on bulk purchases, please contact the Macmillan Corporate and Premium Sales Department at 1-800-221-7945, extension 5442, or write to specialmarkets@macmillan.com.

First Edition: March 2015

10 9 8 7 6 5 4 3 2 1

*For Rose, who saw something in my writing
and decided to take a chance*

Acknowledgments

This book was a marathon. And not a shopping marathon, which I could totally get behind. Not one of those half marathons, either, or one where people walk for the majority of it. Oh, no. This book was a sweaty, chaotic, disorienting, sometimes puke-inducing, hot mess of a marathon. And yet somehow I made it across the finish line unscathed, with a pretty, complete manuscript to show for it. How did that happen? No matter how many times I've done this, it still feels impossible when I'm looking at it, at the beginning, or when I'm in the middle of it, sure I'm never going to get out. But get out I did, because I have some amazing people in my corner.

Thank you to my editor, Rose Hilliard, for reading something else I'd written and thinking I'd be the perfect author to tackle this concept. Your blind faith in me is refreshing and encouraging, and something that kept me going when I thought this manuscript was going to get the best of me. And thank you to everyone at St. Martin's Press, for a wonderful and inclusive author experience, from start to finish.

Thank you to my agent, Mandy Hubbard, for knowing right

off the bat that Rose and I would hit it off, for falling in love with this idea the same exact way I did, and for being the perfect sounding board to bounce ideas off of. Sometimes just typing an e-mail out to you helps me see everything clearly.

Thank you to my Plot Whisperer, Christina, for helping me more than any other person in the history of the world has ever helped another. Exaggeration? Pfft. Ghost and Maddie came to life through the thousands of texts pinged back and forth between us, and I have no idea how I would've tackled this without your input. I would be lost without you.

Thank you to Kristin and Jess, who were my always encouraging cheerleaders during the many, many, many . . . many writing sessions via gchat. Thanks for listening to me whine. A lot. And a special thanks to Kristin, for giving me the idea of a hot teddy. Maddie appreciated it.

Thank you to my critique partner, Jeanette Grey, who talked me down from countless ledges and told me, *of course you can do this*. Hopefully I'll get out of this crazy habit of writing up until 7 P.M. on the night of deadline so I can get your notes in my margins again (not a euphemism), because I miss them.

And last but not least, to my guys. My little ones, who gave me cheers of encouragement when I'd have an exceptionally productive writing day. And my big one, who, like my CP, repeated (daily), *of course you can do this*. I love you all.

Captive

Chapter One

MADISON

Sometimes I wanted to go to sleep and not wake up. I'd lie awake in bed, wondering, wishing, *hoping* that I'd close my eyes and then I just . . . wouldn't open them ever again.

Sometimes I wanted to wake up but wake up someone new. Someone different with a different life and a different family in a different city with a different future mapped out for her.

And every morning when I actually did wake up, when I looked around this room that was too grand, too elaborate, too luxurious with its vaulted ceilings and silk curtains and canopied bed, I felt guilty for daring to think like that at all.

No matter how crushing that guilt, though, I couldn't help but feel like I had the weight of the world on my twenty-year-old shoulders. And then I felt like a spoiled brat—like I personified every cruel, hate-filled whisper uttered about me by people who were never really my friends—because I thought of all those who had it so much worse than I did. Of those who maybe had an absent, workaholic father and a lush of a mother, but who were living my life in a one-bedroom apartment on the south side instead of the mansion in Kenilworth I called home. Maybe they were completely alone, fighting with the demons of their life, and as much as I hated that others sometimes had to help, the fact of the matter was there *were* others around if I needed them. People my father employed, people who were paid to keep their mouths shut and forever keep hidden the secrets behind these walls.

I wasn't truly alone.

But I always felt like I was.

I sighed and glanced at my alarm clock, seeing I had an hour before I needed to be out the door to make it to my first class on time. It never took me long to get ready—I'd learned long ago not to bother much with my appearance—but the other responsibilities I had always ate up a good chunk of time. I threw back the covers and forced myself out of bed, robotically going through my morning routine.

Once I was showered, my hair brushed out straight and left to air-dry, I rummaged through my clothes to find something I wouldn't feel self-conscious in all day, though I knew that was futile. No matter what I wore, the judgmental whispers of my subconscious would crowd my head. I finally settled on a pair of jeans and a shirt I hoped was flowy enough to distract from all the parts of me I wanted to hide.

I slipped my MacBook into my messenger bag and slung it over my shoulder, tugging at the hem of my shirt, trying in vain to make it a little longer, a little looser. I didn't know why I let any of this bother me. I could show up to my classes wearing a potato sack and no one would bat an eye. I wasn't someone people paid attention to, and I simultaneously reveled in and begrudged that fact.

My door clicked shut behind me, and I walked down the long hallway and across the catwalk until I got to my parents' wing of the house. I knew before I opened the master bedroom door what I would find, but I never failed to hope for something different every time I reached for the doorknob.

The overwhelming stench of alcohol filled the stuffy room, the heavy curtains all drawn closed to cloak it in near-blackness. The light from the hallway illuminated a path so I could see inside. My parents' bed was obnoxious in its grandeur, the massive, dark wood four-poster frame standing prominently in the middle of the room. Expensive linens made of silk and Egyptian cotton lay crumpled in heaps on top of the mattress, no doubt concealing my passed out mother.

I dropped my bag by the door and shuffled inside, cleaning up the scattered things I found along the way. Just because my father employed people to do this didn't mean they should be subjected to my mother's complete disregard for anyone else. She didn't care what she left in her wake or who had to clean it up. All she cared about was getting drunk enough to escape her life for a little while. The day I found vomit all over the Persian rug below their bed was the day I decided no one else needed to see this and took it upon myself to clean up after her.

The empty bottles I gathered from the nightstand—she didn't even bother with a glass anymore—clinked together as I tossed them in the trash. I wasn't concerned with being quiet, of masking my presence. I knew from experience nothing short of a bomb going off would wake her until she was good and ready.

I shuffled back over to the bed, adjusting the blankets so she wouldn't suffocate under the piles. As I pulled on the bed coverings, expecting to come across the slumped form of my mother passed out in all her splendor, I found nothing but rumpled sheets and heaps of blankets. My eyes darted to every corner of the room, even though I'd already walked through the entire space picking up after her. I knew she wasn't in here, and my anxiety spiked, my heartbeat thumping against my chest so loudly, I swore I could hear it in the too-quiet room.

By the time I noticed the light spilling out from the closed door of the en suite bathroom, every worry I'd had this morning, every anticipation of what I might find when I got in here, had flown through my mind, and my palms grew sweaty at the possibilities. In all the years I'd been checking on her in the mornings, I'd been greeted with this sight too many times—an empty bedroom, a closed bathroom door, and God knew what beyond it. My stomach churned as the memory of the last time came to me unbidden, when she'd nearly drowned because she'd passed out in the bathtub and was frozen to the bone from being in there for hours before I had found her.

Anxiety clawed at my insides as I reached for the handle, not bothering to knock before attempting to turn the knob. Locked. Of course. Knocking several times, my fist slamming harder with each pass, I worked to keep my voice level. "Mom, open the door." I waited for several moments before I pressed my ear to the solid wood, hoping to hear something, rattling the knob as I tried it again. Louder this time, my voice shaking, I said, "Mom! This isn't funny. Open up."

When I heard no movement on the other side, my instincts kicked in, forcing me away and toward her freestanding jewelry chest against the far wall of their bedroom. Last time I'd had to break into the bathroom, I'd hidden a key in here, in a drawer I knew she never went in, because I'd always known that wouldn't be the last time I'd be in this situation.

Once I had the cold metal clutched tightly in my shaky hand, I rushed back to the closed door, steadying myself enough to fit the key in the lock, and pushed through into the bathroom.

The scene before me was too much to take in at once, my eyes flitting to every corner as I absorbed what I was seeing. Prescription bottles littered the countertop, the tub was filled to the brim with water, some having spilled over to the floor, and my mom was collapsed in a heap in the middle of the pristine white marble tiles, her hair obscuring her face, her legs bent at an odd angle.

"Mom . . ." I couldn't help the shakiness of my voice as I rushed to her side, slipping on the flooded floor in my haste to get to her. I crashed down hard on the tiles, but I barely felt the pain radiating up from my knees. I grabbed her, probably harsher than I should have, and brushed her hair back from her face. A bold slash of red broke up the weathered skin of her forehead, the blood in the gash long since dried, the skin around it already bruising. "Oh, God. Mom!"

I leaned down, pressing my ear to her chest, and prayed to feel it rise and fall with her breath. In those brief seconds I waited for confirmation, I hated myself. Hated every bad thought I'd had in my twenty years—every time I'd wished to be alone, wished to be born into a different family, wished to be anywhere but here. Even though logically I knew it wasn't my fault, I couldn't help that whisper from creeping up and making me wonder if my harsh thoughts had somehow caused this to happen.

After concentrating, I finally felt her chest rise and fall, albeit shallowly, against my ear. I slumped against the wall, pulling her head into my lap, uncaring of the cold water from the overflowed tub as it seeped into the back of my jeans.

I let my head fall to the wall and closed my eyes, exhaling for the first time in what felt like a year. She was fine. Everything was fine. It was all going to be *fine*.

Except it wasn't. This was the norm—this crazy, screwed-up morning was the start of just another day in the life of Madison Frost. Daughter to one of the most prominent businessmen in Chicago, who didn't have time for anyone but shareholders and CEOs, and a woman who loved vodka more than she loved her only child.

Sister to no one.

Friend to no one.

Confidante to no one.

And though there were no doubt half a dozen people milling about in the house, I felt how I always did.

Completely and utterly alone.

Chapter Two

My fear got the better of me, and the tears I fought hard to keep at bay clogged my throat, making my voice shaky as I called out for our longtime housekeeper, the only other person I could trust to see something like this.

By the time Sylvia came rushing in, my throat was scratchy from yelling for her, my body exhausted. Her eyes were wide, taking in everything, and I looked up at her, feeling like I was ten years old again and completely lost. Except I wasn't. Of course I wasn't. I'd done this before. I'd been in this situation a dozen times, and I knew the drill by now. Clearing my throat a couple times, I swallowed and attempted to make my voice even. "Can you help me clean her up?"

Her eyes, solemn and full of pity, landed on me. "Oh, Maddie. What happened?" She stepped carefully inside to avoid slipping on the wet tiles and knelt in front of me.

"I don't know. I found her on the floor. I think she must've slipped and cracked her head on the vanity."

Sylvia tenderly touched the broken skin on my mother's

forehead, then moved to stand. "I'll be right back. We'll get her fixed up and moved to the bed."

She was back before I could blink, all the supplies she needed clutched in her arms along with a few fresh towels. With some cotton balls and hydrogen peroxide, she made quick work of cleaning up the cut, making it look less ghastly in the blink of an eye. "It doesn't look too deep. I don't think she'll need stitches."

She glanced up at me, and a thousand things were spoken between us in those few seconds. She knew as well as I did that going to the hospital was only to be a last resort. Heaven forbid we show the public anything less than perfection, especially when my father was finessing a buyout.

As I sat, staring off into space, Sylvia got my mom situated with little help from me. She pulled away the soaking wet robe clinging to her petite frame, toweled her off, and redressed her in a dry nightshirt.

"Okay, do you think you can help me lift her to the bed?"

Numbly, I nodded. It wouldn't be a problem. My mom weighed all of a hundred pounds—as if our differences weren't already glaringly obvious, it was just another reminder how we were polar opposites.

Once she was settled back in the now neatly made-up bed— Sylvia must've straightened out the crumpled bedding when I'd zoned out—she continued to sleep peacefully, as if she hadn't tipped my whole world upside down with her behavior. I stared at her, hating her more than words could say, knowing all the while my love for her held me prisoner.

She looked haggard, her mouth hanging open, the fine lines on her face showing her to be so much older than the forty-three years she was. She used to be pretty. In my childhood, I remember her as this gorgeous, *glowing* woman with her long, blonde hair, her bright blue eyes, and her free-flowing smiles. The antithesis of everything I was. My hair, my eyes, even my build came from my father. Where she was rays of sunshine, I was a slab of concrete. As if I didn't feel enough of a freak for being so much younger than everyone in my class, so much smarter than everyone in my class, they made sure to remind me just how different I was from my beautiful mother.

Except she wasn't beautiful anymore. Her hair, once shiny and lush, had turned lackluster and brittle. Her eyes, once always sparkling, had grown tired and dull. Her smiles had come less and less frequently until I couldn't remember the last time I'd seen one. It seemed like it'd always been like this—like *she'd* always been like this, even though I knew that wasn't true. It never used to be this bad. And I didn't know what made everything change.

Sylvia's soft voice interrupted my reverie. "I'm sorry, honey. I hate that you have to do this. You *shouldn't* have to do this."

I shook my head before the words were even out of her mouth, because really . . . if I didn't do this, who would?

She heaved a deep sigh and stood beside the bed. "Maddie, how many times am I going to have to help you with this? How many times will it take before you get out? Before you go off and live your life?"

"When my father is here enough to take care of his wife."

She scoffed. "Is that your plan, then? To stay here for the rest of your life? Because you and I both know your father's wife is his *business,* and your mother is second place. She has been for a long time. He's not going to be here to look after her any more than I'm going to fly to Paris tomorrow."

"I can't just leave, Sylvia. I can't leave her behind. She's my mother."

Her voice was barely above a whisper and beseeching as she said, "She left you a long time ago, Maddie. And now she's draining the life from you. I wish you could see it. I wish I could say something to make you see it."

I turned away from her, from the desperate eyes pleading with me to see her point of view.

But I did. I saw it. Every day, every morning when I woke up dreading my life, when I walked down the hall and checked on my mother, every night when I put my earbuds in to drown out her drunken escapades. I saw it and yet I was helpless to stop it, trapped in a life I never wanted because I loved someone who didn't love me back.

Since I was already late for my first class, I took my time as I peeled off my wet jeans and changed into dry clothes. With my mother tucked safely in bed, none the wiser of the scare she'd given me, the overwhelming sense of resentment I'd been pushing away hit me like a tidal wave, washing over me until I was nearly consumed by it. The hate I'd felt guilty for not even an hour ago was back in full force, and this time, I didn't attempt to stop it.

Sylvia was right. Just like she'd been right the dozens of times before when she'd told me the same thing. I shouldn't have to do this, and I hated that I was the one who did. That my father slept in another room most nights and never bothered to check on his wife before he left for work. That I was the one who had to walk over every morning, feel for the pulse in her neck to make sure she was still alive, that she hadn't died of alcohol poisoning or choked on her own vomit or drowned in the bathtub. That she hadn't slipped on the wet floor of the bathroom and cracked her head open on the corner of the vanity.

I resented both of them for everything I sacrificed in my life because of their selfishness. That I never made friends easily because I was too embarrassed and ashamed to bring anyone home to see my mother in all her drunken glory, dancing on coffee tables or singing too loudly to music better suited for a strip club. That I couldn't go away to school, to start a new life somewhere else, because despite how much I hated her and the mockery she made of my life, I still loved her, and I wasn't sure anyone else would look after her the way I did. I *knew* no one would.

I'd give up the too-large home, the fancy electronics, the drivers and chefs and housekeepers if I could just have a moment— one single moment—of an ordinary life. Where I could be a carefree college student whose only worry was passing her next exam.

Except I knew that even without my mother's sickness and my father's absence, deep down inside I'd still be me. A little naive. A lot closed-off. And above all else completely unprepared for life outside these walls.

I grabbed my bag and once again slipped out of my bedroom, shutting the door behind me before I descended the back staircase that led directly to the kitchen. It was my favorite room in the house, the only one that made it feel like this place was more of a home than a mansion. It was large—too large, probably—but it was bright and warm with pale yellow walls and dark maple cabinets. Fresh flowers were always perched on the round table in the breakfast nook, and being in here made me feel a little less alone.

When I came around the corner, Sylvia was already there waiting for me, her all-knowing gaze landing on me as she offered a sad smile. Normally I avoided her eyes in the morning because I was sure she knew exactly where I'd come from—that I was the only one who checked on my mother, that a grown woman couldn't look out for herself and her daughter had to do it for her. On any given day, I was embarrassed by my family. Today, however, was a thousand times worse. I was ashamed of what she'd had to help me do, ashamed that I had to let anyone else see this screwed-up part of our lives.

"Morning," I mumbled, like nothing at all was unusual. Like I hadn't thought my mother was dead, like Sylvia hadn't helped me carry her slumped form to the bed because she was a drunk and didn't think of anyone but herself.

Sylvia didn't acknowledge any of what had gone on upstairs— her acceptance of what I was and wasn't comfortable talking about was one of the many things I loved about her—and instead said,

"I just plated your omelet, so it should still be warm. I'll get your fruit in just a minute."

My stomach rumbled an answer for me, and I offered a smile of thanks—for the breakfast, for her help upstairs, for being my only friend—as I placed my bag on the floor next to me and took a seat at the table before digging into the food.

"Your dad left you a note this morning." She pointed to the folded white piece of paper off to the side of my plate. My full name was scrawled across the front in my father's unmistakable handwriting, and no matter how many times he left these, it didn't ease the ache I felt at never having him around in the first place. "He headed out earlier"—she cleared her throat and lowered her eyes to the counter—"before."

Of course he did. I was surprised half the time he even bothered to come home at all. I grabbed the note and stuffed it in the front pocket of my bag without reading it. I didn't need to. It'd say the same thing it always did. That he missed hanging out with me. That maybe this weekend we could catch a movie. That he'd try to be home early from work tonight so we could eat dinner together. The truth of it was, I'd eat dinner by myself like I always did, with Mom upstairs drinking her meal and Dad still at the office, doing whatever he did to make sure we were able to remain living in the lap of luxury. The luxury I didn't even want.

After swallowing a mouthful of eggs, I said, "I have my study group after classes, so I won't be home until later."

I glanced up at her, and she fixed me with a level stare, her words unspoken, though I heard them anyway. She'd keep an eye on my mother today, make sure she didn't have a concussion and need to see a doctor, in case my father didn't make it home early like he promised to every night.

"Studying on campus, right? Not going to anyone's home?"

"Yeah, at the library. You've told me a million times not to go to anyone's house, but I really don't think there are any serial killers hanging out at Northwestern just waiting for an overweight, too-young junior to walk into their lair."

Like always, she rebuked me. "You're not overweight, you're *healthy*." I snorted and she continued as if I hadn't interrupted, "And you're young because you're so smart. Someone might want to exploit that, you never know. People are hard to judge, Maddie, and you should know that better than anyone. What you see isn't always what you get."

A soft smile slipped across my face for the first time today. Her concern was like a balm to my heart when I felt split open and raw. I loved her a little more because she seemed to be the only one who tried to act like a parent to me. She'd been employed by my father for as long as I could remember—always a steady fixture in my life. She'd gotten grayer and rounder over the years, but her stern, yet gentle way with me had never changed.

And she couldn't have been more right. When people looked at our perfect little family of three, they certainly didn't see the demons we worked hard to keep hidden.

Chapter Three

Even though I was less than five miles from home, I felt like I was in another world. All day, I'd watched the clock while in my classes, counting down the minutes until I'd be able to head home. I'd called Sylvia four times throughout the day, and each time she answered my questions about my mom's safety with patience and understanding. She didn't think there was a concussion, but she'd been diligent in checking on her anyway.

Study group finished earlier than we'd planned. A few decided to stay behind, but I was anxious to get home so I headed out with two of the girls who were ready to leave. While it was nice to be surrounded by people, especially when it was dark on campus, I always felt more at ease when I was alone. I never knew what to say, what to talk about, how to interact. Being so young—having just turned twenty more than halfway through my junior year—meant there were a lot of experiences my classmates had had that I hadn't yet. Being homeschooled for the entirety of high school on top of being young meant there were an *embarrassing* number of experiences I hadn't had yet. Add that to the fact that I didn't want to talk about my home life, and my love life was worse than my so-cial life, and I went blank any time there was silence.

But after nearly three years here, I'd learned to fake it. I of-fered a small smile and nodded along with the girls who walked with me as we exited the library and descended the stone steps. They were talking about an upcoming party that weekend at their sorority house, and even though I knew they didn't intend to make me feel isolated, the effect was still the same.

The early March air was frigid, this winter longer and harsher than it had been in years, and I huddled further into my scarf, stuff-ing my gloved hands into my pockets to retain some heat. I kept my head down as we walked, not wanting to be rude by walking away, but feeling more out of place than ever.

"Thanks for your help this afternoon, Madison. I'd probably still be in there if you hadn't stepped in."

I glanced over at Ashley and offered a shrug, my lips quirking up at the corners. "It was no problem."

She reached out and tugged on my coat sleeve, her eyes bright, her smile brighter. "Hey, you should come by this weekend if you're not busy. The party's Friday night. I'll give you the details tomor-row in class." As we came to a T in the path, they slowed, both of them moving to head in the opposite direction from me. "We're over this way. You'll be okay by yourself?"

"Oh, yeah. Of course. See you tomorrow." I gave an awkward wave as I turned to leave, and their voices trailed off behind me. As I traversed the sporadically lit path, my thoughts were on the invitation I was sure had been given more out of a sense of obliga-tion and guilt than anything else.

During my first month at Northwestern, I'd made the mis-take of venturing to a Greek party. I'd thought I could wipe the slate clean, start over in a place where no one knew me. Except just because I was ready to step out of the box I'd been put into for the previous seventeen years, that didn't mean people were ready to accept me. While my body had developed early—both a blessing and a curse—I couldn't fool many people into thinking I was any older than I actually was. I didn't fit in with anyone, and five minutes at a party certainly couldn't turn me into a social butterfly. I got shunned, just like always. Only then it felt a thousand times worse because I'd been expecting something different. I'd been *counting* on something different. And the snide comments and barely hidden glares just proved how very wrong I was.

I told myself it didn't matter—those people didn't matter. But when I sat alone in my bedroom, no one to keep me company but the people my father paid to be there, I knew I was only lying to myself.

My toe caught on a raised crack in the pavement, and I stumbled before righting myself, my heart speeding to a gallop after my near-fall. I glanced around, hoping no one had borne witness to my clumsiness, and exhaled a relieved breath when I saw my surroundings were deserted. Pulling my phone from my pocket, I checked the time. Ronald wasn't due to pick me up for another twenty minutes. Although judging by his years of punctuality while working for my father, he might already be there waiting. I shot him a quick text, just in case, checking if he'd be able to come a little early.

While I waited for a reply, I decided to call home once more, even though I'd be there within half an hour, to see if Sylvia needed me to pick up anything on my way. I hit the speed dial and waited as it rang.

"Frost residence."

"Hi, Sylvia."

"Maddie, are you done already?"

"Yeah, we just finished. I'm walking to meet Ronald now, but I wanted to check in. Should I stop to get anything on my way home? Has she woken up completely yet?"

"Yes, a couple hours ago. She's fine, Maddie. Nothing her usual cocktail of Percocet and vodka couldn't cure."

"She's drinking already? Is that a good idea with her head?"

"You and I both know it'd take a force of God to take it away from her."

Her reply, though true, struck a nerve, and I closed my eyes against the embarrassment I always felt whenever talking about my mother's addiction. I could hear the clang of pans in the background, and forced my voice to be even as I said, "You sound busy. I'll talk to you when I get home."

"Okay, honey. I'm making your favorite tonight. We'll see you soon."

"Bye."

I exhaled a deep breath, the dread I always felt settling in my chest at the thought of going home. It was a precarious balance I had, this need to be there fighting with the constant urge to flee. But it was something I'd felt for as long as I could remember, and I stuffed it down before it could suffocate me. It was just another part of me now.

I'd just slipped my phone back in my pocket, exhaling a deep breath when the hairs on the back of my neck stood on end. Before I could contemplate what that meant, before I could even begin to feel any kind of terror, a sickly sweet smell surrounded me as a solid body pressed along my back.

The whole thing took three seconds, maybe less. An arm came into my vision, tattoos snaking down the wrist and onto his hand, and then a rag covered my mouth as the man pressed me back unyieldingly against his chest.

I didn't even have time to scream.

Chapter Four

Even coming to slowly, a thick fog shrouding my mind like I was waking up from anesthesia, I knew something wasn't right. I was pitched on my side, my arms in an awkward position behind my back. It wasn't until I tried to move them that I realized they'd been bound together, the ropes scratchy and harsh against my wrists. I tried to force my eyes open, but they felt so heavy, like they were glued shut, I eventually gave up and let them remain closed. My stomach rolled, nausea overwhelming me, and my head was spinning.

Fear, so potent I could taste it, crept through my bloodstream, making my heart beat as wildly as a hummingbird's wings.

I tried to concentrate, to calm myself enough to think of the last thing I could remember. I recalled this morning, finding my mother in the bathroom, cleaning her up with Sylvia. Calling to check in several times throughout the day. There were classes, then study group. I knew I'd left the library with Ashley and Marie and called home once more to check in, but that was where my memories ended.

The steady motion I hadn't been aware of until it stopped made my stomach churn, and I dry-heaved. There was a muttered curse from somewhere in close proximity, and then the sound of a door slamming. My terror had me struggling to open my eyes, to sit up, to do *anything* other than lay here like a waiting victim. My struggles were in vain, though. I could barely move, could manage little more than the fluttering of my eyelids. Terror gripped my throat, and as much as I tried to stay awake, to take in my surroundings, listen for anything that might help me in the long run, I couldn't quite manage coherency. I finally stopped fighting to open my eyes and let them slide shut just as I felt a cold draft on my legs, then my ankles were being yanked, and the world tipped upside down.

My eyelids fluttered open, no longer weighed down, and I blinked until something other than darkness greeted me. A faint yellow light illuminated the small room I was in. I was on my side once again, the fabric under my cheek much softer than the last time. My world was still spinning, though not as much as before, and my nausea seemed to have subsided a little. My terror, however, was nearly choking me. I was disoriented but aware enough to know I shouldn't have been here. As I quickly took in my surroundings, I knew I didn't recognize this place. The walls were dark brown— maybe even logs—the floors beat-up hardwood. The room was scarcely furnished; the only thing I could see was a woodstove in the corner, a small fire burning inside.

Despite the fact that I couldn't hear anything else besides my heavy breathing, I had the sense I wasn't alone. I darted my gaze to every inch of the room, wishing I could see something in the darkened corners, anything that would clue me into what was happening and who was behind this. The single thought that continued to run through my mind was, *why me?* I hoped it was just a sick joke. God knew I'd been the butt of enough of those in my life, but I didn't know anyone who held enough of a grudge to go through with something like this. Somehow, I knew this was different.

This was worse.

So much worse.

I tugged at the restraints on my wrists, pulling until my muscles ached and it felt like there was a heavy weight pressing on my chest. With no give at all in the ropes, my panic increased tenfold and my breathing picked up, the sound harsh and too loud in the otherwise quiet room.

"You're not going to be able to get out of those ropes. I tied them tight for a reason."

I jumped at the sound of the voice, rough and deep, definitely masculine, and that flutter in the back of my mind that said this was all just a mistake died right where it had sparked. The words were quiet, but I'd heard them plainly, which meant he was close. Closer than I was comfortable with, especially considering I was lying on my side, hands tied behind my back. Completely vulnerable.

I scrambled to shift into a sitting position, swinging my feet over the side of the couch and pushing off to move upright. My head swam, and I had to close my eyes and lower my head until I didn't feel like I'd topple right over again. Waves of nausea rolled through me, and I had to concentrate not to throw up.

When everything was still and I felt like I wasn't going to vomit at any moment, I glanced around, noting few details. It was a nondescript room that could've been a hundred different places. A large window off to my right showed only darkness beyond it, no streetlights interrupting the black, so I knew we were no longer in Evanston. I twisted, whipping my head left and right as I tried to get any more details I could use to find out where I was being held.

"I'm not stupid enough to leave shit around to clue you in to where you are, little girl."

I snapped my head in the direction the voice had come from. There was a dark alcove in the corner, and I could just make out the outline of a person leaning against the wall. The tone of his voice, even and calm, contradicted his harsh words, and that he seemed so unaffected only increased my panic.

I swallowed the lump of terror in my throat. "Who are you? What do you want?" I tried to push my words out fiercely, but they came out scratchy and weak, shaky with fear.

"We're going to work this on a need to know basis. And you don't need to know either of those things right now."

Not willing to be shut down, not when I had nothing to go on, I tried another question. "Why am I here?"

He was quiet for a moment, and I didn't think he'd answer. I stared into the darkness, willing him to respond, to give me anything I could use to help me, whether he knew it or not. Finally, he said, "Someone wants you out of the way for a while. I'm the one making sure that happens."

His words stoked the fear already spreading through me. Who would possibly want me out of the way and for how long? And *why*? My life, despite being lavish, was nothing of consequence. I had no high-profile contacts, no political or powerful allies or enemies, nothing of value to give to anyone. That was all my father. And no one dared cross him.

After years of having people use it against me, I tended to keep my status a secret. I didn't openly share who my father was, what family I came from, but I didn't know what else to do now. It was the only card I had to play, the only way I could strike back, possibly evoke some fear in my captor, and I was going to use everything in my power to do so. Putting as much authority in my voice as I could, I said, "Do you know who my father is?"

The quiet rumble of a laugh that came from him startled me. "Not even five minutes and you're already pulling the daddy card. I don't know why, but I somehow expected more from a smart girl like you. I assumed you got into Northwestern so young for your brains, but maybe it was just the buckets of money your father has. What'd he do, donate an entire fucking wing to the school or something?"

My mouth went dry while the palms of my hands grew clammy. The fear I felt at him having knowledge of my life was nothing compared to what gripped me when my captor stepped out of the shadows. I barely held in a gasp at the sight of him. My eyes grew wide as I took him in, my fight-or-flight instinct kicking in as panic beat a rapid drum against my rib cage. Except I knew I could never fight him. Not fight him and win. And he'd be on me in three quick strides if I attempted to run. He was tall, massive in every sense of the word, his arms corded in thick muscle, every inch of which were covered in dark ink. I followed the interwoven designs down, seeing that the tattoos trailed all the way to his wrists and extended to his hands, and I remembered the glimpse of ink I'd gotten on campus before everything went black. I snapped my gaze to his face. Dark hair cut close. Jaw hard and shadowed in stubble. Angry-looking scar cutting through his left eyebrow. His eyes were pale blue and cold as ice as they appraised me in something close to contempt.

He looked lethal.

And I was scared for my life.

Chapter Five

Despite wanting to remain brave—for what purpose, I didn't know. It wasn't like I was going to be able to convince my captor I was a martial arts expert or anything—I couldn't stop myself from scooting as far from him as I could get. When my hands reached the far corner of the couch, I stopped, swallowing down the knot of uncertainty that had taken up permanent residence in my throat. I'd never felt fear like this. I'd been scared, sure. But never bone-deep terror for my life.

A question thrummed in my mind, and I wasn't sure I wanted to know the answer, wasn't sure if knowing a strike was coming would be better than being blindsided, but I had to ask. I was an academic. Information was what I thrived on. Knowing things ahead of time helped calm me, prepare me. My eyes, wide from panic and fear of the possible answer, stayed rooted on him as I swallowed and forced the words out through a sandpaper rough throat. "Are you going to kill me?"

He lifted a single eyebrow, the one with the scar slicing it in half, his entire body radiating apathy. How could he be so indifferent about this when my entire world was at stake? He answered my question with one of his own. "Are you going to give me a reason to?"

Just like that. Like I'd asked him if he could run to the grocery store or if I could borrow a cup of sugar. Like I wasn't talking about something as important as my *life*.

My head barely moved, but he saw the subtle shake, and the smile he gave me was anything but warm. Condescending and patronizing, but more than that, it was chilling. "No, I didn't imagine you would. You're scared as a little mouse."

Of *course* I was scared as a mouse. And that was exactly what I felt like, huddled and quivering in the corner while the stealthy cat paced in front of me, just waiting to pounce.

"I've been kidnapped and taken to a strange place with a strange man, and my arms are bound behind my back. I can't imagine there are many people who wouldn't be scared in my situation." I clamped my mouth shut, hoping that didn't sound as snotty to him as it did to me. The last thing I wanted to do was anger this man. I swallowed, trying to get myself back under control, and asked, "If you're not going to kill me, why am I here? Are you really just going to let me go? I've seen your face."

"You've also seen too many shitty TV shows. I don't give a fuck if you've seen my face." He leaned against the wall, the picture of utter ease, and crossed his arms against his chest. "I wouldn't get very far if I worried about every target seeing my face. It won't stop me. Hasn't ever stopped me before."

"You—you've done this before?" Hearing my voice come out weak and small made me cringe internally. Somehow, the fact that this wasn't a onetime thing—that he was a skilled and hired man—made this situation worse than I'd originally thought. While I may not have been able to outrun or outfight him, I might've been able to outsmart a first-timer. But someone who did this often? I wasn't so sure.

Then he smiled at me, and though I thought his eyes had been like ice before, they had nothing on the chill I got from looking into them now. He regarded me hollowly, like he was staring right through me. Like I meant nothing, like my *life* meant nothing.

"Definitely didn't pop my cherry with you, princess."

He shifted suddenly, reaching into his back pocket to extract his phone, and glanced at the lit-up screen. His entire demeanor changed, his shoulders going rigid, jaw clenching, eyes narrowing, and I couldn't believe the looks I'd been given before were his *pleasant* expressions. Whoever was on the other end of the line wasn't someone he was happy to speak with. He twisted away from me, his hulking frame moving down the hall as he answered. "Yeah."

His voice was pitched low, and all I could catch was the overall cadence of it. The tone said he was mad, but I couldn't make out what he was saying. I strained to listen, scooting away from the corner of the couch and closer to him, hoping to hear something, anything, that would help me. Help me how, I didn't know, but I certainly wasn't going to sit back and wait for whatever was coming for me. Despite the fact that he wasn't a one-timer, that he may very well have done a kidnapping every day for the last ten years, I couldn't do *nothing*. So I was going to do what I knew. I was going to approach this like I would any problem. Look at it from all angles, dissect it, and come up with a solution. I knew I wasn't a match for him, and I'd probably fail, but I had to try.

I had to fight.

GHOST

Once I stepped outside of the house, away from the prying ears of the girl, I waited until the door banged shut behind me before I spoke again. "What do you mean the plan's changed?" I didn't care that my voice had taken on a sharp edge, that I sounded lethal. This amateur I was dealing with obviously needed to be scared. He could take a lesson from the princess inside.

My breath came out in white puffs against the cold March air, and out of habit, my eyes darted to take in my surroundings. Snow and trees as far as I could see. This cabin was so desolate I couldn't hear anything but the wind. I crossed my arms against my chest, uncaring of the chill, and narrowed my eyes at the words that had just come out of this guy's mouth. I pressed the phone closer to my ear, thinking I'd misheard him. Surely this dumbfuck couldn't be this stupid.

"Say that one more time."

"I need you to hold her. A week, minimum. Maybe two, I'm not sure yet."

"And you didn't think to tell me this before the capture? You didn't think that was good information to have?" Except I knew exactly why he hadn't told me any of this during our meeting last week. Because he thought I wouldn't have taken the job. Little did he know, if I hadn't wanted this job, him simply calling me to switch plans wouldn't have done anything to prevent that.

"Things changed since we last spoke."

"Yeah, here, too," I replied. I lowered my voice, inflicting it with as much authority as I could. It had taken a bit during our meeting for him to realize exactly who was in charge, and it seemed like he needed a refresher. "Now listen very carefully, Mr. White, because I don't like having to repeat myself, and all my patience is gone. You're going to drive out here. Tonight. You're going to get in your car, and you're going to hit your safe on the way, and you're gonna bring me triple my original down payment."

"Oh—oh, no, I'm not sure I'll be able to come out there tonight. I don't think it'd be smart for me to be there."

"I don't give a shit if it'd be smart or not. I'm not fucking around, and you know it. Let me put this in a way you can understand: if you don't get your ass out here in the next three hours, this is done. *I'm* done. I'm dropping her off on her front step with everything her daddy will need to know to nail you to the fucking wall. Unlike you, this isn't my first time, and I sure as shit have covered my ass. Have I made myself clear, Mr. White?"

He paused for a couple seconds, then cleared his throat. "Crystal. I'll be there by midnight."

"Damn fucking right you will," I muttered to myself as I hung up without bothering to respond to him. I forced myself to pocket my phone when what I really wanted to do was smash it against the porch. This change fucked everything. All the planning I'd put into this capture, all the specifics I'd pored over, making sure every last detail was foolproof. All of it was a waste. I had to start over while in the middle of the fucking job.

This was supposed to be a quick grab and drop. Over and done within twenty-four hours. It was bad enough I was out of my element with this capture—girls like Madison Frost weren't high on the shitlist of the people who employed my services. Corrupt businessmen? Yes. Guys who thought they could skim a little money from their bosses? More times than I could count. But an innocent girl? A girl, period? Never.

Seeing the fear on her face when she'd realized where she was had made it pretty fucking clear I wasn't dealing with the assholes I usually did. Watching them squirm, knowing they'd fucked over thousands of people employed by their companies was cathartic. They were getting what they deserved. But her? Despite her being a spoiled princess—the kind of person I'd loathe on the street simply for being born with a silver spoon in her mouth—she hadn't done anything except come from the wrong family.

But I knew if I didn't take the job, some other asshole would. And while she certainly wasn't going to enjoy her time around me, I didn't have the sadistic side some of my colleagues did. Spoiled princess or not, she didn't deserve to be tortured simply because of what she'd been born into.

And not only was I working a job I had reservations about doing in the first place, but now I wasn't just kidnapping, I was also *holding* her. The job went from undesirable to clusterfuck in the span of five minutes.

I could work it out—I knew I could. I'd done it before. This job, however, was the most precarious, and I didn't like gambling when there were so many variables. When there were so many possibilities for failure. But this kidnapping, for all its troubles, was the biggest payday I'd ever seen, and I was hard-pressed to turn down that kind of cash. Especially now that I'd demanded triple the payment.

Though it'd probably have been smarter to make the necessary calls after Mr. White had come and gone, I couldn't wait. Things needed to be shuffled around, adjusted immediately. I pulled out my phone and dialed my brother Riley to make sure I'd have the shit I needed out here. Since this was supposed to be just a drop, I hadn't planned for more than a single night in a cabin that had nothing but running water, electricity, and a woodstove for heat.

When the line clicked on, I said, "It's Ghost. We've had a change of plans. I'm going to need some provisions dropped off by tomorrow. We also need to make some major adjustments to the original scenario . . ."

Once I'd relayed the change and listed off the things I'd need, I hung up and pocketed my phone once again before turning to head back inside. I wasn't looking forward to dealing with Madison Frost any longer than I had to, because I hated myself a little more every time she rested those terror-filled eyes on me.

There was nothing I could do about it now, except lay low until I got the word to deliver her back. Back to the mansion she lived in, back to her life of luxury.

Chapter Six

MADISON

When he came back in, he stalked straight through the room and disappeared into one of the dark corners. The rhythmic thud of his footsteps told me there were stairs somewhere in the cabin, and I immediately looked up into the darkness. The single lamp lit from behind me didn't provide enough light, and I struggled to see past the tiny room I was in. The floor creaked overhead, somewhere off to the left, and I instinctively looked that way. Suddenly, a soft glow came from above, showing me a loft, separated from the open, pitched ceiling by a thick log railing. I couldn't see what the space contained—couldn't even see my captor from where I was sitting—but I knew I needed to. I needed to learn this whole place, inside and out, so I could figure out how I could escape.

While he was otherwise occupied, I scooted down on the couch toward the other end and tried to see as much as I could from my perch. My ankles weren't bound together, so I could get up and walk around, but something told me I needed to be very careful about how much I showed him I was doing. I didn't want him thinking I was anything other than scared out of my mind, certainly not plotting and planning.

I twisted around, looking behind me, and saw the source for the pale light. A small lamp sat on a side table between the living space and a compact kitchen. Whatever this place was had definitely been designed as a strictly utilitarian home rather than a space for comfort. Before I could peek toward some of the darkened corners, footsteps sounded on the stairs again, and I slipped back to the other corner of the couch, my eyes focused on the area he'd disappeared through a minute ago.

It didn't take long before he walked out from it, his icy gaze landing immediately on me, and my instinct to shrink away from him was something I couldn't stop. His presence alone frightened me on a level I'd never experienced.

But I knew if I was going to make it out of here, I had to bite back my fear. I had to shove it all away, get past it and focus on getting some answers. This wasn't a time for me to be timid, for me to revert into my shell, where I was most comfortable. I started with the most obvious, figuring out why he was so angry when he stormed out of here minutes ago.

"Who was that?"

He stared at me for a moment before walking past me into the kitchen.

Not giving up at his lack of response, I elaborated, my voice shaky, "On the phone, I mean."

When he still didn't answer, I twisted around to see him as he stood in front of the sink, hands braced on the countertop while he stared out the window. After looking outside for a moment, he turned his head toward me. "I can't quite tell if you're hoping I'm going to slip and accidentally tell you, or if you're stupid enough to think I actually would." He turned his body toward me and leaned his hip against the counter, arms crossed against his chest. "Are you one of those book-smart-only geniuses or what? No street

smarts on you?" He shook his head and glanced down, muttering
something that sounded like, "Wouldn't last a fucking minute . . ."

His snap assessment of me hit a nerve, and I felt my cheeks
heat. I knew my lack of experience was going to haunt me, and
while I thought it was always apparent while at school, surrounded
by people my age who'd experienced so much more during their
lives than I had, it was never more apparent than right now, here
with him. I was out of my element, and I was fumbling. And I
hated that he knew it. I hated that my weaknesses were so apparent to him. I felt even more vulnerable than I had already.

So helpless.

And I wasn't sure my will to fight was going to be enough. I
was in over my head, and I wasn't sure I'd be able to find a way
out.

He pushed away from the counter and walked toward me, his icy
gaze never faltering. I couldn't—*wouldn't*—look away, attempting
to show him I wasn't terrified out of my mind. The closer he got,
the faster my heart beat against my chest. My eyes grew wider with
each step he took toward me until I had to tip my head back to
look at him as he loomed over me.

Feet shoulder width apart, arms crossed, steely eyes boring
into mine. He looked hardened, lethal, and it was clear he was
making sure I knew exactly who the authority was here.

Not breaking eye contact with me, he pulled something out
of his pocket. Though I didn't want to look away from his face
for a minute, didn't want to make myself vulnerable like that, I
had to see what he'd taken out. I glanced down just in time to see
him flip open the blade of a pocket knife, and my breathing increased, coming in sharp, fast gasps.

"No paper bags around, princess, so you might want to get
that shit under control."

He leaned over me, his chest right in my face, and I felt like I was being smothered. The closer he got, the harder it was for me to breathe, to think, my mind a jumbled mess of all the possible outcomes. I was going to die. He was going to slit my throat, stab me in the side and throw me out in the snow; he was going to toy with me, drag it out until he got what he wanted.

Wordless pleas left my lips, but he either didn't hear them or paid no attention as he pressed closer to me, too close, until all I could see, hear, breathe was this strange man who was going to kill me. I'd never see my parents again. I'd never have another one of Sylvia's omelets. I'd never backpack through Europe or take a road trip along Route 66 or fall in love.

I was only twenty, and I'd never really *lived*, and now I wasn't going to get the chance.

And then the bindings on my wrists suddenly came loose, and when my brain registered what he'd done—that I was unbound— I scrambled as far away from him as I could, pressing myself back into the corner of the couch once again, my knees tucked up against my chest, curling in on myself. I stared at him, wide-eyed, as he stood to his full height, shaking his head at me.

He regarded me with a single eyebrow raised. "If I wanted to hurt you, I would've done it while you were tied up. Though I've never minded a challenge."

If that was supposed to make me feel better, it did anything but. His words, harsh and unyielding, only served to remind me exactly what kind of situation I was in.

"I think we've already established that you're not going to give me any trouble, so for now the bindings will stay off. But don't fuck with me." His voice was sharp, his eyes sharper, as he pinned me with a glare. The foundation of my plan was shaking under his penetrating stare, and I almost buckled. Almost decided to forget about it, wait it out, see where it got me.

He slipped his knife back into his pocket and walked behind the couch to the adjacent dining area, flipping a chair around and sitting down, his arms crossed over the back. I followed his every movement, looking over my shoulder at him. I didn't dare let him out of my sight for even a second. Not since I knew he carried a weapon—at least a knife, maybe more—on him.

His voice was barely more than a murmur, speaking just loud enough for me to hear, but the authority he commanded hadn't waned at all. "There are a few things you need to know while you're here. You follow the rules and you won't get hurt. One, you don't go outside without me. Ever. We're thirty miles from the nearest town, so if you think you can get there before I catch you, by all means, try. Two, screaming is only going to serve to piss me off. No one's around to hear you anyway." The more he said, the wider my eyes grew, my panic slamming into me like a sledgehammer. "The only working phone is mine, and I keep it on me at all times. Lastly, you don't do anything, go anywhere—not even the bathroom—without asking first. Since you're so smart, I don't imagine you're going to have trouble following the rules, right, princess?"

With only the slightest quaver in my voice, I asked, "Why are you doing this?"

He contemplated me for a moment, then when he spoke, his voice was low and gritty. "I do it because I'm paid to. And because I'm damn good at it."

His words hardened my heart, all hope I'd allowed to bubble up fizzling out to nothing. I didn't know if he was telling the truth about how far we were from another town, or the fact that no one would hear me scream, but I wasn't sure I was prepared to test him. What had once seemed like a plausible solution crashed and burned at his words. What could I do? Fighting him wasn't an option. He had more strength in one arm than I did in my entire body. And even if I did manage to somehow sneak away, I knew he wouldn't be far behind. Outrunning him was laughable. I'd run a total of ten minutes my whole life, and it looked like he lived his life bench-pressing cars for fun.

He was too much. Too large, too tall, too muscled. Even completely silent, he screamed.

Never in my life had I met someone like him. And never had I felt as if I'd been entirely too sheltered throughout that life than I did while in his presence. I didn't know men like this existed— hard-bodied men covered in tattoos with angry dispositions who snatched unsuspecting girls for something as simple as a payday. Something noble I could maybe understand, forgive even. But doing this to someone's life simply for money? That I didn't— *couldn't*—comprehend.

I glanced over at him. He looked completely unaffected while my entire world was crumbling around me.

"Why me?" My voice was quiet, though I'd managed to get the tremble under control.

"I don't make the rules. I don't know why, and I don't really give a shit. I just do what I'm paid to."

"And it doesn't bother you? To—to do this, just for money?"

He pinned me down with the weight of his icy stare again, his eyes seeming to go right through me. "Where I'm from, you do what you gotta do to live. Though I wouldn't expect you to understand that. Just know not everyone was born with a silver spoon in their mouth."

His cold, harsh words seeped over me, and I sank down in the couch, attempting to hide as much as I could, trying as I always did to make myself smaller. An impossible feat.

With only my eyes peeking over the back cushions, I studied him. The tattoos that were so incredibly intimidating to me disappeared into the short-sleeved shirt that was wrapped tightly around too-large muscles, and they extended down to his wrists, wisps of ink spilling onto his hands. Small bits curled up his neck over the top of his t-shirt, and I wondered if his entire body was covered with them. I wondered where he'd gotten them. Had he ever been in prison, like his persona suggested, or was he just a product of the streets, hardened through life?

His gaze made me nervous, his eyes cold and hard, ice-blue and unrelenting, and I wanted nothing more than to close mine and hide. I couldn't do that, though. Covering my eyes and pretending he couldn't see me would only leave me blind and vulnerable. I needed to learn everything I could about him, because I had to hope that one day I'd be able to use that information to help the police catch him. I had to hope that someday, I'd be free.

Mustering up all the courage I could, I asked, "Have you ever been to prison?"

"That's what you'd assume, isn't it?"

Could he blame me, really? Men like him didn't frequent the streets of Kenilworth or Evanston. Sure, some of the guys on campus had tattoos, some of them even covering both arms, but this man's entire persona was so drastically different from any of them—from anyone I'd ever met. He could be stripped of the ink completely, wearing khakis and a polo shirt, and I'd still feel terror in his presence. It wasn't the trimmings on him, it was *him,* straight down to his bones.

Without waiting for me to utter another word, he said, "I'm too good at what I do to get caught."

That was what I was worried about.

The silence hung in the air for a few moments. Even when I wasn't looking at him, I felt the weight of his stare on me. Finally finding my voice again, I asked, "What's your name?"

He raised a single eyebrow at my question, but answered anyway. "People call me Ghost."

The way he said it sent a shiver of fear racing up my spine, and I swallowed back the dread that'd crept into my throat. "Why?"

His eyes gleamed as he regarded me. "Because they don't know I'm there till it's too late."

Chapter Seven

The cabin was smaller than I'd imagined. Those darkened parts
I'd seen from the couch had merely been corners or alcoves leading to nowhere. The only other rooms besides the living space and
kitchen I'd already seen were the postage stamp–size bathroom
and the loft upstairs that contained a double bed and a small table
serving as a nightstand.

Ghost was standing in front of the staircase that led downstairs, his stance taking up as much room as possible, and he was
overwhelming in this tiny space. I turned away from him and
looked around, walked over to the railing that overlooked the
main room. I could tell why he—or his boss—had chosen this
place. There was very little privacy.

"This is where you'll sleep."

I whipped my head in his direction, surprised that he'd given
me the separate room with the only bed. "You . . . oh." I glanced
at the bed again, then back to him. "I assumed you'd take it."

He stared at me like I was stupid, then shook his head and
turned around to walk away, down the steps and to the main
room. And that was when it finally clicked. If he stayed up here,

I'd have unencumbered access to the front door, be able to slip out before he was even down the steps. Though I wouldn't have put it past him to vault right over the side of the railing and jump into the main room of the cabin to catch me, if need be.

The hours I'd spent downstairs, sitting next to him in silence, feeling the way he watched me, studied me, cataloged my every movement, only served to make me question my plan. I'd stared outside, trying in vain to see the outlying environment so I'd know what I was up against if I decided to make a run for it. It was too dark, though, the cloud-covered moon giving off little illumination, and with no other light as far as I could see, I was sure he was being honest about the cabin being desolate. *How* desolate, I didn't know. I didn't know if he'd been exaggerating or not, and I needed to decide if I was willing to chance it and see where I could get.

Of course, if I got caught—God, I couldn't even think it. Would he kill me? Torture me? Call whoever had hired him and get the orders to dump my body on the side of the road, after cutting me enough so I'd bleed to death?

I sunk to the bed, my head hanging down as I hunched over and finally gave in to the sudden onslaught of tears. I hadn't cried since the beginning of this entire nightmare, too busy trying to figure out who and what and why, but now, as the possibilities came to me unbidden, I couldn't stop the tears from running down my cheeks. I tried to be quiet, tried to muffle the sobs I knew he could probably hear, but it was no use.

I thought about what I'd left this morning, how ungrateful I'd been for my life, wanting something else—anything else— other than what I had to deal with every day. And I got it. What I wouldn't give to be back in my luxurious home, surrounded by things I didn't want or need, but safe.

How long had Ronald waited before he figured out something was wrong, before he knew I wasn't coming? Had Sylvia called my father yet, letting him know I hadn't come home? Was my mother even cognizant enough to understand what was happening or was she already drunk and numb to everything? Had they called the police, reporting me as missing?

Were they as scared as I was?

Chapter Eight

GHOST

It was almost midnight, and the girl's sobs had ceased about an hour ago. Listening to her cry herself to sleep had been a kind of torture in itself. If I'd had any doubts before about how different this capture was from every other one I'd ever done, they fizzled and burned right then and there. I'd been bribed, I'd been threatened, I'd even heard grown men beg, but I'd never heard the quiet, desperate sobs of a girl.

What the fuck had I gotten myself into?

White would be here soon, and I wanted to make sure the girl was really sleeping so I didn't risk her overhearing any of our conversation. Quietly, I climbed the stairs, being diligent to skip the one that creaked, and crept my way into the loft space. She was turned on her side, her back to me, her breathing slow and even. I walked to the other side of the bed and turned on the lamp on the side table. Her dark hair was tangled on the pillow, her cheeks flushed, full lips parted, and *girl* probably wasn't an apt descriptor of her. Despite her being more than four years younger than me and a thousand years more innocent, she was all woman.

The light hadn't caused her to flinch, not even to flutter her eyelids, so I was satisfied she was well and truly out. Even though it'd taken longer than I wanted, she'd finally cried herself to sleep.

Shaking my head, I reached over and shut the light off, then descended the steps and waited by the front door. I just wanted this whole thing over and done with. I wanted my money and I wanted her back in her mansion and I wanted to go the fuck on with my life. The sooner that asshole White got here, the sooner I could figure out when I'd be able to do that.

With my arms crossed against my chest, I stared out at the night through the slim window next to the door. A quick glance at my watch told me he had less than ten minutes to get here before shit got real. And in the time since I'd talked to him, since I'd told him exactly what I would do, I'd only grown more aggravated. One thing he needed to learn about me: I didn't make idle threats. Ever. In all the years I'd been doing this, I'd found people lost respect for you if you didn't follow through.

I *always* followed through.

Which meant if that slimy asshole didn't get here in the next several minutes, I was taking Madison back to her mansion in Kenilworth and leaving everything I could to make sure Mr. White got nailed to the fucking wall. And it would be no hardship for me. Even only getting half my payment, in one night I'd still end up making nearly as much as I'd made all of last year, and I wouldn't have to deal with my conscience nagging at me about keeping Madison here.

It was a few minutes later when I heard the sound of an engine rumbling down the otherwise deserted path, and then the flare of headlights swept through the window and across the small hallway. I didn't wait until the car was parked before I slipped outside and shut the door behind me.

Once I was standing on the top step of the porch, Mr. White got out of the car, leaving the headlights shining, and slammed his car door. Squinting my eyes, I looked in through the windshield, attempting to see if he'd bothered to bring the hired muscle he'd tried to use to intimidate me at our last meeting. Not that it had worked.

Before he was even around to the front of the car, I said, "Are you alone?"

"Yes." His answer was clipped, his tone sharp, and my hackles rose. I knew how this meeting was going to go—much like the first one where I'd had to remind him who he was dealing with. I had no problem putting people in their place—had to do it more often than not. What I *did* have a problem with, though, was stupidity. I didn't know if it was a pride thing with this douche bag or if he was really as dense as he seemed to be. Regardless, he was wasting my time, and my time was at a premium. Unaware of the part he played in my mounting anger, he continued, "I told you, no one but you and I know the location of this. I wasn't lying." He shuffled his way over to me, the headlights shining behind his back, and I descended the steps until we were only a couple feet apart.

On a good day, I had an ant's piss worth of patience for people like him, but after leaving me to stew in my anger for several hours? Any ounce of what little patience I had for him was long gone. He needed to know exactly how unhappy I was with this change in plans, and I was going to make that fact crystal clear. Keeping my voice low and even, I said, "I don't appreciate being played. I know you've never done this before, so I'm willing to cut you a little slack. But just so we're completely fucking clear, White, that slack is gone."

He looked taken aback, and I was still astonished at the balls on this guy. "Cut *me* some slack? I think you're forgetting who's paying whom."

"And I think you're forgetting just who the fuck I am. Don't test my limits. You won't like what you come up against. Your little stunt already pissed me off, and it's going to cost you." I took a step closer to him and noticed with satisfaction as he took half a step back. Keeping my voice even, I said, " 'Cause, see, the longer I sat out here, in this deserted cabin you made sure I was in, the more I got to thinking. You're a planner, White, and the fact that this hadn't come up during our initial meeting doesn't quite sit right with me. So you know what I think?" I tilted my head down and lowered my voice. "I think this was the plan all along, and you thought you were going to fuck me over by backing me into a corner and getting me to agree with it."

"No—no, that's not—"

I lifted my hand to cut him off, not caring for his excuses. My mind was already made up. "The entire original quote, not just the first half, is tripled. And I want a ten-thousand-dollar bonus wired to this account by tomorrow morning." I passed him a piece of paper with the information written on it.

He sputtered a bit, his eyes growing wide, and if he hadn't angered me so much, I would've reveled in the sweat I saw beading on his forehead. He sure as shit wasn't hot—it was barely twenty degrees out here. "That's—that's too much. That's— No. No, I can't do that." He shook his head, his wide eyes darting from me to the cabin and then back again.

Stepping closer, I towered a good six or seven inches over him. I used my height to my advantage whenever I could, and now was no different. I could see the fear in his eyes the closer I got. "Are you seriously this fucking stupid? This isn't a goddamn negotiation. You're not in charge here. It's triple. *Period*. You're lucky I'm letting you stick with the original payment schedule instead of demanding it all upfront. Because I'm a nice guy, the remaining half will still be due upon completion. But don't mistake that generosity for being a pussy, because if you fuck with me, I swear to Christ, you'll wish you'd never called me in the first place. And because you seem like the kind of guy who needs shit spelled out for him, what I mean by that is I'd hate to have to pay *your* daughter a visit." He froze, his eyes growing wide, and I offered my first smile of the night. "You didn't think I'd take a job without doing some homework of my own, did you?"

His voice was tight as he said, "You'll be paid, Ghost."

"Good." I held out my hand for the bag he carried, and he passed it over. "Now, I need details on what's to happen."

He gave a stilted nod, his eyes flicking back and forth from the cabin to me. "The timing's changed. I'll need you to stay here for the next week, maybe two. Once you've received word from me, she can be delivered back to her home, in whatever condition you deem necessary."

"And if I haven't heard from you after two weeks?"

He leveled me with an unwavering stare. Right. He didn't care what happened to her, but she wasn't to be allowed to return home, and he was to be left out of it.

Clearing his throat, he glanced behind me toward the cabin again. "The capture went well, then?"

I stared at him for a beat, wondering if he was being this dense on purpose. "Well, I'm sure as fuck not out here by myself. Jesus Christ."

"Where is she?"

"In the loft."

"I want to see."

I ignored the unfamiliar hesitancy I felt at allowing him into the loft, alone, with Madison. Raising an eyebrow at him, I stepped to the side and gestured toward the cabin with an outstretched arm. "Be my guest."

He walked ahead of me and waited on the porch as I climbed the steps, then unlocked the door. Once inside, he didn't wait for me to show him the way, heading straight for the stairs and climbing them until he was in the loft. While he quenched whatever curiosity he had, I stood prone on the landing, my eyes pinning him in place as he stared at her from the top of the steps.

I didn't like him, and that was saying something considering all the people I'd dealt with in my years doing this. But he was slimy, conniving, and I didn't trust him. He was one of those assholes who always had something to hide, someone who wore a mask at all times. I'd rather deal with someone who was a stone-cold killer, but who was honest about it, than deal with someone who put on a show for everyone, all the while making kidnapping deals for innocent girls in the dark.

Almost immediately he stomped back down the stairs. "She's passed out."

I exhaled and relaxed my stance. My voice flat, I answered, "Getting dosed with chloroform will do that to a person."

"And there's—there's no permanent damage from that?"

I stared at him for a moment, not knowing why I was so shocked by his ignorance. "Before you talk to me, do you try to insult me as much as you can, or is it a natural gift? This isn't my first fucking time, White. I know how to use it." I raised an eyebrow at him. "Wanna see?"

A small smile crept over my lips as he backed his way toward the door. "N-no, that's fine. I'll be in touch."

With that, he turned and left, waddling down the front steps and to his car. I kept the door open and leaned against the frame, watching until all I saw was the faded red of his taillights, then I pushed off and went inside. Once everything was locked back up, I headed to the main room. I didn't expect Riley to have someone out here until tomorrow with the supplies I'd asked for, and Madison would probably be out for the night. Normally, on a standard kidnapping, I'd stay awake for the duration. Surprises weren't something I wanted to deal with, and I needed to be ready for anything that might come up. I'd never been in a situation where I'd had to capture *and* hold someone, and figuring out a sleeping schedule while making sure there were no escapes was going to be challenging. I slept lightly enough, though, that I'd wake up at the slightest noise.

Though I didn't think I had anything to worry about with her currently passed out upstairs. She was scared, intimidated by not only me but the situation—everything I'd already known she'd be after studying her file for weeks. After living a life where the scariest thing she had to worry about was what to wear every day, she was completely out of her element here, and that was exactly how it had to be to make sure this whole thing went smoothly.

And there was no way she was brave enough to attempt something against me.

Chapter Nine

MADISON

The slamming of a car door had jarred me awake, and I'd crept to the window to peer out, seeing a car pulled up next to the old SUV I'd seen when Ghost had first shown me the loft. The window had been secured shut, so I'd pressed my ear to it, but it had been no use. I hadn't been able to hear anything, and the harsh shadows provided by the illuminated headlights hadn't proved helpful, either.

When Ghost and the other man had turned to come into the cabin, I'd scrambled back to bed, lying as still as possible as one set of footsteps echoed up the stairs to the loft. By the heavy, clumsy fall of them, I knew it wasn't Ghost coming to check on me, and I'd worked hard to even out my breathing and remain as motionless as I could, all the while desperately fighting the fear that had crept up in my throat, nearly choking me. Fortunately, all the man had done was stand by the stairs. He never came close to me, which was both a blessing and a curse. Had he gotten close, he probably would've been able to see that I was faking sleep. However, with him remaining in the far corner, I hadn't been able to see his face, but I hadn't needed to see him for every warning alarm in my body to go off. He creeped me out on a level I hadn't yet experienced, and that was saying something considering my last several hours.

Somewhere between crying myself to sleep and lying still as stone while a strange man came into my space, my fear had been shoved in the back of my mind and was instead replaced by determination. Despite Ghost's threats, I was still going to try. I *had* to. I'd never been a quitter, and I certainly wasn't going to start now—not when the outcome really mattered.

Sure, the man hadn't done anything that time, but what about next time or the next after that? When would looking at me no longer be enough? Was Ghost the kind of man who would sit by and let whoever his boss or partner was come in and do whatever they wanted? What if they tried to touch me? What if they tried to hurt me? I couldn't let that happen. I couldn't *allow* that to happen.

I waited over an hour after I heard that man leave and then saw the light disappearing from my window until I got up and tiptoed down the stairs. It was well after midnight, darkness cloaking the cabin. While I didn't plan to do anything tonight, I wanted to be prepared for whenever I felt like the time was right, and that meant some sneaking around. I wanted to know as much as I could about Ghost's routine. How heavy of a sleeper he was and where he was planning to sleep. I needed to know every inch of this cabin and study the surrounding area as much as possible. Tomorrow, once the sun shone on the land around us, I planned to spend a lot of time staring out the window in the main room as well as the one in the loft. They both looked out in opposite directions, and I hoped it would give me a clue on where to go.

When I was on the third step from the bottom, the wood groaned loudly, and I paused, cringing as I clenched my eyes closed. I held my breath, feeling my heart thud in my throat.

"Thinking of going somewhere, princess?"

My eyes snapped open at his voice. I didn't know where he was, couldn't see him, but from how low he spoke and how well I heard him, I figured he was close. His voice was so calm, so collected, like he didn't have anything to worry about. Like the thought of me trying to escape was preposterous. That lit a spark of anger, a fire inside me I hadn't expected.

And then I realized he'd already written me off as someone who wouldn't attempt anything against him, and I could use that to my advantage. He wasn't suspecting me of anything, and certainly wouldn't be suspecting me of scrutinizing every inch of the place in preparation for an escape.

Clearing my throat, I looked in the direction I'd heard his voice come from, seeing nothing but blackness. "I, um, I need to use the restroom."

I gasped and gripped the stair rail as he stepped out of a darkened corner, having been invisible to me only a moment ago. His pale blue eyes burned straight through me, and I had to force myself not to look away. Not to flinch or curl in on myself, despite the way he made my stomach clench in uneasiness.

"Go ahead." He stayed rooted in his spot, and I nodded and made my way toward the bathroom. Once inside the privacy of the small room, I leaned back against the door, my eyes flitting to every corner in the space. Much like the rest of the cabin, it was cramped and strictly utilitarian. There was a square shower stall, a toilet, and a pedestal sink.

With extra care, I quietly pulled open the door to a freestanding compact cabinet next to the sink. It held three bath towels and a single roll of toilet paper. No medicine, no toiletries, nothing but the stark basics.

How long ago had this place been in use? Probably not recently, as there wasn't much around. No magazines, no books, no newspapers, though Ghost could've removed those before he'd brought me here.

I spun around in the space. No windows. A quick glance at the doorknob showed me there was no lock. With the closed door, I had the illusion of privacy, the illusion of safety, but it was nothing more than a mirage. Because I had no doubt Ghost was standing on the other side of that door waiting for me. And I had no doubt he'd come barreling through if he felt he had a reason to. Even though I knew the probability of being able to escape through the bathroom had been slim, I was still defeated when I realized the chance was a bleak zero.

Once I got my disappointment under control and used the bathroom, I opened the door and stepped out. Just as I'd thought, Ghost was leaning against the opposite wall not more than two feet away, standing in his usual stance with his arms across his chest, his expression showing nothing but boredom.

But I knew better. In the short time I'd spent around him, I'd already realized that no matter what he was doing, what he was projecting, he was always scrutinizing, his eyes taking in everything, and I had to be careful with how I went about studying this space in its entirety.

"Can I have some water?"

He stared at me for a beat before he pushed off from the wall and gestured for me to walk ahead of him. Once we got to the end of the short hallway, I went to the right and into the open kitchen. When Ghost walked past me and to a cabinet, I darted my eyes to every inch of the space. There were no doors in here and only one way into it, from the hallway, so I wouldn't be able to use any aspect during my escape. The rest of the cabin, though, with its small, darkened alcoves . . . I'd have to be diligent in studying them tomorrow.

I knew that while he was awake, he was going to be watching me like a hawk, and the conclusion I'd already come to, that I wouldn't be able to fight or outrun him, was still very much true. My only hope was going to be if I could manage to sneak out while he was asleep. My plan was to spend what little hours we had left before morning waiting, watching, listening, and figuring out his patterns. Then during the day I'd learn this cabin inside and out, studying the outlying area, figure the best way out and the most sensible direction in which to flee.

And then tomorrow night, I'd wait for Ghost to fall asleep.

And then I'd run.

One hundred and twenty nine minutes. That was how long I'd lain here, waiting, listening, barely moving. It was like I could *feel* him, his presence having gotten under my skin somehow. I hadn't stayed downstairs long after I'd gotten my water, deciding instead to bring it upstairs with me.

I was exhausted, mentally and physically drained, but I couldn't give into the sleep that was trying to pull me under. I had things I needed to do, details I needed to uncover, and I didn't want to push it back another day, too fearful of what tomorrow or the next day or the next might bring.

After just over two hours of listening to nothing but silence, I finally slipped out of bed, tiptoeing my way to the thick wood railing separating the rest of the house from the loft. I stopped before I got to it, and as quietly as I could, I peeked over it and peered into the main room. Ghost was sprawled out on the couch, his arms in their ever-present home across his chest as he lay on his back. The dim lamp from the far side of the room was still lit, but the shadows it cast across his face made it difficult to see if his eyes were closed or not. Based on his stillness, though, it appeared he was sleeping.

I took a step backward, my eyes still trained on his form, and the floor under my feet creaked. His entire body suddenly came alive, humming with awareness. It was a series of subtle movements—the muscles in his arms tensing, his entire body going rigid—but ones I saw all the same, and I held my breath as I moved farther away until I could crawl silently onto the bed.

I'd been hoping, praying, he was a deep sleeper, that a door opening, let alone a creak, wouldn't wake him. Now that I knew he wasn't, there was no denying my plan would have to be flawless. I had less than twenty-four hours to learn every nook and cranny of this place, every creaky floorboard, every possible exit. Because with him being in a constant state of alertness, I knew the only way I'd be able to slip past Ghost unnoticed was to become a ghost myself.

Chapter Ten

It was both the longest and shortest night of my life. Despite my exhaustion, sleep didn't come easily for me, even at three in the morning. I found myself staring at the ceiling, a thousand thoughts flitting through my mind as I prepared for today. I slipped in and out of restless sleep, never really feeling like I was getting any kind of actual rest. When the sun finally shone through the windows, I pushed myself off the bed and made my way downstairs, being diligent to take in every inch of my surroundings now that it was daylight. However, even with the sun out, the cabin was naturally dark. The log walls and overhanging porch roof ensured that it remained mostly shadowed inside. There were still dark corners, places I couldn't quite make out, and I needed to explore them.

Once I was at the bottom of the stairs, I paused, listening. I couldn't hear any movement inside, and I walked a few steps over to the front door. The window next to it was skinny, but it still provided an adequate view. I glanced outside, seeing Ghost sitting on the front porch steps. His shoulders were hunched, his elbows resting on his knees as he stared into the distance. I didn't know what he was doing out there, if he was waiting for someone else to come, but I couldn't concern myself with that now. With him otherwise occupied, I knew it was the perfect time to learn as much as I could. And I had to hurry, because I didn't know how long he'd be out there.

Not wasting another second, I walked every inch of the space, scrutinizing it. The darkened corners, the hall closet, the alcove next to the fridge . . . not a foot was uncovered, and it was both a blessing and a curse that it didn't take me long. The cabin was tiny. There were no secret doors, no hidden passages. No basement or attic. It was just the main room, the kitchen, bathroom, hall closet, and the loft. And despite the cloak of darkness that seemed to settle on certain parts of the cabin, it was so open. Exposed. It made me feel more vulnerable than I expected.

Hiding was out, though I'd already pretty much figured that. With another quick glance over my shoulder in the direction of the front door to make sure Ghost was still occupied outside, I walked to the main room, past the couch and to the large picture window that overlooked the back of the property. An inch or two of snow still covered the ground, and the bleakness of it all felt overwhelming. As far as I could see, there were no other homes or barns or garages, no structures at all, just like he'd said. There was a small body of water—a pond or lake—maybe twenty yards down from the house, and trees. So many trees, in every direction. My chest felt tight, the very real possibility of getting lost in them pressing down on me. Even if I did manage to escape Ghost, that was only the first step. The first of many. If he was telling the truth about all of it, I had a long hike in front of me, through possibly miles of wilderness. In March. In the dead of night.

I didn't even know where my coat was.

I felt helpless and out of options. But despite all that, I wasn't giving up. I couldn't. Not if the possibility of getting out existed.

While on constant alert, I rummaged through the kitchen drawers, careful to keep an ear out for the front door opening, looking for anything I could find that might help. He must've taken out all the knives because there wasn't one to be found anywhere. No scissors, either. Most of the drawers were barren, save for a couple. There was a notepad, a few pens, and a flashlight in one. Quickly, before I could second-guess myself, I grabbed the compact flashlight and stuffed it in the front pocket of my jeans, making sure my shirt covered the bulge it made. I didn't know if the thing worked, didn't even know if it had batteries in it, but if it did, it would come in handy when I got to the coverage of the trees after nightfall.

I moved away from where I'd been, anxious at the thought of Ghost finding me in there and somehow knowing what I'd taken. Just as I moved past the hallway into the main room, a gust of cold air rushed in as the front door opened suddenly, and I jumped, whirling around and watching him come in. The way his eyes settled immediately on me, pinning me in my place, was like he'd known I was there all along. Like he knew my every move. I swallowed as the tension curled around my shoulders, holding me rigid.

He walked toward me as he peeled off his jacket, then tossed it over the back of the couch. His gaze was penetrating, unwavering, and despite what it cost me, despite my hands shaking in fear, I held it, refusing to look away.

He moved past me and into the kitchen, and his voice, when he spoke, was gruff. "We've got some food, if you're hungry."

I snapped my head toward him, eyes wide. I didn't know why the simple offer of food surprised me so much, but it did. From the very beginning, I'd assumed he was heartless . . . cold. And I hadn't been proven wrong. Until now.

But as soon as that thought flitted through my mind, it was pushed aside by another, and that was when the panic set in. Because if there was plenty of food, that meant this wasn't going to be quick. It wouldn't be a day of him holding me. He'd planned to keep me for an extended period of time.

He must've taken my silence as something else entirely, because he said, "Sorry, princess, no maid or chef here. You'll have to figure out how to cook it on your own or you don't eat."

I pushed back my wave of fear, focusing on what he was saying, thinking of what I needed to do instead of the impending, looming possibilities. "I . . . I know how to cook." Kind of. "I was just surprised."

"By what?" His question seemed to be an afterthought, something you asked but didn't particularly care about the answer. His back was to me, so I couldn't see his face, but the boredom in his tone spoke volumes.

"I didn't . . . I wasn't sure I could eat. That you'd, you know, that you'd *let* me."

He froze, his entire body stiffening, then he slowly turned around to look at me, his expression unreadable. "Why the fuck wouldn't I let you eat? Jesus Christ, I'm not going to starve you."

"I just—I didn't know."

"Well, let me set your mind at ease: I'm not into slow torture."

He didn't say anything more, just continued into the kitchen and opened the fridge, then bent over and disappeared behind the door.

Rather than be relieved at his words, all they did was strike a fire inside me again, fear at everything he *wasn't* saying. Because if he wasn't into slow torture, I had to wonder what kind of torture he preferred. What kind he'd used on all the other people he'd taken before me.

And I didn't want to stay long enough to find out.

Chapter Eleven

Knowing what awaited me once night fell, I retreated to the loft as soon as I'd finished the apple and bowl of cereal I'd found, wanting to get some rest since it had evaded me last night. And, if I was being honest, I wanted to get away from Ghost. He unsettled me with his unwavering stare that seemed to see right through me. And the cryptic, off-hand comments he made didn't help.

I stared out the window in the loft, looking toward the front of the property. Much like the back, there were trees everywhere, except here they were split down the middle by a winding driveway. How long was it? How far to the main road? And what kind of road was it? I knew I wouldn't be able to follow it, though. At least not directly. If I wanted to stay hidden, to stay safe, I needed those trees as coverage.

I just hoped and prayed that once I got to those trees something was out there for me to find. All I needed was a phone so I could call for help.

Ghost had a phone, but he carried it with him at all times—I'd watched. It was always slipped into his front pocket, and there was no way I'd be able to extract it from him without him knowing.

I heard him downstairs now, walking around, soft murmurs of conversations to someone on the phone, but nothing concrete made its way up to me. Exhausted, I curled in a ball on the bed and willed my mind to be silent so I could rest.

Despite my best effort, my mind churned—thoughts of my escape, possible problems, possible outcomes. I knew it was a real possibility that I could get lost in the woods and then I'd be the victim of my environment. But at least that way, I'd be a victim on my own terms.

I closed my eyes and images came to me unbidden. Pictures of my mother and father . . . of Sylvia. I wished I could call them, just to tell them I was okay, that I was alive and breathing. That I had a plan, and that I was fighting.

A tiny part of me—a part I'd silenced on a daily basis—wondered how much it had affected them. Sylvia was the only one I had contact with day-to-day, despite living with my parents as well, and she was more of a parental figure than either of the two who shared my blood. She, I knew, would be distraught. My parents? I didn't know. Was my mother still drinking herself into a stupor despite my being gone? Was my father still off at work, uncaring of the situation at home?

The uncertainty settled deep in my chest, the pain at their avoidance of everything for as long as I could remember eating away at me. It had always been there, a thorn in my side, but I'd soldiered on, pushed through and slapped a smile on my face, pretending everything was okay. Except it wasn't okay, and now there was a real possibility that all that time I'd spent taking care of other people would be the only life I'd get to live.

And I wanted to live for so much more.

I wanted to make friends and study something that made me happy, and I wanted to meet a guy who made me laugh. Who made me forget about everything weighing me down, who didn't care about where I came from, the money my family had or the addictions that afflicted our house. I wanted to fall in love.

I wanted to be happy.

Silent tears ran down my cheeks, my heart breaking for a million different things. Would I get out? Would I see my family again? Would they care?

But above all that, more than anything, there was only one question that weighed most heavily on me. Only one that ate away, repeating itself over and over again until it was all I could think about.

What would Ghost do to me if I got caught?

My heart was thudding in my chest, the vibration nearly shaking me. My palms were sweaty, my legs shaking, my breath coming in short gasps.

This was it.

I'd asked for my coat earlier, thankful my hat and gloves had been tucked inside, using the excuse that I was cold, and though he'd stared at me for a moment, he'd eventually relented and pulled it from the hall closet before handing it over. It *was* cold in the cabin, the only heating element the tiny woodstove in the main room, so my request was plausible. I just hoped I hadn't made him suspicious.

After I'd asked, I'd moved right back into the loft and lay down, pretending to sleep when really I was replaying my plan over and over again until I was certain I had every nuance of it planned out. It was simple, really. I just needed to wait long enough after he fell asleep, when he'd, hopefully, be in the deepest state, then slip out the front door. I now knew which squeaky steps and floorboards to avoid, and I was confident I could make it outside without alerting him. But even if he heard, my plan was to get the door open and haul ass to the trees. Once I got under their cover, I knew it'd be harder for him to find me.

I'd been quiet up here, listening and watching when I could. Ghost had come up a few times to keep an eye on me, and I'd feigned sleep each and every time. I didn't know if he bought it, but he never came to my side of the bed to check. And now, he was on his back on the couch, arms crossed over his chest, face turned toward the back cushions. I didn't know the exact time he fell asleep, but I'd been watching him now for fifty-seven minutes, and the clock was ticking down. Each minute brought me closer to the decision I'd made.

I was scared—terrified beyond belief. But I was ready.

With that, I pushed off from the side railing and tiptoed along the floor, avoiding the creaky spots. Once I reached the bed, I silently slipped on my coat, hat, and gloves. All this bulk was awkward, but I knew there was no way I'd survive long outside with just my jeans and shirt.

With my back pressed against the wall by the railing, my heart beating so loud I was certain he could hear it, I crept down the steps, skipping the third from the bottom, and landed on the main floor without a sound. I poked my head around the corner, verifying he was still in the same spot, then slipped over to the door. The knob dug into my back as I pressed up against the door, my eyes trained on the motionless form of Ghost. I reached behind me and felt for the dead bolt, then slowly twisted it until it was unlatched. With shaky hands, I grasped the doorknob, and with a small twist the door was released. My breathing rapid, my heart beating wildly, I pulled the door open the smallest bit, but one thing I didn't count on, one thing I hadn't even noticed earlier but now sounded as loud as a gunshot in the room, was the squeaking of the hinges. It was just a peep, the barest of whispers, but I watched in horror as Ghost's entire body tightened.

I had a millisecond to make a choice.

Run or stay.

Run or stay.

Run or stay.

Run.

Chapter Twelve

Uncaring of noise now, I whipped open the door and pushed through the threshold. Just before my foot landed on the porch, I heard a muffled curse from Ghost, and I knew I'd have minutes to get away—*seconds* more likely.

So I ran.

It was past midnight so the sky was dark, but the moon was almost full, and tonight, clouds didn't cover it. It illuminated the landscape enough to guide me until I got in the shelter of the trees. I didn't want to turn on my flashlight until I absolutely had to. It might as well be a calling beacon for Ghost. Instead, I gripped it in my hand and flew off the porch, pumping my arms and legs as hard as I could, as hard as they'd ever been worked. Adrenaline was rushing through my veins, pushing me to go harder, faster. Thoughts bombarded me—the desire to be free, the fear of what was waiting back at the cabin, who was chasing me right now—and I couldn't look back. No matter what, I couldn't look back. I could hear him, his pounding footsteps behind me, but I refused to turn around. I knew if I did, I'd stumble, and I couldn't afford even a second's time lost. Instead, I focused in front of me, on the picture of freedom I found in the ever-closer patch of trees.

Thirty feet.

My breath was coming out in pants now, the white mist puffing out in front of me with every exhale.

Twenty.

I didn't even feel the cold, the harsh wind against my face. All I could feel was the hammering beat of my heart, threatening to thump right out of my chest.

Ten.

Almost. I was almost there, almost safe in the cover of the trees, so close I could nearly reach out and touch the rough bark of the branches.

But as the trees came upon me faster, the louder the footsteps behind me grew, closer and closer until they were *too* close, and then it was too late. Steel bands wrapped around my waist, the force jerking me back and knocking the wind out of me. Before I could even make sense of what was happening, before I could even build a scream in my lungs to protest, Ghost had lifted me, his shoulder digging harshly into my stomach and his arm locked tight around the backs of my thighs. Without a pause, without a moment to even catch his breath, he turned in the direction I'd just fled from and ran back toward the cabin.

No. *No.* This wasn't happening. This *couldn't* happen. I couldn't go back in there, couldn't let him keep me, and I refused to give up now. Not when I was so close.

I tried to push myself up, pressing my palms against his back and locking my elbows, but with a shift of his arm around my thighs, pushing me back farther, I was tumbling over his shoulder again. I tightened my hands into fists and pounded against his back, all the while kicking my legs as hard as I could, but his grip was unrelenting.

I pinched, dug my nails in, scratched and clawed, pressed my face against him and bit whatever skin I could find. I screamed through my sobs, thrashed around as much as possible. But in the end, none of it mattered.

None of it mattered, because in thirty short seconds we were once again inside the cabin, in my tiny prison, and I wasn't free.

And as he marched straight to the kitchen and grabbed something out of a high cabinet, I knew this was going to be different. Whatever freedoms he'd afforded me before were gone.

My throat was dry, scratchy, and raw from yelling, but I still managed to speak. I begged, pleaded . . . I broke. Into a thousand shattered pieces, I broke. I didn't care how pathetic it made me, begging for my freedom. Showing him just how scared I was. I didn't care. Everything I cared about was out that door, and he'd ripped it away from me.

He ignored my pleas and dropped me onto the bed in the loft, then straddled my waist, pulling my arms over my head in one easy motion. His movements were fluid and practiced, quick and efficient, and I felt bile rise in my throat at the thought of how many others there'd been before me. How many times had he restrained someone else?

When my wrists were bound and secured to the headboard, he turned around and repeated the movement on my ankles. Then he pushed off the bed and moved to stand with his back to the railing, his eyes focused intently on my face. Despite running after me in what had to have been a dead sprint to get to me so quickly, and then carrying me all the way back, he wasn't even breathing hard. Meanwhile, my breaths were coming in pants and gasps, my lungs screaming from the exertion of running, of fighting. My eyes were scratchy, tears still leaking from the corners, and if I'd thought I was terrified before, it had nothing on the fear that was now creeping its fingers along my body, clutching me by the throat as I stared at Ghost.

"Why the fuck would you do that? When I told you to try if you thought you could make it, I wasn't serious." His voice was low, controlled, and I wondered if anything ever rattled this man. But then I got my answer a second later as he closed his eyes and shook his head, muttering, "Jesus fucking Christ. God*dammit*, Madison." When he lifted his head again, his arms behind him on the railing, all I could do was stare wide-eyed at him. His tone sharper than before, he said, "Get comfortable in these ropes, princess. You just sealed your fate."

And then he pushed off the railing and crossed the room, taking the stairs two at a time until he was at the bottom.

And once again, I was all alone.

GHOST

I couldn't believe she'd tried to escape. I'd never—not once—had a captive attempt that before. They'd begged, they'd pleaded, but they'd never once had the balls to run. Not like her. Seeing the fire in her eyes, that spark of determination as she took off like the hounds of hell were after her, sent a wave of appreciation and, if I was being honest, attraction through me. Not to mention anything about hauling her over my shoulder, feeling her against me . . . none of it should've registered at all. And I hated myself that it did.

She was a mark, plain and simple.

A mark I'd underestimated. Because I never thought she'd have it in her to run. Maybe I'd pegged her all wrong. Maybe she wasn't the delicate, spoiled girl I'd assumed she was. Because the person I'd pegged her as sure as shit wouldn't have attempted escape, not with so many variables. Not with the unknown waiting for them outside these walls.

This couldn't happen again—*wouldn't* happen again.

Considering how long she needed to be held, I'd hoped I wouldn't have to keep her tied up. She shot that plan straight to hell. All she had to do was sit tight and wait. That was all we were doing here, waiting for a phone call, and now I had no choice but to keep her bound.

And what pissed me off the most was that I actually felt *bad* for her. Empathy was an emotion that never came into play while I was on the job, and yet I couldn't deny I was feeling it now. She didn't deserve to be terrorized like this. Worse than her being terrorized was that the terror came at my hands, and that disgusted me.

I blew out a breath, reminded myself this was just another job, and paced in the living room. I needed to call this in, to let him know. I also needed to call Riley and have him get a different lock for me to install. One that you had to have a key to open, because this standard dead bolt wasn't going to cut it for the week or more we'd be stuck out here.

I pulled out my phone and dialed the number I needed as I walked back down the hallway and out the front door. She didn't need to hear any of this conversation.

It rang three times before the call was answered. "Yeah."

"She tried to run."

He must've pulled the phone away from his mouth because his voice came out mumbled and soft, then I could hear rustling in the background as I assumed he moved to a different location. When he spoke again, his voice was clipped and short. "She what?"

"I'm not going to repeat myself. You told me I wouldn't have to worry about that, and because of it I underestimated her." I paused, scrubbing my hand over my face. "*You* underestimated her."

"Do not tell me what I did or didn't do with her, Ghost."

I clenched my jaw at his tone but decided to let it go. Considering what had just transpired, I wasn't in any position to pull rank. "Whatever. It won't happen again; I'll make sure of that. I'm gonna have a new lock installed out here, one that has to have a key. For now, she's secured to the bed."

"Fine. Do whatever you need. And I better not get another call like this again or I'll find someone else to do your job for you."

And with that, he hung up. *Fucking prick.*

I slipped my phone back in my pocket and braced my hands on the porch railing, my eyes focused on the line of trees encasing the property. It was dark, but the light of the moon allowed me to see it well enough. As I stared, I knew without a doubt the girl had studied this very thing. From everything I'd come to learn about Madison Frost, the one thing that was overwhelmingly apparent was her intelligence. This wouldn't have been an offhanded attempt. She would've learned everything she could. And even so, I knew she hadn't been outside before tonight, so as much as she'd prepared within the cabin, staring out the windows probably, she was still running toward the unknown.

I knew better than most the lengths you'd go to when pushed far enough, when your back was up against a wall. Sometimes the unknown was better than what was staring you in the face.

The thing that pissed me off was that I should've expected this. For as long as I'd studied her file, I should've seen it coming. Just from the minimal pieces of information I'd gotten on her—some notes and a dozen photographs—I could read more about her than most people in her daily life knew. After eight years of doing this, I knew how to read people better than most, how to profile a person in a matter of seconds. When I'd studied the pictures, I'd taken in her stance, her clothes, every nuance to her I possibly could. And from those mere photographs, I'd figured out she was skittish and timid. Studious. Not athletic. Self-conscious about her body. And unhappy.

What the photos hadn't told me was how affected I'd be by her in the flesh. Her face was all sweet innocence despite that fire in her eyes I'd witnessed, and her body was lush with curves and made for sin.

While the images had told me she was someone easily captured and easily held, what I got in person was so much different.

And the fact that I hadn't seen it coming, that she'd taken me by surprise, didn't sit well with me. I was always prepared for any situation, and I should've expected this from her. Moreover, that bastard who hired me should've warned me she might do it. If I knew her file inside and out, he knew her ten times better.

Knowing if I allowed myself to focus on that any longer I'd get even more pissed, I pulled myself out of that train of thought and grabbed my phone once again. I needed to call Riley and get him to send someone out here before any other botched escapes were attempted.

Not even a full ring later, he picked up. "Hey, man. What's going on?"

"I need a runner out here again. As soon as fucking possible."

"We forget something?"

"No. An issue came up."

"Okay, what do you need?"

"A double cylinder dead bolt and the tools to change it."

"Miss Priss giving you troubles?"

"Don't worry about it. Just bring the fucking lock."

His chuckle was easy and unrepentant. "Got it. Give me a few hours."

I hung up and pocketed my phone once again, then went back inside. I took the stairs two at a time up to the loft and found Madison exactly where I'd left her, her head turned to the side, though now she was asleep. Her hair was a rat's nest on top of her head, her face a mess. Her eyes were red and swollen, her cheeks still wet from all the crying she'd done.

And through it all, through every ounce of terror she'd felt—and I was certain terror was exactly what she'd been feeling—she fought. Without exception, without pause. I never took her for a fighter, and I'd be willing to bet no one else ever had, either.

Even though she'd managed to earn my frustration with her little stunt, I had to admit she'd earned a little bit of my respect while she was at it.

Chapter Thirteen

MADISON

It felt like I lay there for hours, drifting in and out of a fitful sleep, my eyes burning from my tears, my throat raw from my screams. Dreams of attempted escapes and nightmares of what was to come jolted me awake more times than I could count. With my hands tied to the headboard above me, the tension on my shoulders was unbearable, and combined with the events of the last thirty-six hours, I was working my way toward a vicious migraine.

The sun filtered too brightly into the room, and I turned my face away, attempting to cover my eyes with my arm. The sharp pounding behind my eyes seemed to get worse by the second, exasperated with even the slightest move I made. I tried to go back to sleep, hoping that doing so would alleviate the pain. Before I could drift, there was clanging downstairs, and I realized what had woken me up in the first place.

Metal clanked together, then the whirring sound of a drill drifted up the stairs. It felt like it was drilling straight into my skull, and I whimpered against the sensory onslaught.

Sleeping wasn't going to be an option, and even if it was, this migraine had gotten bad enough that, unless I got my prescription, nothing was going to help it short of cutting my own head off. I usually kept at least two pills with me at all times, just in case I was struck with one unexpectedly, so, assuming Ghost hadn't thrown out my bag, relief was somewhere in the cabin.

I waited until there was a pause in the noise from downstairs, then called for him. Even the soft timbre of my voice made my head thrum in agony, and I moved restlessly on the pillow, yearning for relief even when I knew none would be found.

After a few moments with no response, I tried again, louder this time. "Ghost?"

Still no response, but I could tell he was moving around. I heard the door shut and metal clanging against something, and then footsteps. I prayed he was coming up here, and fast. The nausea was setting in, and I needed to get my meds in me before I threw up or this was going to be a bad one.

"Ghost, please. Can you get me my medicine?"

"Jesus Christ, give me a minute!" His voice was loud—too loud—and I cringed back into the pillow, waiting as my head pounded in time with my heartbeat.

Tears leaked from my eyes, and I did nothing to stop them. I didn't resist them and I didn't succumb to them—either would only make the throbbing worse. Instead, I lay as still as I could, willing the nausea pushing at me from all sides to subside. But it didn't. It only grew worse, in the shortest amount of time I'd ever experienced.

"Ghost, I'm going to be—" I couldn't even finish my sentence before I felt it overwhelming me. Saliva rushed into my mouth, and I rolled to the side as much as I could, coughing and sputtering as I lost every small bit of what was left in my stomach over the side of the bed.

Somewhere in the midst of it all, I heard Ghost come in with a muttered curse, and then my hands were being untied from the headboard, then my ankles.

"Why didn't you say you were gonna puke?" His voice was frustrated, irritated, but I caught a note of something else, as well. Something softer, something almost contrite.

I wanted to tell him I'd tried, but I didn't bother. I couldn't think about speaking, even in whispers. Instead, I kept my eyes closed, my face pressed to the pillow, and I didn't even care if I smelled like vomit. I didn't care if I was covered in it. I didn't want to get up, didn't want to move.

"What's wrong?"

When I didn't answer, he pressed his fingers to my forehead, then asked again, "Madison, what's wrong?"

"Migraine." My lips formed the word, but it was nothing more than a breath, and I wasn't sure he heard me.

"You need to go get cleaned up. Take a shower."

I hadn't had a shower in two days, and it sounded like heaven as much as it sounded like hell. I wasn't sure I'd be able to stand, let alone actually wash myself, but my olfactory senses were so sensitive, I knew now I wouldn't be able to lay here with the overwhelming stench all around me and get back to sleep.

My movements were labored, slow, as I rolled to my side, then paused before I pushed myself to a sitting position, my head hanging. I waited for the fresh, intense wave of pounding to subside to a less-potent throb, then stood and shuffled behind him to the stairs. By the time I was at the bottom, he'd already moved to turn the light on in the bathroom and grab a towel out of the cabinet for me, which he thrust in my direction.

"My bag?" My voice was barely above a whisper, but anything more than that felt like I was shouting through a megaphone.

I hadn't raised my head to see his expression, but I could hear the skepticism in his voice. "What do you need in there?"

"Medicine."

Without waiting for him to respond, I walked into the bathroom and shut the door as much as I could while still allowing a bit of light to filter in, then I flipped the switch off, cloaking the room in darkness and sighed. It'd be difficult to shower in nearly pitch black, and I wasn't even going to think about the fact that Ghost would be just outside a partially opened door while I was completely naked and exposed in here. It didn't matter, anyway. I couldn't think about anything but the bed waiting for me upstairs and, hopefully, the medicine Ghost would bring to me.

GHOST

I felt like a complete ass.

But, really, how the fuck was I supposed to know she was going to be sick? The first time she'd called down for me, I figured she just needed to go to the bathroom, and she could wait five minutes until I finished installing the new dead bolt. So I ignored her. I was still so frustrated with her after her attempted escape last night. And I was frustrated with myself for noticing things I had absolutely no fucking business noticing. The more time I spent here, the more I hated that I'd taken this job, that I'd let myself be backed into a corner to do so. She was innocent, and that was only one of the ways she was different from a standard job. She was also braver than any other person who'd been a mark.

I was trying to make this as comfortable for her as possible—I knew it wasn't going to be a vacation at the Ritz, but it didn't have to be hell, either—but after her attempted escape, how could I let her wander the cabin freely?

Combine all that with the shit Riley had given me when he called to make sure the equipment had been dropped off, and I was in no mood to deal with Madison.

And then when she became more persistent, I thought she was actually going to try something again. Despite everything that had happened not even eight hours earlier, I thought she was attempting to get out of her binds . . . to flee.

Instead, she was sick, and I was an ass.

The water came on in the bathroom, and I turned and walked away, very aware of the six-inch gap the door hung open to allow a sliver of light inside. It was still dark in there, but I had no doubt I'd see more than I should if I looked in. Which was the last fucking thing I needed now.

And I was a lot of undesirable things, but I wasn't an asshole who got my rocks off from unsuspecting women. When I had a woman, I wanted her to participate.

With the double cylinder lock in place and the key stuffed safely in my pocket, I felt comfortable leaving her unattended. I headed straight to the hall closet and pulled her messenger bag out of the safe, making sure to remove her cell phone and laptop and stuff them back into the safe. Once that was locked again, I walked the few steps back to the bathroom. I stopped just before the door opening and yelled in to be heard over the shower. "Where are the pills?"

She whimpered, the sound nearly lost among the shower spray. Then she mumbled something that I couldn't hear, so I stepped closer, closing my eyes and slipping my head into the space offered by the open door. The steam from the shower drifted over to me, the fresh scent of the soap filling the air, and my dick twitched in my jeans.

Jesus Christ. "I didn't hear you."

With obvious effort, she said, "Quiet please. Loud noises make it worse."

"Sorry."

"S'okay. Pills are in the front pocket."

I didn't wait for any further instructions before I yanked my head back from the door, nearly clipping my ears in the process. I needed to get out of there, because I was seriously fucking losing it.

Shaking my head, I dropped her bag on the table, then flipped up the front flap and rummaged around inside the pocket, looking for a pill bottle. I pulled out a couple loose slips of paper and a few pencils, then found a small tin. I unscrewed the lid and saw several small, round, white pills inside. After setting them down on the table, I began stuffing everything back into the pocket. The notes were scattered across the table, and I gathered them all up, my motions freezing when I saw Madison's name across the front of one of the pieces of paper.

Glancing back toward the bathroom, I confirmed the shower was still on, then turned back to the thick paper in my hand. I flipped it open, reading the few lines inside. There wasn't much written, just the date—the day of her capture—and a couple sentences. To the average person, it might have looked like a bullshit note to toss aside. But I knew more than the average person, and I read into everything. This was no exception.

Let's talk soon about your mother. I've found a few options for where we can admit her. It's not fair to you to keep taking care of her like this. I'll make it right, Madison. Just give me a little more time.

~Dad

Get her mother admitted? To where? What secrets were they hiding in that house? Because I knew everything there was to know about Madison Frost—or I thought I did. But I didn't know this. Her mother, what I knew of her, went to the appropriate charity functions, accompanied Madison's father to dinners out and parties and whatever the fuck rich people did. But this note . . . this said something entirely different.

I looked over my shoulder toward the bathroom again, making sure I hadn't missed the water being shut off, then stuffed everything back inside the pocket and flipped the flap closed.

The note didn't mean anything, really, except that it was a piece of a puzzle I was beginning to realize I hadn't had all the pieces to from the beginning. She was much more complex than I'd originally pinned her as, much more than the spoiled daddy's girl who didn't have to work for anything in her life. And though our lives couldn't have been more different, I was beginning to wonder if maybe there weren't some similarities there, too, both of us forced to do shit we didn't want to because of the families we'd been born into. Both prisoners in our own ways.

Shaking those thoughts from my head, I headed to the hall closet and pulled my own bag out. There was no way she was going to want to stay in her puked-on clothes, and unless she carried around extra clothes in her bag, she was going to need something to change into.

I dug around and found a long-sleeved Henley and a pair of basketball shorts—she'd be cold, but they'd have to do until her clothes could be washed—then I turned to the bathroom and tossed them inside the space just as I heard the water shut off. She was quiet as she stepped out and dried off, and I felt like a fucking pervert for standing there listening to her.

"I left you some clothes in there, since yours are dirty."

There was a pause, not even the sound of her towel against her skin, then a soft, "Thank you," barely loud enough for me to hear. The light from the hallway poured into the bathroom, and I saw a flash of creamy white skin and the curve of her shoulder, and spun on my heel before grabbing some sheets from the closet. I took the stairs two at a time up to the loft and made quick work of the bedding, tossing the dirty sheets off to the side, then cleaning up the mess on the floor, all the while trying—and failing—to not think about what I'd seen a minute ago.

It was nothing.

Nothing more than a PG peek at something I wasn't interested in anyway. Except I felt like a Peeping Tom because every time I thought of that glimpse of skin, my dick grew a little harder until it was steel in my jeans.

With a harsh curse, I closed my eyes and made myself calm the fuck down. This was a girl—a child, really, compared to what I'd been through in my life—who I'd kidnapped for money. I had absolutely no business getting wood over her. I had no business thinking about her like that at all. And I needed to get that through my thick fucking skull, or this was going to be a very long two weeks.

Chapter Fourteen

MADISON

It was stuffy in the bathroom, even with the door open as far as it was, but the hot water helped my head a little. A very little. If nothing else, at least I felt more human now that I was cleaned off.

I shuffled over to the spot where Ghost had tossed a couple pieces of clothing inside, then looked to my pile of dirty laundry. I hoped he'd let me throw them in the washing machine, because those five pieces of clothing—a bra, a pair of underwear, jeans and a shirt, and my coat—were the only things I had to get me through however long I was here for. In all my fighting and flailing last night, I must've lost my gloves and hat somewhere along the way.

Unable to even think about the exertion it would take to do the laundry, nor the ever-present anxiety I had when thinking about what the future held, I dropped the towel, then gingerly squatted to pick up the clothes, diligently not moving my head more than absolutely necessary. I held the bottoms between my knees while I pulled on the shirt he'd left. Normally I wouldn't be caught dead without a bra on, too self-conscious of my large breasts, but I needed comfort now more than anything. And I was heading straight back up to the bed to try and sleep this off, anyway, not running around the cabin.

After pulling on the shorts, I tugged at both garments. Despite Ghost's massive frame, the clothes weren't nearly as big on me as I'd have liked. The shirt pulled tight against my breasts and hips. The shorts, while hanging nearly past my knees, were snug in the butt. Closing my eyes, I took a deep breath and pushed the thoughts out of my head. It didn't matter anyway. What I looked like didn't matter. Here, of all places.

I grabbed a washcloth from the cabinet and ran it under hot water, then pulled my fingers through my hair, combing it as delicately as I could. I was going to pay later for leaving it wet, but the thought of using a comb right now made my head throb. With a deep breath, I opened the door, then blocked the onslaught of light with my hand. I'd been standing up for too long, and the exertion was wearing on me, my migraine a constant torment.

Keeping my eyes downcast, I made my way to the stairwell and up the steps, my warm washcloth clutched in my hand. The higher I got, the darker it became, and I realized the curtains must have been drawn. I removed my hand from over my eyes and turned to move to the bed, set on lying down as quickly as possible and sleeping this off.

Except where I expected a rumpled, *empty* bed, I found a freshly made one with Ghost perched on the far edge, phone in hand, eyes studying me. I froze, the sudden movement causing a crashing wave of pain to radiate through my head, and I cringed, closing my eyes and pressing my fingers against them.

"Your pills are over there with some water." His voice was rough but low, and I silently thanked him for remembering that the quiet helped.

"Thank you." I shuffled over to the side of the bed I'd been sleeping on—the side I'd been tied up on—and darted a quick look in his direction before I sat and took my pill. I didn't know what to do now. He sat in the bed he'd told me I was to use, and all I could think about was lying down, resting my head on a soft pillow, and drifting into a blissfully pain-free sleep. But he was here— too big, too much—and I didn't know why.

He cleared his throat. "I thought, with the migraine, you might be more comfortable without the ropes."

Slowly, I turned my head to look at him over my shoulder and gave a subtle nod.

"Because you're not secured, I'll need to stay in here."

My eyes grew wide, my heartbeat increasing. He didn't say anything about my escape attempt, but his frustration and irritation were prevalent in his unwavering stare. And how was I supposed to relax enough with him *right next* to me? How was I supposed to trust him being so close?

My expression must've given away my fears, because quietly he assured me, "I'm not going to hurt you, Madison. I know it doesn't seem like it, but you're safe here."

And, no, it didn't seem like it. But when I thought about it, when I removed myself from the situation and looked at it from an objective position, he hadn't hurt me. He hadn't laid a hand on me, despite having a dozen different opportunities to do so.

Satisfied with his vow, I gave another nod and pulled the bedding down, then lay down and settled on my back under the covers, as near to the edge as I dared. Carefully, I placed the warm washcloth over my eyes, hoping for relief.

I wanted sleep to take me under immediately, but my mind was working too fast for that to happen. The bed was small under the best of circumstances, and Ghost was huge, not to say anything about me at all. The space between us wasn't nearly enough, and though we weren't touching, I *felt* him. He wasn't doing anything to make his presence known—he wasn't jostling the bed or making any noise—but I was aware of him all the same. What we were doing—sharing a bed—felt intimate, despite that he was on top of the covers and I was under . . . despite a million different reasons why I shouldn't feel this way. It felt more intimate than I'd been with anyone, save for the one and only time I'd ever had sex. But even that hadn't felt like this. This was more, but I didn't know why or how.

I lay as still as I could, willing myself into sleep, but it refused to come. Immersed in my attempts to force it, I didn't notice Ghost had moved at all until I felt a slight pressure on the washcloth and then the now-cool piece of fabric was gone. I stopped moving, stopped breathing, as the bed lifted when he got out. His footsteps echoed down the stairs, then I heard the water running in the bathroom. Thirty-seven breaths later, he was back, the mattress dipping gently as he sat down, and then there was once again warmth covering my eyes. The relief was palpable, and I sank further into the bed.

Despite the flurry of questions that had just erupted in my mind, eventually the even cadence of his breathing lulled me into sleep.

GHOST

Madison slept hard. For hours, she didn't move from her spot on the bed. She was on her back, hands clasped over her stomach, face slack.

She looked like she was dead.

I'd never had a migraine, but everything about her body language was screaming at me to back the fuck off. With the exception of rewarming her washcloth, I stayed on my side of the bed and kept myself busy checking in with my brother, making sure everyone else was pulling their weight so this elaborate plan could be pulled off. Riley told me things were going fine on the outside, that everything was going accordingly, but I was still uneasy. I didn't know if it was because the plans got changed so late in the game.

If it was because this was an entirely new situation to me. If it was because I was uncomfortable having a girl for a captive. Or, more probably, having Madison specifically. This unwanted attraction that had taken me off-guard hadn't waned at all in the time she was sick. If anything, it'd gotten more potent, this foreign desire to protect her—to take *care* of her—blindsiding me. And then there was the whisper of a voice, my instincts kicking in, saying it was something else entirely. I needed to be diligent while here. Completely focused. I'd been doing this for too long, had it come too easily to me, and I'd gotten comfortable. But I needed to be on top of everything, especially when I had a captive who was ballsy enough to attempt escape. Would she try it again? I didn't know, but I'd do everything in my power to make it nearly impossible for her to do so. An attempted escape would only be more dangerous for her in the long run.

Even knowing that, I couldn't stop thinking about that note, about what this girl's life was like behind closed doors. And the more I thought about it, the more I wanted to kick my own ass. Because I was starting to get inside her head even more, starting to learn things about her that made her not so different from me. And that was a very dangerous path to go on. I couldn't afford any distractions. Not with the person who was the reason for this entire fucked-up scenario.

And definitely fucking not the person indirectly responsible for my obscene payday.

MADISON

I woke fuzzy, disoriented, my head cloudy and heavy. The still-warm washcloth was covering my eyes, and I reached up to pull it away. I blinked, my eyes gritty, my eyelids feeling like they had weights attached to them. The sun was on the other side of the cabin by now, and the loft was dim with the exception of the light coming from Ghost's phone. It illuminated his face, drawing attention to the sharp angles. He was still there, his back against the headboard, his legs propped up on the mattress and crossed at the ankles, looking for the whole world like the picture of ease.

I was anything but.

Memories of what he'd done before I'd drifted off to sleep bombarded me, and I darted my eyes to his. I was confused, uncertain, and now that the migraine wasn't infiltrating my every thought, I was able to focus on the details I hadn't been able to before. The reassurances he'd given that I was safe here, with him. Then the gentle way he'd pulled the washcloth from my face. How he'd rewarmed it for me, thinking I'd already been asleep. How he'd obviously sat here, stock-still, for the entirety of the time I was out, making sure not to disturb me.

It was a glimpse of consideration I hadn't expected—not here . . . not now—and I didn't know how to digest it.

"Feel better?" His gritty voice pulled me out of my thoughts, and I looked up toward him.

"Yeah." It came out in a croak, and I cleared my throat before folding the blankets back. I slipped my legs off the side of the bed and pushed myself up to sit, my back to Ghost. Pausing and closing my eyes, I prayed the incessant pounding I'd had in my head for the last however-many hours wouldn't make another appearance. When there was only a dull ache in the back of my skull, I breathed a sigh of relief. The migraine was on its way out now. I needed to drink a lot of water, maybe have some toast, and it'd be good by morning. This wasn't my worst migraine ever, but it'd been bad. Of course, based on the events of the last couple days, I should've seen it coming.

I reached for the glass of water and downed it all before placing the cup back on the nightstand. While I wasn't in my restraints anymore, I didn't know the new rules. I assumed he'd tie me back up at some point, though I hoped he wouldn't. I wasn't stupid enough to try and escape again, not now. Not when I'd ruined my chance at it in the first place. The only thing I'd had going for me was the element of surprise. Now though, he was on high alert, even more so than before, and there'd be no way I could slip something by him again. My only choice now was waiting.

Waiting and watching and hoping for someone to find me.

Chapter Fifteen

I braced my hands on the bed and held my shoulders rigid, remembering what he'd said to me about him being my shadow, going everywhere I needed to go. Without turning toward him, I said, "I'd like to use the bathroom now."

When he didn't say anything, I turned my head to look at him over my shoulder. His forehead was creased, his whole face morphing into a scowl that was becoming very familiar. He didn't answer me, but he swung his legs over the side and walked to the steps, pausing briefly to look at me before he slipped down the stairs. I followed him, shuffling my way along, still groggy from all the sleep. And even though my migraine was fading away, they always left me drained for the rest of the day no matter what.

Ghost didn't stand outside the door like he'd done before, but instead went to the end of the hallway, bracing his shoulder against the wall where the space opened up into the main room. I didn't know where this newfound freedom he was allowing me was coming from, especially after last night, but I wasn't going to question it.

I slipped into the bathroom and shut the door, cringing at the bright overhead light. While my eyes were adjusting, I used the restroom, then headed to the sink to wash up and splash some water on my face. When I lifted my head to stare into the mirror, I cringed at what I saw. My hair was unruly, the result of laying on it wet, and I knew from experience just how painful it would be to comb through. My face was free of makeup, though that wasn't anything usual. But I hadn't brushed my teeth in more than two days, and I felt like the walking dead. I didn't even know if I had anything in my messenger bag—anything that could make me feel a little more human—but it wouldn't hurt to check. Pulling the door open a couple inches, I called out for Ghost.

"Yeah."

"Can you . . . I mean, can I have my bag, please?"

A shadow filled the hallway, and I looked up in time to see him come into my line of sight. His arms were crossed, his eyes narrowed. "Why." It wasn't a question as much as a demand.

"I just . . . I need to see if I have any, um, personal hygiene things."

His eyebrows lifted as he watched me silently, his eyes dropping to slowly take in every inch of me, his gaze pausing somewhere on my legs, his brow creasing. I looked down to see what he was staring at, not noticing anything, and by the time I looked back up, his face was wiped clean of whatever I'd seen there. Then he turned on his heel and was back a second later, my brown leather messenger bag in his outstretched hand.

"Thank you." I grabbed it from him, then shut the door again and rummaged around inside, hoping I'd somehow slipped something in here at one point and forgotten about it. But I wasn't that girl. I'd never been that girl—the one who carried a tote bag full of makeup and hair spray and glittery body lotion and whatever else girls lugged around with them when they were concerned about their appearance. It'd never been an issue for me, so why should I bother?

Except now I was wishing I had, because all I had inside here were two textbooks, the paperback I was reading, some pens, and a handful of loose papers. Ghost must've taken my laptop and phone out of here and either tossed them somewhere or kept them hidden from me. I knew a laptop wouldn't help me now, but I would've given anything to get my hands on my phone. Just to call home once . . . I sighed and closed the flap of my bag, knowing I'd have to ask for help again and hating every minute of it.

Setting the bag down by the door, I cracked it open again. More tentatively than last time, I said, "Ghost? Are there . . . I mean, is there anything I can use here?"

"Like what."

"A comb? And maybe a toothbrush?"

He pushed off the wall across from the bathroom and pressed his hand against the door before pushing his way past me and into the small room. I stepped to the side and watched as he reached above the stacked washer and dryer and pulled down a plastic bag. He rummaged around inside, and then handed it over to me before leaving without a word, shutting the door behind him.

I stared at the wood of the closed door, the bag hanging from my fingers. I didn't understand him. I didn't understand this whole situation. But something had changed since my first night here. I knew I wasn't in a good place, but I no longer feared for my life.

After closing the lid on the toilet seat, I sat down and propped the bag in my lap. There wasn't much inside, but there was enough. Travel-sized items—toothpaste, deodorant, shampoo and conditioner—plus a comb, toothbrush, and . . . tampons? I grabbed the pink box, and despite how hard I tried to imagine Ghost buying them, I couldn't form a mental image of it. I glanced up and looked at the door, wishing there was a two-way mirror in here just so I could watch him without him being aware, because none of this made sense. *He* didn't make sense.

I couldn't stop a thousand questions from popping into my head. When had he gotten these things? And why? Were they for me, or were they here from some other time . . . some other kidnapping? And what kind of person kidnapped people for a living? Did he do it for ransom, or was he some kind of hired hitman?

Almost as soon as the second possibility popped into my head, I discarded it. Something in my gut told me this wasn't a man who killed for money. Maybe it was his quiet reassurances, the hints of softness that I'd caught glimpses of, or simply an unexplainable inner knowing, but I knew Ghost wasn't a killer.

After I'd combed out my hair and brushed my teeth, I felt more human. More human, but still scared, uncertain, nervous. More than anything, though, I was confused, and it was a welcome relief from the all-consuming terror that had been taking over every bit of rational thought I had.

Tentatively, I slipped out of the bathroom and stepped down the hallway into the main room. Ghost was in the kitchen, slapping some deli meat on a couple pieces of bread. He glanced up, his eyes roving over me quickly before he looked back at his sandwich.

I tugged at the T-shirt he'd lent me, attempting to pull it away from the swell of my hips. Then I crossed my arms against my chest, overwhelmingly aware of the fact that I wasn't wearing a bra.

"I wasn't sure you'd feel up to eating after your migraine."

"Um, yeah, I could eat. Something light, though."

"Knock yourself out." He gestured to the space around him, and I walked that way, sliding my eyes to him every once in a while.

I pulled a paper plate from the stack on the counter, then took two pieces of bread from the bag. Glancing around, I hoped to find a toaster but didn't see one. "Is there a toaster here?"

"Yeah."

Before I could move, before I could even take half a step back, he was there, his whole body eclipsing everything in my sight. He towered over me as he reached around me to the cabinet above my head, his arm grazing my breast as he did, and everything in me stilled. I froze, my breath caught in my throat, but I wasn't scared. This wasn't the same feeling I'd had the first time he'd towered over me when he'd cut my bindings. No, this was something else entirely. Despite my brain firing off warnings that I should be scared, should be terrified by this man who'd less than twenty-four hours ago carried me back here against my will—*again*—my body reacted all on its own. Goose bumps erupted on my arms and my nipples hardened, and what the *hell* was that about?

Unaware of the war raging inside my head, he pulled the toaster out and set it on the counter. Then, as if he realized how close he was, his eyes darted to mine, then lower, and I felt utterly naked under his stare. When his eyes met mine again, his gaze was penetrating and heavy.

Almost as quickly as the entire thing happened, the moment was over. Ghost broke eye contact and stepped away from me, grabbing his plate before settling in at the small dining table.

But I was still frozen, barely breathing, in the aftermath. It was nothing, really, nothing but an accidental brush of his forearm against my breast, but just as with lying in the bed together, it *felt* different. It felt like something more.

And that scared me almost more than anything.

I'd been down this road before, feeling things I shouldn't have for a man I shouldn't have felt them for. I'd been here, in a passive position where I fell for the guy who was all wrong for me, who I *shouldn't* be with, but despite my instincts screaming at me that it had been a bad idea, I'd leapt anyway. And I'd gotten burned.

I wasn't about to allow that to happen again. And certainly not with the man who was my captor.

GHOST

I devoured my sandwich while Madison made her toast. She was flustered, her cheeks pink and her hands shaky as she spread peanut butter on the bread. All from a brush of my arm against her. At first, I took her reaction for fear, considering the situation. But after I looked closer, I realized it wasn't fear at all that was making her breath come quickly. It wasn't fear causing goose bumps to pop up all over her arms. And it sure as shit wasn't fear making her nipples hard.

She inched her way toward me, my clothes showing off more of her than she had yet . . . probably more than she was comfortable with. And for once, as I swept my eyes leisurely along every bit of her body, I didn't fight it. Finally—*finally*—I allowed myself to look. She was tall—taller than average, anyway, probably only a head shorter than my 6'3". And she was . . . lush. That was the only word I could think of to describe her. Despite being in my clothes, they pulled tight across her tits, and the shorts clung to her ass. She wasn't frail, all skin and bones. She had the kind of body women hated and men wanted, all creamy white skin covering curves made to be gripped. She looked like the kind of woman I'd fantasized about when I was a thirteen-year-old, jacking it to dirty magazines.

It was a testament to my rules for a job that I hadn't allowed myself to truly focus on her until now, because Madison Frost had the kind of body that got me going every time.

Before she sat down, I lowered my gaze to take in her exposed legs, my eyes narrowing once again at the massive bruises covering both her knees. The right was harsher, more prominent, but they were both noticeable, especially against her pale skin. Unless she'd fallen hard in the cabin the couple times I was outside, those hadn't happened while she was here. And I wanted to know what the fuck they were from, if maybe she was getting pushed around at school or at home. The thought had me clenching my jaw, anger boiling up in me. Yeah, I pushed people around for a living, taught them lessons that sometimes had to come by way of my fists, but not a woman. *Never* a woman.

When I raised my eyes, she was staring at me, uncertainty showing on her face; I'd let my anger bleed through to the outside and show in my expression. I grabbed the last bit of my sandwich and took a bite, then said, "What happened?"

Her eyes widened. "Wha-what do you mean?"

I tipped my head toward her legs. "To your knees. What happened."

Her brow creased as she glanced down. "Oh." She extended her right leg out to get a better view of the bruise, then she shrugged. "Nothing."

Sitting back in my chair, I crossed my arms and continued to stare at her. I wasn't new at this game, getting people to do what I wanted, and everything about what we were doing was new territory for her. She'd break eventually.

"It's not a big deal," she mumbled around a bite of her toast.

I continued my silence, knowing it was the best way to fluster her. She'd work to fill in the quiet when she got uncomfortable enough, and judging from the way she shifted restlessly in her seat, that was going to be any minute.

"It's really not. I just slipped."

"Slipped, huh? Did anyone 'help' you slip?"

"Help me sl— Oh, you mean push me? No, nothing like that."

"Where'd it happen?"

Her eyes lifted to connect with mine for a second, then she lowered her gaze to her plate once again, still not saying anything.

"If it's not a big deal, why can't you just tell me what the fuck happened?"

"Because it didn't happen here, and you have no need to know anything else about my life." Her tone was clipped and haughty, and I smiled at her ignorance.

"Princess, I know *everything* about your life."

She snapped her head up, her eyes wide, lips parted. She was panicked, nearly more so than I'd ever seen her, and that was saying a lot, all things considered. What secrets was this girl hiding?

"No you don't." But she didn't even believe the words she was saying. Her voice was shaky, her tone lacking conviction.

"Try me."

"What?"

"Ask me something about your life. We'll see if I know it."

Staring at me for a moment, she picked at her toast, never taking another bite. "Okay, um, what'd I get on my SATs?"

"Math, Reading, or Writing?" I asked with a raised eyebrow.

Her eyes widened slightly. "All of them."

"750, 780, 770, respectively."

She swallowed, never dropping her gaze from mine. "Who's our driver and when does he show up to get me?"

"Ronald, and he's there every day, twenty minutes before you're due to meet him. And, yes, he was waiting for you Thursday night. C'mon, you can do better than that. Something a bit more personal, maybe?"

"When did I get accepted into Northwestern?"

I shook my head. "That's not personal. And I have a better question for you. Why did you only apply to Northwestern? Smart girl like you . . . seems like you'd have tried for Harvard or Stanford . . . Princeton or Yale, maybe. Or, hell, all of them. And yet you sent off one little application. That's it."

Her eyes grew wider with each word I spoke until she looked like she was ready to bolt at any minute. Instead, she shot another question to me. "When did I begin seeing my tutor in high school?"

I leaned forward and rested my elbows on the table, my eyebrows shooting up. I didn't even care that it was obviously a diversion to get me focused on something else, because this . . . this I hadn't expected. "You dated your tutor? How old was he?"

She relaxed back in her chair, her shoulders slumping as she exhaled. "Dating isn't exactly the right word. And does it matter?"

"Fuck yeah, it matters. How old were you? Fifteen? Sixteen?"

"Sixteen. Barely."

"And he was?"

"I don't know. Twenty, I'd guess. Twenty-one, maybe."

"Jesus Christ. Your parents let that go on?"

She blew out a disbelieving laugh and shook her head. "See, you don't know everything there is to know about my life. If you did, you'd realize what a stupid question that is."

"Oh, yeah? Why's that?"

"Because my parents haven't been involved in my life in a very, very long time. If anyone's looking after anyone, it's the other way around. At least with my mother." She averted her eyes and pressed her lips together, as if she could keep the words trapped inside through sheer force.

"What about your mother? From everything I learned, she's the picture-perfect North Shore housewife."

"Well, at least it's working," she mumbled.

"What's working?"

"The lies and elaborate tales we weave to keep people from knowing what's truly going on in our house." She stared straight at me as she said it, her voice hard but monotone, and it only served to stoke my curiosity.

I knew I had to play this casual if I was going to get her to talk, that intimidating her into telling me wasn't going to work. I relaxed back into my chair and propped my ankle on my opposite knee. "So what's her deal?"

She shook her head, staring back at her half-eaten toast again. "Nothing anyone else has to worry about."

"No one else but you, right?"

She lifted her eyes to look at me again, a thousand questions swirling there.

"Yeah, I know what it's like. I mean, I've never lived in a fucking mansion, but I know what it's like to be dealt a shitty hand in the family department."

"How so?"

"Ah ah, tit for tat, princess. If I tell you, I expect the same."

Chapter Sixteen

MADISON

I let his words sink in as I studied him. Then, before I could second-guess myself, I gave a subtle nod, and the corner of his mouth twitched.

"I'm holding you to that."

My back straightened, my ire igniting. "I'm not a liar. If I said I'd do it, I'll do it." My voice was harsh, harsher than I'd used yet, and he drew back, his eyebrows raised. I held his stare, even though I had to clasp my hands together to keep them from shaking.

"Yeah, well, it's just me and my brother now, but when I was younger, there were a lot of years of hell. Never knew my dad—or even if my brother and I have the same one—and my mom was a junkie. She'd been hooked on heroin for as long as I could remember. Riley's only a year younger than me, and when I was four, I was already taking care of him. We'd crash a lot at friends' houses because whenever we'd get a place of our own, we'd get evicted before too long. While our mom was strung out, I made sure Riley was fed. That we went to school when we could. It got harder the older we were, especially when I could do something to get us out of the situation we were in."

His life, everything he was telling me, was just like the scenario I'd think about every morning when I'd wake up hating my life. Ghost was living that—or a version of it—and he wasn't doing it in one of Chicago's most affluent suburbs. He wasn't doing it with a staff of people at his disposal or unlimited funds in his checking account to help him. He'd been all on his own, with a younger sibling to look after on top of it. "Is that why you"—my voice was shaky and I cleared my throat and tried again—"why you do . . . this?"

"When you've got no roof over your head and you find your mom dead with the needle still sticking in her vein, you find you'll do a lot of shit you might not otherwise."

His words conjured a picture up in my mind, and I saw the entire scene—a frail woman, skin and bones, sprawled out on a stained couch in a dirty, dark apartment somewhere, and Ghost finding her, syringe hanging from her arm. And then suddenly it morphed into what I'd seen a few mornings ago, finding my own mother on the floor of the bathroom. Of the dozens of times I'd found her in similar states. Those initial moments of panic where I'd thought that was it—she was dead and gone, and every time, I'd been simultaneously devastated and relieved. What kind of person did that make me? To be relieved at the thought of her mother's death?

Had it been the same for him? Had he felt overwhelming relief that his responsibility was no longer weighing him down, holding him captive?

I swallowed, looking down as I picked at my toast. "My mom's an alcoholic. And sometimes, when that's not enough, she throws prescription pills in the mix. I check on her every morning to make sure she's still breathing. The day"—I lifted my eyes to his briefly, then glanced back down at my uneaten toast—"you took me, I found her that morning crumpled on the floor of her bathroom with a huge gash on her forehead. I checked on her before my first class. I thought she was dead. The bathtub had overflowed, and I slipped trying to get to her, landed hard on my knees. Marble's pretty unforgiving. That's what the bruises are from."

"Why didn't your dad find her before he left for work?"

"Because that would mean he'd have to pay attention to his family. My dad hasn't been a father to me in a very long time, and he certainly hasn't been a husband to my mother."

"So it gets piled on your shoulders."

I looked at him, allowed myself to truly look at him for the first time. There was something different in his icy blue gaze, something that looked like respect. I'd never had friends growing up, and I'd certainly never had someone who could empathize with me. Even Sylvia, though she meant well and she had my best interests at heart, didn't truly know what it was like to have this burden placed on your shoulders. But Ghost did.

He did. He knew. He knew the hope and the dread and the overwhelming guilt at wanting something else, at yearning for something more. And even though we'd come from two different paths, at the core, we still dealt with the same pain.

And that bit of information tied us together in a way I'd never expected.

GHOST

With her arms wrapped around her stomach, she looked at me with wide eyes, almost as if she were seeing me for the first time. I'd shared one of the worst stories of my life, and yet she was looking at me like I was more than just the kid of a junkie, more than just someone who'd been cast aside. And I couldn't deny that a part of me—a bigger part than was probably good—liked it.

"Sounds like we've both had shitty home lives."

"Yeah . . ." She held my gaze for a moment, then turned to look out the window over the sink. "How old were you when your mom died?"

"Fifteen."

"So young . . . What did you do?"

I shrugged. "I did what I had to. Riley and I stayed with friends, couch hopping for a while. I dropped out of high school, started doing some shit to make enough so he didn't have to drop out, too. In the end it didn't matter, though. I had to look into other things to make ends meet, and though he graduated—barely—he's mixed up in it now, too." The thought had my jaw clenching, how hard I'd worked to get us both out—and how I'd failed.

"Other things like . . . kidnapping?"

I leveled her with a stare. While I did a lot of shit I should be ashamed of, I did it because I got paid, because I had myself and my brother to take care of, and I wouldn't apologize for that. I did what I had to, but I did it for someone else. These were never my plans I was carrying out. As much control as I had over a situation, deciding what jobs I wanted to take, in the end I was just a puppet, nothing more. "For hire, yeah."

"What else do you do? Besides kidnapping, I mean."

"Whatever I need to."

"You'd . . . you'd kill someone?"

"If it was my life or theirs, fuck yeah, I'd kill them."

She was looking directly at me, her eyes curious but with a surprising lack of fear. Then she leaned forward with a shake of her head. "I don't believe you."

"Excuse me?"

She shrugged. "I don't believe you—that you'd kill someone."

I cracked my knuckles one by one, then rested my elbows on the table. "And why wouldn't you believe me?"

"I just don't."

"You don't *just* anything, Madison. You've got a brain in that pretty little head of yours, and you're always using it. Now why not?" I asked as I leaned toward her.

Her gaze dropped to my arms, her eyes roving over my biceps for a moment, lips parting, before she snapped out of it and met my stare. "I think you put up a front. A façade."

I raised an eyebrow.

"But you're not an evil person," she continued. Her voice was stronger than I'd ever heard it, and listening to her defend me, even to myself, was something I hadn't counted on. I hadn't counted on my reaction, either, on the warmth that spread through my chest with each word. "You've hurt people, I have no doubt of that. But if you were truly evil, if you were truly a killer, you wouldn't have removed my restraints when I had my migraine. And you wouldn't have cleaned up after me. Or gotten me my medicine. Or kept the washcloth warm on my forehead. Or made sure I had basic necessities." She swallowed and matched my posture, elbows on the table, leaning toward me. "And you wouldn't have reassured me that I was safe here. With you." She lowered her voice, murmured words between us. "You wanna know what I think? I think underneath all that muscle, you have a heart. You just don't want anyone to know it."

She was perceptive, just like I knew she'd be. And knowing she saw more of me than I wanted her to should've had me locking shit up tight again, checking my actions. But it didn't.

With my voice just a low rumble, I said, "You know better than anyone that people aren't always what they seem. There's more than what you see at first glance."

"Most people don't look at me long enough to see more than what I allow them to see."

I locked eyes with her, seeing more in her gaze than I'd allowed

myself to before. Seeing someone who carried a lot of the same bag-
gage I did. "Looks like we've got another thing in common."

MADISON

"Are you going to eat the rest of your toast?" Ghost asked after
several minutes of silence.

I glanced down at my forgotten food, not as hungry as I thought
I was. I meant every word I'd said to him—yet he still didn't make
sense to me, not even a little bit.

Without warning, he stood from the table and grabbed both our
plates. After dumping them in the trash and cleaning up the kitchen,
he walked toward me and leaned against the wall behind his chair.

"We've got some issues we need to discuss."

His voice had gone hard, stern, and I swallowed as I nodded.

"That stunt you pulled is to never happen again, do you
understand? *Never.*"

"I'm not going to run again."

"Good. That still doesn't change the fact that you did, and
now shit has to change."

"Like what?"

"You've got a couple options. I can restrain you again. The
only time I'll relieve you of the bindings is to use the bathroom
or shower."

I didn't want to be tied up again—didn't want that ever-
present feeling of incapacity, of vulnerability—and would do just
about anything to avoid that. "And the other?"

"You never leave my sight."

"I never leave your sight now."

He shook his head, pushing off the wall and gripping the back
of the chair as he leaned toward me, the muscles in his arms flexing
and reminding me exactly how strong he was, exactly who I was up
against. "This is different. If you need to use the bathroom, I'll be
standing right outside. If you're hungry, we're both in the kitchen.

When you sleep, I'll be right next to you. You go nowhere without me, and vice versa. We'd be attached at the fucking hip."

I swallowed, worried about what that would mean. Not just for lack of privacy, but what it would mean based on my reactions to him so far. I didn't know if I could push it. If I *should* push it. But I knew I wasn't going to allow myself back in those ropes. Not if I had the ability to stay free of them.

I gave a subtle nod. "Okay."

"Which one, Madison?"

"I don't want to be bound again."

He stared at me for a moment, then pulled out the chair and sat again. He contemplated me, his head tilted to the side ever so slightly, and I shifted under his gaze. It was quiet for a long time, so quiet that when he did finally speak again, I startled.

"Why did you?"

"Why did I what?"

"Run."

With my brow furrowed, I regarded him. "Why wouldn't I?"

"Even after I told you there wasn't anything close? Even after I told you it was thirty minutes by car to the nearest town?"

"Even then. I was more scared of what was waiting for me here than I was of what was outside."

"And now . . . you're not going to try anything stupid like that again, correct?"

I opened my mouth to answer but found I couldn't. While I didn't have the bone-deep fear of Ghost I'd once had, the truth was I still didn't know what was waiting for me at the end of my time here. I didn't know who the man was who'd come to the cabin; I didn't know who'd hired Ghost to do this or why they had. And not knowing all those things terrified me.

"Correct?" he asked again, his voice deeper, more commanding now.

I nodded my head, but I doubted either one of us believed it.

Chapter Seventeen

There wasn't much to do in the cabin. There was no TV, no radio. I didn't have access to my phone or my laptop, and I was going a bit stir crazy. I needed to keep my mind active at all times, so after half an hour of doing nothing, I asked Ghost if I could get my book from my bag.

True to his word, he followed right behind me while I retrieved it, then joined me on the couch when I sat down. He'd grabbed a sketchbook and a pencil and was drawing something now. His right leg was crossed, his ankle propped up on his left knee, and with the way he had the paper angled on his leg, I couldn't see what he was working on.

And I tried.

While I pretended to read the book I'd already read nearly ten times before, I was actually spending more time trying to sneak a peek at what he was doing instead of the words on the page.

"I'll just show you, you know."

My head snapped up, my focus moving from the back of his sketch pad to his face, my eyes wide. He wasn't looking at me, though. His head was still tilted down as he watched the lines his pencil made across the paper. I opened and closed my mouth to say something but found I was at a loss for words. Eventually, he lifted his head enough to peek at me, then he tilted the paper in my direction.

And it . . . was not at all what I'd expected.

Where I'd assumed he'd be creating something dark—skulls or guns or garbage-littered back alleys—it was none of those things. Instead it was the view out the back window. The snow-laden trees, the frosted-over pond, the acres of wilderness. I stared at the paper, then turned to look out at the view beyond the panes of glass. It was a near-perfect replica, yet I hadn't seen him look up even once since he'd started drawing.

"That's . . . amazing."

He tipped his head in my direction, the only acknowledgment of my words he gave, then went back to the paper.

"You're really good. How long have you drawn for?"

"As long as I can remember. I don't get a lot of time to do it, but there's nothing else to do out here."

"Do you only do landscapes?"

"Nah, I can do just about anything."

"Even people?"

"Especially people."

I didn't understand why someone with his talent—and it truly was a talent—would waste it on the life he'd chosen. "Why didn't you go to an art school or something?"

He snorted, his focus still on the drawing. "You heard when I said I dropped out of high school, right?"

"Yeah, but there are ways around that. You could get your GED. You could do something with your life besides"—I paused and gestured around us—"*this*. You could still do it now."

"And who would pay for that? We're not all like you, princess. We don't all have a daddy footing the bill to a fifty-something thousand dollar a year school."

"But . . . but there are scholarships. And financial aid."

"So I can draw pretty pictures? C'mon, princess, you're smarter than that. You think I can keep a roof over my head and food on the table with this?" He waved his sketchbook in the air with a mocking glint in his eyes.

I shrugged. "Maybe. There are a lot of people who support themselves through creative pursuits."

He just shook his head and went back to his work. As I watched him, I couldn't reconcile his stance with my own desire to do *anything* but be stuck where I was. "So this is all you want?"

He looked up at me, his eyes boring into mine, and I couldn't look away. There was so much in his gaze. Pride and stubbornness and determination, but there was pain there, too. And the barest flicker of regret.

"Maybe not, but it's all I deserve."

GHOST

And that was what it all boiled down to. I'd done a lot of shit in my life . . . a lot of shit most people would be ashamed of. And the truth of it was, I wasn't.

Or I hadn't been.

But ever since I'd taken this job, ever since I'd gone against every instinct I had and accepted this kidnapping, witnessed the terror on Madison's face, I was wondering what the fuck I was doing. What kind of screwed-up life I'd made for myself. But not just for me—for my brother, too. Why I hadn't pushed for something more. And deep down, I knew the reason I didn't strive for any of that was exactly what I'd told her. After everything I'd done in my life—things she'd be horrified to learn about—I didn't deserve it.

Rather than ask more about that, rather than give me bullshit reassurances, she looked down, focusing once again on my sketch pad. "Is that full of your drawings?"

"Yeah."

She shifted on the couch, turning toward me, her left leg bent and tucked under her. "Could I look through them?"

"That depends. Are you going to spout off about how I should be in college doing this when you're done?"

"Not if you don't want me to."

I nodded, then mimicked her position on the couch, turning toward her, and handed over the sketch pad. While it wasn't something I intentionally hid from people, the fact was, no one ever knew me well enough to want to see any of my drawings. My brother was the only one who knew I sketched. I didn't mind her looking at it—there wasn't anything groundbreaking or personal inside there.

And the truth was, I wanted to see her reaction.

I studied her as she flipped to the front of the sketchbook, then took her time as she turned each page. Studied every drawing. Her eyes were wide, full of . . . wonder, maybe? Full of something I wasn't used to seeing from anyone. And definitely not something directed at me.

About halfway through, she lifted her head and smiled while she turned the pad toward me to show me whatever she was looking at. But I couldn't look at the drawing she was showing me, because I realized this was the first time I'd ever seen Madison smile. Ever. Not just since she'd been here, but in every picture I had in her file, in every instance I'd seen of her prior to the capture, this was the first time the corners of her mouth had lifted up, the first time her eyes had brightened.

"—really like this one. Do you always re-create what you see, or do you freehand sometimes?"

Finally, I glanced down at the drawing she was referring to. It was one I'd done a few months back, a view of the Chicago skyline. "I can do both, but I generally draw what I see."

She accepted my answer with a small nod, then continued slowly flipping through the book, her attention entirely captured.

Rather than watching what she was looking at, I was looking at her, studying her reactions, hoping I'd see another one of those rare smiles. Instead, after a few minutes, I got a sharp gasp and wide eyes as her hand flew to her throat.

Even though I'd drawn it not long ago, I'd forgotten it was in there. Or maybe on some level I just didn't care if she saw it. Maybe I wanted her to.

She didn't look up, didn't glance at me, didn't take her eyes away from the page in front of her. Tentatively, she reached out and traced something on the paper as she exhaled a deep breath.

When she spoke, it was so quiet, I wasn't sure it was actually meant for me. "This is how you see me?"

I glanced at the paper, at what I could see of it, then back to her face. She was still completely focused on the drawing. "That's how you *are*, Madison. How else would I see you?"

MADISON

His words, while sweet, weren't true. They couldn't be. Because the girl—the *woman*—he'd drawn was . . . breathtaking. And breathtaking wasn't anything I'd ever imagined myself as. Not by any stretch of the imagination. But in this drawing . . . on this piece of paper, recorded permanently, I was.

The sketch must've been done when we'd first sat down. In it, my head was bowed, my eyes focused on the book in my hand I'd been pretending to read. He'd drawn everything—from the window behind me to the couch I was sitting on, from the top of my head straight down to my toes—like he'd taken a snapshot of the scene. My hair, which I always thought was limp and flat, cascaded over my shoulders, a few strands resting against the curve of my breast. He'd lessened the roundness of my face, instead playing up the fullness of my lips and the subtle slope of my nose. My body, curled into itself, my legs tucked beneath me as I'd leaned against the arm of the couch, was a beautiful blend of soft edges and sensuous curves. Nothing at all like the inches upon extra inches I wished away every time I looked in a mirror.

I shook my head, still not believing it, still not believing someone could see me like this. That maybe I *was* like this, despite what I saw every time I caught a glimpse of myself.

"Someone sure did a number on you." His voice snapped me out of my trance, and I looked over at him, eyebrows lifted in question. He extended his arm toward me, resting it on the back of the couch. "I already told you, I draw best when I sketch what I see. That isn't fabricated. Yet you're looking at it like you've never seen that girl before."

"That's because I haven't."

He stared at me for a moment, his eyes taking a path down my body that would usually make me squirm with unease. This time, though, it made me squirm for another reason altogether. Knowing what he saw when he looked at me, knowing he was seeing it *right now*, sent shivers up my spine, had a tingle growing low in my belly.

Finally, his eyes rested on mine once again. "So who was it?"

With my brow furrowed, I asked, "Who was what?"

"The asshole or assholes who made you think that about yourself?"

I huffed out a disbelieving laugh, shaking my head. "Who *wasn't* it?" Shrugging, I continued, "Kids are cruel. Being younger and smarter and richer than them made for some vicious playground taunts."

He nodded. "Yeah, maybe, I can see that. But what about when you got older? When you were homeschooled and not subject to the playground taunts? Didn't your parents work to change that?"

"I already told you . . . my parents didn't put a lot of effort into parenting me. As long as they could tote me around to the right functions and I didn't cause trouble, they didn't want to be bothered."

"Fine, what about that guy you were seeing?"

I shook my head, thinking back to Marc. The only thing he'd been interested in was being the first person to get in my pants, and my insecurity had only played into that. He'd filled a void. I'd been lonely, and he'd used that to his advantage. "Whispering sweet nothings wasn't exactly his style." I shrugged. "I guess when something's been burned into your brain enough, it's what you start to believe—it's all you see."

"Well, it might be all you see, but it's not what you are."

Chapter Eighteen

I awoke to rare rays of sunshine streaming in through the window. Blinking against the brightness, I lifted my head and realized I was still on the couch, curled up against the far end. I glanced to my left and saw Ghost still sleeping. I knew I had only minutes, probably, before he'd wake up, and I wanted to study him without his ever-watchful eyes on me. Especially after what had transpired yesterday. The entirety of the day had been confusing on levels I hadn't yet experienced—from him taking care of me when I had my migraine, to his confession about his mother, and finally to the drawing he'd done of me. I'd spent the rest of the evening with my stomach in knots, my palms sweaty. He'd been so fervent, it was hard not to believe his words.

Between what he'd said and the way he'd been acting, I was on a slippery slope. Yesterday, it'd been easy to forget I was being held captive when it was just the two of us here. When we were talking or reading side by side. It was like we were safe in our own little bubble, and it was effortless to pretend this was something else. That I could *allow* it to be something else.

But the truth of it was, I *was* being held captive. I was here against my will, and despite the fact that his orders came from someone else, despite there being a bigger bad than he was, Ghost was the one who put me here . . . the one who kept me here.

I studied him now, surreptitiously. The back of his head rested against the top of the couch cushion, and his face was turned slightly toward me, his legs sprawled out in front of him, feet resting flat on the floor. His arms were, as always, crossed, the pronounced curve of his biceps stark against the black of his shirt. Seeing him like this, so closed off . . . it was like he always kept his guard up, even in his sleep. But his face . . . his face was smooth and free of the hardness that was usually there.

I took in the wide breadth of his shoulders and the black wisps of ink that spilled over the top of his collar, pointing the way to his jaw. Where it had initially only held the barest hint of stubble, now it was scruffy, covered with several days' worth of growth. His full lips were parted, his nose crooked, his too-long, dark eyelashes out of place on his rugged face. But the scar cutting through his eyebrow fit right in.

I didn't know if it was because he wasn't awake and aware right now, able to put up that shield he always had, or if it was because of what I'd learned about him over the past few days or because of how he made me feel yesterday . . . Or maybe it was a combination of it all, but he looked different to me now than he had the first time he'd stepped out of the shadows, when all I'd seen was a criminal. Now I knew there was so much more to Ghost than met the eye.

And that fact both scared and delighted me.

While he was the one holding me, he wasn't the one behind this kidnapping, that much I was sure of. There was someone else behind the scenes pulling the strings, and I wanted to know why. I wanted to know *who*. I wanted to know what that person wanted me for, why I'd been kidnapped. If it was for ransom or blackmail or something else entirely. Ghost said he didn't know, that he just

did what he was paid to, but I wondered how true that was. He
didn't seem like the kind of guy to jump blindly into anything,
and I couldn't imagine he'd done that with this job.

I shifted on the couch, trying to work out the kink in my
neck, and just like I'd assumed, Ghost's body stiffened right before his eyes snapped open. They sought me out immediately, blue
ice looking straight through me—*seeing* me—and I couldn't look
away. I'd never been close enough with anyone to wake up next to
them, and despite the situation, despite how wrong it should have
felt, it made my stomach twist in knots. And it wasn't anxiety doing the twisting.

His eyes never left mine, and the silence was killing me. I
shifted uncomfortably and said, "Sorry I fell asleep down here."

Finally, he broke the stare and shrugged as he lifted his arms
over his head to stretch much like I had. I stared at him, completely
riveted by the strength shown in his body, the muscles flexing in his
arms . . . the sliver of stomach peeking out where his shirt rode up.

Snapping my eyes away, I stood quickly—too quickly, because
the blood rushed to my head, and I had to rest it on my hand and
close my eyes for a moment.

"You okay?"

"Um, yeah. Fine. I need to use the restroom." I avoided looking at him, keeping my eyes locked on the hallway beyond us, but
I could still see him in my peripheral vision. He pushed himself
off the couch, then walked ahead of me down the hall, stopping
just outside the door.

Keeping my head down, I allowed my hair to provide a cur-
tain of separation between us as I walked in, then turned around to
shut the door behind me. I glanced up just before it was latched
and caught his eyes for the briefest moment. And even in that barest instance, butterflies erupted in my stomach.

Once I was safe in the enclosed space, I turned on the light as
well as the fan. I didn't care how little privacy it actually provided

me. I needed space to breathe and being able to hear every move of his body on the other side of the door wasn't going to help.

I walked over to the sink and braced my hands there as I stared at myself in the mirror. What the hell was I getting myself into? This unwavering pull I felt toward him was only because of the circumstances. It was a product of the environment I was in and nothing more. We didn't fit, didn't mesh. We came from two very different places and barely had anything in common. It was *wrong*, this attraction I felt toward him.

But the more I repeated those things to myself, the less I believed them.

GHOST

I was dead fucking tired. I leaned my head against the wall as I stood outside in the hallway, waiting for Madison to finish up whatever she needed to do. In my line of work, I was used to getting by on little sleep, but the events of the last four weeks were wearing me down. And only a couple hours of shitty sleep on an uncomfortable couch didn't help on top of everything else.

After Madison had fallen asleep, I'd waited an hour to make sure she was out before I double-checked the locks, then did the shit I needed to that I couldn't while being attached to her hip— showered, made calls to everyone I needed to for check-in, dug for any new information on what was going to happen in the next week. And the fact that there weren't solid plans in place brought up about a dozen red flags in my mind. I didn't know if it was because I wasn't used to working a job I hadn't planned out to the minute or if it was something else altogether. Whatever it was, I didn't like it. And it was making me tense.

Add that in with the fact that I'd spilled my fucking guts to Madison yesterday, not to mention our exchange over my drawing of her, and I was testy and on edge. I didn't know what had compelled me to tell her all that. My past wasn't something I shared freely with people, and certainly not with a mark. But I'd wanted to know about her mother, and I figured that was the easiest, surest way to get her to spill.

And as much as I didn't want to admit it, the truth was I was starting to look at her as something more than just a mark. I'd *been* looking at her as something more. If I was honest, I'd never looked at her as a captive—how could I when the people I was used to holding were hardened men who'd done everything in their power to scam the system, to cheat and steal and lie . . . kill, sometimes.

There was something different about the way she looked at me after I told her about my past, too. Something I hadn't seen before. And though she'd been fighting it ever since, it was still there, hiding in the depths of those green eyes. I saw it in the way she averted her gaze quickly, the way she kept herself as far away from me as possible. She was interested, despite attempting to deny it . . . to avoid it. Her body, without question, was interested.

I just didn't know what would come of it. If I should *allow* anything to come of it.

The fan shut off right before the door swung open, and she stood in the threshold, her eyes tentative as she appraised me. "Is it okay if I use the washing machine? I forgot to put my clothes in yesterday."

With a nod, I said, "Go for it. Soap's on top."

"Thank you."

After turning around and heading back in the bathroom, she shut the door enough to get to the machine situated behind it. Her clothes were still in there from when she'd had her migraine yesterday morning. It was only a second later that I heard the rush of water and then the clank of the lid closing. When she came back into the doorway, she was tentative all over again, and I didn't know why.

"Your head hurt again?"

She glanced up at me in confusion. "What?"

"Your migraine. Did it come back?" I darted my eyes to every inch of her face, looking for the tenseness I'd seen there when she'd been suffering from her headache. Her eyes were bright, though, and no creases marred her forehead. Before she answered, I already knew that wasn't what was bothering her.

"Oh, no. It's fine." She didn't elaborate any further, just went to the kitchen to grab a bowl of cereal.

I followed behind her, not even trying to stop my eyes from taking in the curve of her ass as she walked, then glanced at the clock on the microwave, seeing how early it was—not even ten— and cringed. I was getting bored out of my fucking mind out here, and there was no relief in sight. I didn't know how long we'd be stuck out here, and this space was already feeling too small. It wasn't just having nothing to do, it was also being surrounded by Madison with nothing else to occupy my mind. "There's not much to do around here. I could look for some cards or something."

"Oh. Sure." She shifted her spoon around in her bowl, and while her attention was still focused on that, she said, "Do you have my laptop here?"

I raised my eyebrows, wondering where she was going with that. "It's around, yeah."

"Because I have some movies on there we could watch." She glanced up at me. "If you want."

There was no Wi-Fi out here in this godforsaken cabin, and even if she had a hotspot on her phone, she didn't have access to it, so I knew I didn't have to worry about her getting online and sending a message to anyone. I didn't see any reason we couldn't use it. And a movie sounded like fucking heaven after four days of doing nothing but staring at the walls.

"Yeah, I want." I left her standing in the kitchen and went to grab her computer from the safe inside the hall closet. Carrying it with me, I got back in the kitchen just as she was putting her bowl in the sink.

"You want to do it down here or in bed?"

She sputtered, choking on the bite of cereal she was still chewing, and spun around to stare at me with wide eyes. "Wha-what?"

I appraised her with a raised eyebrow. Her response definitely set some things straight. She was thinking about things she probably wished she wasn't. Things between the two of us. Instead of pressing her, instead of calling her on it, I said, "I'm not sure how easy it'll be to see it if we're both on the couch without a coffee table or anything to put the laptop on. We could set it up at the foot of the bed, though."

"Oh. Um, sure. Yeah, that's fine."

I nodded, waiting for her to finish up, then walk ahead of me up the stairs. Except as I watched her ass sway in front of my face as she climbed the steps, I wasn't sure this was such a good idea. It was one thing when she was sleeping in the bed and sick with a migraine, three layers of blankets separating us.

It was going to be another thing altogether to both be awake and aware.

And I knew without a doubt I'd be unbelievably aware of her.

Chapter Nineteen

MADISON

He was too close.

This bed was too small, his body overwhelmingly large, and I was focused on the three inches of skin on my arm that his shoulder would brush against with the barest of movements.

I'd barely watched a total of ten minutes of the entire movie, because I couldn't concentrate on anything but him taking up all my space. We were both sitting with our backs propped against the headboard, our legs crossed at the ankles outstretched in front of us. On the foot of the bed, resting between our legs, the laptop sat open and playing one of the handful of movies I had stored on there.

But I wasn't watching. I couldn't watch. I was too busy trying to manage the fluttering in my stomach, trying to get the constant questioning and uncertainty in my head under control. Nothing was working.

I couldn't help it. Puzzles had always kept me captivated, and he was no different. He had my full attention whenever he was within arm's reach. He had my full attention when he was in another room entirely.

While the movie played on in the background I studied him, even with my eyes focused unseeing at the bright screen in front of us. I studied his breaths—low and even. I studied his movements, how he shifted once in a while, uncrossed and recrossed his legs. Reached up to scratch his jaw, the sound of his short nails against the light growth there nearly silent except that it echoed around me as if we were in a cavern.

I was frozen, stock-still, and I could hardly breathe.

I didn't know when I'd gone from feeling nothing but utter terror in his presence to feeling something else entirely, but I had. At some point over the last four days, I had. I'd stopped looking at him as the scary man who'd kidnapped me and started to see him as Ghost. Just Ghost.

Except *Ghost* wasn't who he was anymore. Not to me. Not after the small things he'd done for me—seemingly inconsequential things, but nothing was inconsequential with him. He did everything with purpose. Ghost, in name, was the man who'd brought me here. Ghost was the man who'd lived a hard life and had all the wrong contacts and whose job was outside the law. Ghost wasn't the man who offered me comfort and took care of me when I was sick, who drew pictures of me that made me feel beautiful for the first time in my life.

Before I lost my nerve, I asked, "What's your name?"

He paused for a moment before replying. "Ghost."

I turned my head toward him to find him looking at me, his eyes boring into mine, and it was clear he knew exactly what I was asking. "That's not what I mean, and you know it."

He shook his head and looked back at the movie. "No one's called me that in a long time."

I exhaled a deep sigh and turned away, staring unseeing straight ahead. It wasn't a big deal if he didn't want to tell me his name. It didn't mean anything.

Except it felt like it did.

It made me feel foolish, like this . . . *pull* between us was something one-sided. Was something only I felt. It made me feel like I was sixteen all over again, stumbling headfirst into a situation I wasn't at all prepared to deal with.

"It's Gage."

The soft cadence of his voice rumbled between us, and I snapped my head toward him, finding him already looking at me. I took in everything about him, as if I were seeing him for the first time. His dark hair, piercing blue eyes, full lips, completely imposing presence, and yeah, I could see him as that.

"Hi, Gage."

His lips parted when his name left mine, his eyes dropping to my mouth, and it felt like he'd sucked the air right out of my lungs. Suddenly we were closer than we were a second ago, his shoulder flush against mine, and I let my eyes flutter closed the moment I saw him lean toward me.

In the back of my mind, my conscience was screaming at me, telling me this was a bad idea, I shouldn't be doing this—not with him. But my body had other ideas. My body wanted this, and right now, I was letting that part of me lead.

I met him in the middle, the first brush of our lips tentative. Only a whisper of flesh upon flesh, and when I didn't pull back, he leaned in again, pressing his mouth firmly to mine.

And his kiss . . . his kiss was an unexpected contradiction of the man I'd come to know. The softness of it surprised me, considering the rough edges of *him*. His lips were tentative, questioning in their exploration, and I answered every unasked question, moving with him without hesitation. When my tongue licked against the seam of his lips, he groaned, a deep sound resonating from his chest, and then his hands were on me. He cupped my face, pulling me closer to him as he opened his mouth to me, slid his tongue against mine.

It was everything I'd ever imagined and yet nothing I'd ever

experienced. He was consuming me, every single one of my senses
honing in on him. The scruffy whiskers of his beard were long
enough that they didn't chafe so much as brush softly against me.
His hands were rough, the tips of his fingers marred by calluses
that ran across my cheeks, down my neck. He smelled like fresh
soap and laundry detergent and the scent I'd grown accustomed
to that was all him. Every time a groan echoed in his chest, I felt
it against my own, and I could barely hold in a reply.

And his taste . . . God, the way he tasted. His tongue swept
into my mouth, sliding against mine as he tilted my head so he
could push the kiss deeper, harder.

My hands were still limp at my sides, but I wanted to touch
him. I inched them over toward him as he continued to kiss and
lick, his teeth scraping lightly against my bottom lip. With one
hand, I gripped his arm, feeling his muscles flex with every movement. Reminding me exactly how much power he had behind his
body, yet showing me how gentle he could be. With the other hand,
I reached over until I found his leg, and as soon as my fingers
brushed against his thigh, he stiffened.

But he didn't pull away.

GHOST

I should've stopped this. I should've pulled back, pushed her away,
retreated to the other side of the bed, the other side of the room.
I should've gotten as far away from Madison as I could, because
this wasn't right. *I* wasn't right. Not for her.

I should've done any one of those things, but I didn't.

There was no fucking way I was stopping this. Not unless
she told me to, and based on her reactions, that wasn't anything
she was going to do.

Instead of doing what I should, I gripped her neck harder and
tugged her toward me. I wanted to feel more of her—I needed to—
but I didn't want to push her farther than she was willing to go.

With everything I knew of her, both what I'd learned while here and what I'd come to find before the capture, her experience level was slim to none, but based on what she'd told me yesterday about her tutor, what little she knew about the opposite sex probably wasn't positive.

While I put gentle but constant pressure on her neck to come closer, she didn't shift over. Instead of climbing in my lap like I wanted her to, she just leaned farther into me. I kissed her twice, then pulled back and looked at her to gauge her reaction.

She was breathing heavy, her lips parted and swollen and dark pink. Her cheeks were flushed, her eyes sleepy, and *Christ,* I was harder than I could remember being in a long fucking time. From a *kiss.*

No, not from a kiss. From Madison.

"Do you want to stop?" My voice was like gravel, rough and harsh.

She tilted her head to the side, her brow furrowed. "No, I like this." And I loved the way I made her voice go all throaty and low.

"Why won't you come over here?"

She looked at the nonexistent space between us. "Over where?"

I patted my lap and raised an eyebrow as I tugged on her hand.

"Your lap?"

"My lap. Come on."

With her eyes wide, she didn't move an inch, staying rooted exactly where she was.

"You don't want to? Is it too much?"

"No! No, it's not too much. I just . . . I've never done that. Won't I be too heavy?"

I snorted. "No, you won't be too heavy. Come on."

Tentatively, she moved to her knees, then inched toward me. Her hands were braced on my chest as she lifted a leg over to straddle me, and my dick could've pounded fucking nails right now. It didn't realize there were still layers of clothes between us, but I did. And I wanted nothing more than to rip them away.

She was looking down, her hair falling forward as she moved her knees to either side of my thighs, and I could feel the tension radiating from her. Reaching out, I put my hands on her hips—on the very hips I'd thought were perfect for gripping, and fucking hell, they were. I wanted to feel her skin, to run my hands all over what I had no doubt was creamy, smooth flesh, but that was too much. For her, I knew it was too much. Instead, I settled for holding her as tightly as I dared and feeling those curves under the cover of my clothes.

I curled away from the headboard, coming toward her and capturing her lips again as soon as she looked up. Her fists gripped my shirt and she melted into the kiss, her tongue sliding against mine, but she still held herself rigid above me, not quite resting against my legs.

So I started to explore. I let my hands travel over the arch of her hips, brushing down the expanse of her thighs. I wanted to slide my hands under the hem of her shorts, slip them inside and reach up as far as she'd let me. I knew for a fact she wasn't wearing any underwear, and it was killing me to know just how close I was to feeling her there. Instead, I slid my hands back up on the outside of her shorts, all the way up and over the hills and valleys of her body, stopping just below her tits. And then I did it again. And again. Enough times that she was finally all but boneless in my lap, and that was when I applied enough pressure on her hips to push her down against me fully.

She froze immediately, but I didn't let her get lost in her head. I slid one hand back to cup her ass and pull her even closer while the other went to her neck. I guided her mouth to mine, and she fell into the kiss once again, her hands resting against my chest. Except this time, it was different. It was more. Because she was pressed up against me, with only my sweatpants and the flimsy material of the shorts she was wearing separating us. I could feel the heat from her pussy, and I wanted to feel it without the restriction of clothing. I wanted to touch it, lick it, fuck it, but even as much of a bastard as this make-out session made me, I wasn't enough of one to do that to her. Not to force her into something like that. And I knew that was exactly what it would be.

Because Madison Frost was intelligent and way too fucking good for some asshole like me. She was from the right side of the tracks and I was all wrong, and under normal circumstances, she wouldn't have looked at me twice.

She would have run from me.

Chapter Twenty

MADISON

I was overwhelmed.

This entire thing, everything about it, was overwhelming me. How Gage gripped me, attempting to pull me even closer to him, though I was as close as I could get. How his mouth moved with mine, his lips soft and tender against my own, my jaw, my neck. The way he felt under me . . . and I felt him. All of him.

I was trying my hardest not to feel self-conscious about being on top of him, and he was doing a good job of keeping my mind otherwise occupied. Without thought, I rocked my hips against him, feeling the delicious pressure the hard length of him provided. We both groaned at the first pass, his fingers digging into the flesh of my hips, and I wanted to do it again. Over and over again until this hunger inside of me abated.

I'd never felt anything like this before—nothing as all-consuming as this. With Marc, it had been lackluster at best. He'd used me as a vessel to get off, nothing more, and I'd let him. But this . . . it felt so much different.

It felt like so much more.

Gage was gentle when I needed him to be, showing me a side of him I wasn't sure many people saw—I wasn't sure *anyone* saw. He'd shown me more consideration in four days while being held here than my own family had my entire life.

His hands swept over my body, making passes from my thighs, up over my hips, all the way up to just below my breasts, and despite being nervous, despite knowing this wasn't something we should be doing, I wanted his hands to move up and cup my breasts. I wanted him to brush his thumbs against my nipples. I wanted to feel his mouth on me, and this intoxication he made me feel was frightening. And thrilling.

Gage added pressure to my hips, encouraging me to keep rocking against him. We got into a slow rhythm, my breathing increasing, his hands roaming more. And through it all, I never once wanted to stop him. I never once wanted to pull away, to put my hand against his lips and block his mouth from me, to peel his fingers from my body. I only wanted more.

And I didn't know what kind of person that made me.

Even worse, I didn't care.

A buzzing came from his pocket, vibrating against my leg, and we both pulled away, panting heavily. We stared at each other for a moment, his gaze flitting all over my face before looking into my eyes. He was flushed, his cheeks red, his lips redder, his eyes hooded and sexy, and I didn't know what the hell I was doing.

Gage reached down, shifting me slightly, and pulled out his phone. One glance at the screen and he let out a low curse. He pressed a button on the touch screen to answer and held the phone up to his ear. "Yeah."

I tried to hear the other side of the conversation, but the other voice was low enough that I could only get garbled snippets. Judging from his facial expressions, though, it wasn't a good phone call.

"When?"

His eyes were locked on mine, his gaze so intense I wanted to glance away. I wanted to, but I couldn't. He was looking at me like . . . like he was worried, and that didn't make sense.

"Fuck. Okay. Thanks for the heads-up."

He ended the call without a good-bye and slipped the phone back in his pocket before resting his hands on my hips. Then he stared. He just sat there, unmoving, unspeaking, and the questions bombarding my brain were driving me crazy.

Finally, when I couldn't keep silent any longer, I asked, "Who was that?"

"My brother."

I was shocked he answered so quickly, with no hesitation. His response was so different now than how it had been initially. "Is he . . . does he know about this? I mean, is he working it, too?"

His jaw clenched, his eyes hardening. "Yeah."

I took in his expression, the rigid set of his body, and said, "But you don't want him to be." It wasn't a question, because I already knew the answer. He'd made that much clear when he told me about his past. Gage wanted something better for his brother, but when this was all Riley knew, what else would he do? Gage didn't answer, but I could see the disappointment—that Riley was doing it, and that Gage had led him to it—written all over his face.

"Is something wrong? Is that why he was calling?"

He took a deep breath and shook his head. "I'm not sure yet. Could be."

"What's going on?"

"We're going to have company pretty soon."

I stiffened in his lap. This was everything I'd feared from the very beginning. That some time, at some point, the guy who'd come up to check on me or some other guy, or maybe three other guys, were going to come back and they were going to do things to me— take me somewhere else? Torture me? Beat me or rape me or kill me?—and I wasn't going to be able to stop it.

How would I stop it?

Would Gage help? Or would he stand back and let it happen?

GHOST

Her entire body went rigid the second the words left my mouth, and I wished I could take them back. I wished she didn't have to hear it, but she deserved to know. But what I really wished was that Frankie had made the trip out here hours later, when she was asleep and unaware. But now, after what Riley had told me, shit could get real, and I needed her to be prepared for that. I didn't think Frankie would try anything while I was here, but I couldn't be sure. Riley mentioned Frankie was spouting off about not getting paid. Money made people assholes. And this guy was an asshole to begin with.

I put my hands on her thighs again, running them up and down until a bit of her tension eased. "You don't have anything to worry about."

She let out a huff of air and shook her head. "That's easy for you to say. I'm the one who's been taken to a secluded cabin and held here against my will for four days. There's already been one strange guy here, and now another is coming. What if he's the guy who wants to torture me? Or rape me? Or kill me?" Her voice got higher pitched with each word that left her mouth.

My eyes narrowed, my jaw clenching at her fears. "You think I'd *let* something happen to you? You think I'd let some asshole do that to you? Even after all this?" I gripped her hips tighter, pulled her closer to me so she could feel exactly what she did to me. Even after the phone call and this conversation, I was still hard as hell, and that was all from Madison. She did things to me I hadn't felt in a long time.

"I don't know!" She put her hands against my chest and pushed off, swinging her leg over my lap and climbing off the bed. She walked around it until she was standing with her back to the log railing. "How am I supposed to know? I don't know anything—not where I am, not why I'm here, not why you were hired, not if I'm supposed to be murdered at the end of this or taken out for fucking ice cream! And despite a few kisses from you, I know that holding me—keeping me here—is what you've been *paid* to do. And you told me very early on you did this because of money. What happens if I get in the way of that?"

I opened my mouth to reply, but before I could, the sound of wheels crunching on the gravel road outside sounded. I got off the bed and went straight to the window, pulling the curtains back. A beat-up car came to a halt next to the SUV I'd used to transport Madison up here, and even before Frankie got out, I was walking toward the stairs. "Stay up here," I said over my shoulder.

"What? No, I'm not staying up here."

I stopped at the bottom of the steps, watching her trail me down. "Like hell you aren't. *Stay up there.*"

"*No.*" She crossed her arms, her eyes narrowed at me, and this was definitely a whole new side to Madison Frost.

"Why the hell not?"

"Because I'm trapped up there!"

"Jesus Christ. You're trapped in this whole fucking cabin, Madison. We both are. Now stay the *fuck* in the loft."

She opened her mouth, no doubt to argue, the same time a knock sounded at the door. I stared at her for a moment, but she was unmoving. When a second knock came, I shook my head and pulled the key from my pocket to unlock the dead bolt, and she slipped past me, down the hall toward the main room. I hung my head, gritting my teeth and mumbling under my breath, "Goddammit."

"Ghost! Open the fucking door, man. It's cold as balls out here."

I looked at her over my shoulder, standing still as a statue at the end of the hall. Quietly, I said, "You do not say a word, do you understand? Not a word." Then I slid the key into the lock and opened the door.

"Jesus, man, what took you so fucking long?" He stepped into the cabin before I shut the door behind him, then clapped a hand on my shoulder as he walked past me and down the hallway.

I trailed on his heels, not wanting him out of my sight with Madison in the same space, but she wasn't standing at the end of the hall anymore. It made me uneasy not being able to see her, especially while this sleazy motherfucker was here.

When we got to the main room, I found her sitting at the dining room table, her back ramrod straight, staring wide-eyed at Frankie.

"So, this is the princess we're going to all this trouble because of, huh?" His lip curled as he took her in from head to toe, and I wanted to shove my fingers into his eyes just to stop him from looking at her. After his lengthy perusal, he turned to me. "Why isn't she tied up?"

I crossed my arms and fixed him with a hard stare. "None of your fucking concern."

He held up his hands in surrender. "Fine, man, whatever. This is your thing, not mine. Course, I already did my thing, and that rich fucker is stiffing me on the rest of my fee. Says things aren't finished yet, so I don't get paid. Well, I call bullshit on that."

I stiffened as he spewed all that information out as if it were just the two of us over a beer. He was a fucking idiot. Madison didn't need to hear any of this, and certainly not the shit about getting paid or who we were getting it from. She was a smart girl. And I didn't need her figuring out who was behind this from an offhanded comment by this dickhead.

Besides making it so she didn't learn the information from him, I wanted him as far away from her as fucking possible. The way he looked at her sent a chill down my spine and had every one of my instincts standing up and taking notice. "Let's go outside and talk about this."

Normally, the guys I worked with were perceptive enough to realize when I'd reached my point, when I was done fucking around, and when you didn't argue with me. This guy wasn't one of them.

"Nah, let's not. See . . . I was thinking. I wonder if he'd be willing to pay up if he saw her get a little roughed up. Think he'd give me the money then?"

He was talking to me, but he was still looking straight at her. Madison kept her wide eyes locked on him, never moving her attention elsewhere. With each word he said in her direction, each sneer he sent her way, she inched back a tiny bit more until her back was pressed against the wall. I could see the terror in her eyes, the realization that she really was trapped now, with a guy standing in front of her and nowhere to go. And it only got worse when he pressed on.

"Back off, Frankie." My voice was hard and forceful, the tone I used when I needed to remind people exactly who they were dealing with.

But instead of listening to me like any sane fucker would have, instead of reading the warning in my tone, he kept right on. "What do you think, little girl. Think he'd be willing to give me my fucking money then? Maybe if I sent him pictures of your face all bruised and bloody. Your clothes ripped to shreds. Or maybe I should take something to bring back to him. Like a lock of hair. Or a finger."

And then he leaned toward her, his arms braced on the table and the back of the chair, and I snapped.

Chapter Twenty-one

MADISON

I was shaking.

As hard as I tried to control it, my entire body shook with the terror coursing through my veins. My back was pressed up against the wall, and I had nowhere to go. Gage was right—I should've stayed in the loft, because I never felt as trapped as I did here, with this man.

This guy . . . he was different than Gage. He had a deadness to his dark eyes that Gage had never had, even at the beginning. Stringy, dirty blond hair hung limply to his shoulders. He was smaller than I'd pictured when I'd heard his voice at the door. He wasn't muscled like Gage, and he wasn't nearly as tall. But he carried himself like he was. There was an arrogance and cockiness that made me uneasy, because he wasn't going to be afraid to try anything.

I wanted to look past him, to focus instead on Gage. To get a read on him, but I didn't dare take my eyes off this guy. I could barely concentrate on what he was saying, my heart beating too loudly in my ears, but his words reached me anyway, and it was everything my worst nightmares were made of.

He leaned farther toward me, and I tried to inch back in my chair at the same moment Gage stepped forward, gripping this guy's arm in his hand.

"You're not going to do shit here, Frankie. This is my job and my mark, and I'm not having you fuck up everything because your dick's bent out of shape. Go the fuck home and wait for your goddamn money just like everyone else."

Frankie pushed off from leaning over me and turned his head around to look at Gage over his shoulder. Though I couldn't see his sneer, I could hear the disdain drip from every word he said. "Why the fuck do you care what I do to her anyway? How would you like it if he was keeping money from you?"

"He's not keeping money from you, you dipshit. He's paying you the same fucking time he told you he would: when the job is done. Does it look like the job is done, asshole? I'm through playing nice. It's time for you to get the fuck out."

Frankie turned to me once again, his face screwed up in an angry scowl. "Don't see what all the fuss is about you. Just an ugly, fat cunt with a rich daddy."

Having heard the words more times than I could even recall, they didn't stun me as much as what Gage did next. Without warning, suddenly he had Frankie shoved up against the wall next to me, his hand gripped around his throat.

"Apologize." Even with the low timbre of his voice—or maybe because of it—Gage's fury was clear.

The guy sputtered, a disbelieving laugh falling out of his mouth. "I'm not apologizing to her. Fuck that."

Gage's arm flexed, his grip on Frankie's throat tightening, then he leaned forward until he was right in Frankie's face. Gage didn't yell, didn't shout or curse. His body was radiating anger, but his voice was smooth and calm. "You're going to apologize to her for calling her that, or I'm going to break every one of your fingers."

"Fine, fine. *Jesus.*" His eyes darted to mine, and his throat worked hard as he swallowed. "Sorry."

Gage stared at him for a long moment, and when he spoke, his voice was steel, brooking no argument. "Now, I've found my hospitality has worn out, so I'm going to give you one more chance to leave on your own. Or you can do it the way I'd prefer. Where I throw your ass out, and then we'll have a little fun outside before I make a phone call you won't want me to make."

When Frankie's attention was focused on Gage, I slipped out of the chair and rushed to the other side of the room, watching the scene from a safe distance away. Gage was in Frankie's face, still towering over him by several inches even though Frankie's feet were barely touching the ground, the tips of his shoes scraping against the worn hardwood floor.

The guy gripped Gage's arms, trying in vain to pull them away. His voice, when it came out, was strained and weak. "Jesus Christ, Ghost. What the fuck is your problem?"

"You are my fucking problem. Now what'll it be? Are you going to leave or are we going to have some fun outside?"

"Fucking hell. Let go, you crazy fuck. I'll go." When Gage didn't loosen his grip, the guy repeated, "I'll *go*, man."

Gage pressed harder against his throat, and I watched the guy's face turn red, his eyes bugging out, hands grappling at Gage restlessly. Gage leaned in close and said quietly, "Don't ever come out here again. And you need to find a new employer, because if I ever see you around, I'm not going to be as forgiving the second time."

Then he let go, and Frankie sagged against the wall, coughing as his eyes darted back and forth between us. It looked like he wanted to say something more, but once he got another look at Gage, he seemed to come to his senses. He shook his head and turned around to walk down the hall, muttering under his breath the whole way.

I watched as Gage followed him out, slamming the door, then I heard the faint click of the lock setting into place, and I couldn't remember when I'd ever felt so relieved to hear that sound. I was suddenly craving the safety the walls of this cabin provided me, instead of seeing them as glorified jail bars.

I still shook—from fear, from shock, from the realization that Gage was the least of my problems. Someone very powerful had orchestrated this for reasons I couldn't comprehend, and there was no telling what he planned to do with me. But I also realized that at some point between when Gage had captured me to now, I had begun looking to him to keep me safe. While not even ten minutes prior I hadn't been sure, the truth came out while I'd had my back pressed against the wall. He was the one I was trusting to keep that guy away from me. He was the one I knew would keep me protected. Not just against the creep he'd just thrown out, but against this whole ordeal turning out very badly for me. I now believed him completely when he'd told me I'd be safe with him. He wouldn't allow anything to happen to me.

Somehow, at some point I'd gone from looking at him as my captor to looking at him as something so much more.

GHOST

It had taken everything in me not to kill that fucker while he stood in front of me. It wouldn't have taken much. A twist of my hands, a tightening of my fingers. I'd wanted to cut out his tongue and feed it to him. I'd wanted to rip off every one of his fingernails, slice off his balls and leave him in the snow to bleed to death. I'd wanted to do one of a hundred different torture methods to him, all because of the way he'd stared at Madison. The way he'd leered at her, spoken to her, the thoughts that went through his head about hurting her.

And it was like a fucking lightbulb going off in my mind, realizing that the only thing that had kept me from doing so—the only thing that had allowed me to let him walk out of here without both his legs broken—was the girl still shaking in the other room. Instead of taking care of the problem and making sure he knew just exactly how serious I was, my focus had been getting him out and keeping her safe.

And thoughts of keeping her safe had been why my anger had ratcheted up so high, so fast while he'd been here. Because if it wasn't me, it was going to be him. The reason I'd decided to take this job in the first place was because I'd known Frankie was next on the list. He was excellent at what he did, though he wasn't as good as me. But he was shady, immoral, and corrupt. Knowing what he'd done in the past, knowing what could possibly await the woman we needed to kidnap, had forced my hand.

Now to see him here, to hear what he wanted to do to Madison . . . to realize he would've been doing those very things to her if I hadn't stepped up in the first place? Fucking *killed* me. Anger rolled through me, boiling over and spilling out as I stood braced against the door I'd just shut behind him.

I was in way deeper with her than I'd anticipated. Way deeper than I'd ever intended.

Way deeper than I should've allowed.

Yet when I walked out to her, when I saw her standing on the other side of the room, her arms wrapped around her shuddering frame, her eyes wide, I didn't pull back or step away or go for a fucking walk like I should have.

Instead, I went to her, stood close enough that I could still see the residual fear in her eyes. I needed to feel her, remind myself she was okay, that he wasn't the one in charge, that he'd never get his hands on her as long as I was around.

I reached out and grabbed the back of her neck, pulling her to me. She came immediately, resting her forehead against my chest, her harsh breaths heating my skin through my shirt. Her fingers clutched the fabric at my sides, and I rubbed circles on her neck with my thumb, running my other hand up and down her back. I was trying so hard to be gentle with her, to be careful, but I was still radiating anger, and I didn't want to handle her too roughly . . . not when she'd just been through that. She was cold to the touch, her body shivering—whether still from fear or from the chill in the air, I didn't know.

The cabin was silent with the exception of her rapid breaths and the faint sound of the movie still playing on Madison's laptop. I shuffled us closer to the couch, then said, "Why don't you sit down? I'm going to turn off the movie and grab you a blanket." I didn't let her argue as I guided her to sit, then turned around and headed down the hallway and up the stairs. I needed the space to calm the fuck down and get a hold of the anger that had been simmering since the first words had left Frankie's mouth and had only grown the longer he'd been here.

I quickly paused the movie, then closed her laptop before grabbing a blanket off the bed and turning to head back downstairs. Except she was standing there at the top of the steps, blocking my way and shaking her head.

Her voice was quiet, but it was stronger than I was expecting. "I don't want to be down there right now."

I stopped, frozen by the end of the bed. I'd faced off against life-long criminals. Gone head-to-head with drug dealers and rapists and whatever else I'd been paid to do, yet this girl . . . this twenty-year-old naive girl was the one who could bring me to my fucking knees. "Okay." I swallowed. "Where do you want to be?"

"Here," she said, her voice just above a whisper. She took a step closer to me, her eyes on mine. "With you."

And just like that, despite the last twenty minutes and the rage that still boiled barely below the surface, with those three little words, she had my dick aching again. It wasn't just her words, though, it was the look in her eyes. She stared unwaveringly at me, and there was no doubt exactly what she wanted to do. What she wanted *me* to do to her.

Despite my body yelling at me to grab her, throw her down on the bed and fuck her until she screamed, I managed to say, "I'm not sure that's such a good idea right now."

Her entire body deflated. Her shoulders sagged, her eyes lowered to the floor, and she nodded in acceptance. Just like that. She thought it was her. She thought I didn't want her, and after everything that motherfucker had said to her, I couldn't let her think that. I couldn't let those be the memories that were burned into her brain.

I tossed the blanket behind me and reached out for her hand, pulling her over to the bed. I sat down and guided her to stand between my legs. "That's not why, Madison. I want you, but this isn't a good idea. Not right now. It's not because of you, okay? It's me."

She snorted and rolled her eyes, trying to push away from me, but I held her tightly by her hips. "I didn't take you for clichés, Gage. You don't need to lie to me. I'm a big girl."

"I'm not lying to you." Not about this. "I'm too worked up right now. I need about three hours, a hard run, and a punching bag before I'm going to calm down. I can't be gentle with you."

She reached up, her fingertips grazing my jaw. Her voice was quiet, her hands continuing down my neck to my chest. "You've been gentle with me, even when I didn't think so. I realize that now. You've always been gentle with me."

"Not now I can't. Not knowing it was going to be him here."

She paused, her fingers halting on my shoulders, and her eyes searched mine. "What do you mean?"

"If I hadn't taken this job . . . it was going to be him in charge of your capture. And the thought of him here with you . . ." My hands tightened against her hips, and I pulled her to me as I dropped my forehead against her stomach.

She curled her hands over on my shoulders and squeezed.
"I'm glad it was you."

It was a simple statement, something she may have said off-handedly, but it shot straight through my chest. I didn't deserve her kindness, her understanding. I didn't deserve the fingers she was running through my hair, I didn't deserve the lush body she was offering up to me. I didn't deserve any of it.

But I couldn't stop myself from taking it.

Chapter Twenty-two

MADISON

"I wouldn't have let him hurt you." His voice was muffled against my stomach, his hands gripping me tightly, and I didn't want to pull away. I wanted to stay locked in this embrace, but I wanted to see his face more. I needed to see the look in his eyes when I asked him this, so I could see the honesty there.

I stepped back enough to get him to raise his eyes to meet my own. "Why?"

His brow creased, eyes narrowing. "Why, what?"

"Why am I here? Why are you still holding me here? Who hired you and what do they want with me?"

He stared at me for a minute, his eyes darting between my own. The silence had stretched on for so long that I didn't think I'd get an answer. Then he said, "I don't know the why of it, but it's one of your father's business rivals. I can't tell you his name, Madison—it's safer for all of us, for you especially, if you don't know that detail." He reached out and grabbed one of my hands, holding it lightly in his. "But I can tell you that my plan has always been to take you home as soon as possible, unharmed and safe. That's the only reason I got drawn into this."

Relief coursed through my veins, reassurances the balm I needed as they settled into my bones. Because even though I felt safe with Gage, even though I knew something different was going on between us, it still settled something inside to hear the words from him. "Why are you telling me this now? And why would you do that down there?" I asked, jerking my head in the direction of downstairs. "Stand up for me and protect me, not just with anyone, but with someone you work with?"

He pushed me back so he could stand up, and then his hands were gripping my face, his eyes intense as he stared into mine. "I don't give a fuck about any of that. You think I'd choose loyalty to a *job* over keeping you safe? That I'd let him put his fucking hands on you? I'd break both of them if he even tried."

He didn't let me answer, didn't wait for a reply before his mouth was covering mine. And it wasn't like before. It wasn't soft or sweet. It wasn't tentative and searching. It was everything I'd thought a kiss with him would be like. It was harsh and demanding, a little rough, and I melted into him as he took control. Even though it was rougher than it had been before, I could tell he was still holding himself back. His muscles were twitching as I gripped his biceps, and though his lips were insistent on mine, he didn't push me. Even though I offered myself up to him, he was the one holding himself in check.

And maybe he was right. Maybe this was a mistake. Maybe this wasn't the right time.

It wasn't. I was intelligent enough to realize that, but even knowing it, I didn't care. Because right now it *felt* like the perfect time. Right now, he felt like Gage to me, not Ghost. Not the man who'd threatened another man's life, not the man who probably would've gone after him and inflicted a world of hurt on him if I hadn't been here.

He was just Gage to me now, and I wanted him, no matter the consequences.

While kissing him, I inched toward the bed until the back of my knees hit the mattress, pulling him along as I went. I was out of my element, being the instigator in this, and I had no idea what I was doing. I was fumbling, unsure of how to proceed, of what to do, how to be, but I wanted this. More than I'd ever wanted anything, and I needed Gage to be certain of exactly how much I did.

When I'd been with Marc, he had initiated everything—the first kiss, the make-outs, the one time we'd had sex, all of it—which was something I now realized had been part of the problem. From the very beginning, he'd been the one to push, to guide, to take— though I was willing, because I thought he was something more to me than he was, he never really asked me.

But Gage . . . he was nothing like that. He was listening to my cues, following instead of leading like I was sure he was used to, and I knew he wouldn't move forward without my complete and utter consent.

And as scary as it was, as crazy and out of control as it was, it was also so, *so* freeing.

I kept my hands locked on his hips and pulled him with me when I sat down, then lay back on the bed. He froze for a second, but when I tugged harder against him, he finally relented, covering my body with his own.

His lips were harder against mine, his tongue sliding against my own before he scraped his teeth along my lower lip. He moved his mouth to my jaw, to my ear, down my neck, across my shoulder. I couldn't keep track of all the places he traced with his lips, all the skin he nipped with his teeth, but when his mouth met mine again, I was panting, every inch of me aching with need. With want.

"Gage . . ." I let my hands settle under his shirt, against his skin. I'd never felt anything like it. Raw power radiated from the flesh-covered muscles, his abdomen taut and rippled, and I wanted to see it. I wanted to see, to feel, every inch of him. His body was a drug, and I craved more. I pushed his shirt up as he continued kissing me, until finally he pulled away and reached behind to yank it off.

He knelt at the edge of the bed, looking down at me, but I couldn't meet his eyes. I was too busy tracking every inch of skin he'd uncovered. Like I'd imagined, his tattoos continued to more than just his forearms. They arced up over his biceps and massive shoulders, trailing down his chest, several littering the ridges of his stomach. Some wrapped around his sides, and I could only imagine what I'd find when I looked at his back.

He groaned. "Christ, Madison. You need to stop looking at me like that." He came down next to me this time, his body half covering mine, the evidence of exactly how much he wanted me pressed into my hip. He slid his hand to my waist and down to my hips before he moved under my shirt. Slowly, so slowly I ached, he continued and allowed the piece of cotton to bunch up against his wrist, his thumb tracing soft circles as he went. And the whole time, he watched me. His eyes never left mine, and the intensity in them stole my breath.

When his hand came in contact with my stomach, I stiffened. I couldn't help it. My body was always a source of embarrassment for me, the source of ridicule from peers, and I was self-conscious, especially when the sun still shone through the back windows of the cabin, casting enough light into the loft to see everything perfectly. Especially when Gage was lying next to me, his muscled body stretched out along mine, the epitome of a perfect physique.

"It's okay." His hand moved from under my shirt, and he smoothed it down. But I still wanted the warmth of him against me again, despite my fears.

I swallowed down my anxiety and opened my eyes to look at him. His lips were resting against mine, his eyes open and studying me. Against his mouth, I whispered, "Keep going."

He shook his head, dropped a kiss on my lips. "We don't have to. I'll still make you feel good like this. I can make you feel so good like this."

I nodded, closed my eyes, and took a deep breath. "I know you can. You *are*. But I want you to keep going. I want more. I want everything."

GHOST

As soon as the words left her mouth, my dick throbbed, begging to be let out. Begging me to take her, to claim her, but that wasn't how I was going to play this. Every single sexual encounter in my past had been about getting off, nothing more. Sometimes angry, always frantic, it had never been about anything more than pleasure—usually mine. I'd never taken the time to appreciate the body of the woman I was with.

But I wanted to do that with Madison. She was a contradiction—on the outside she was all soft, sweet curves and delicate creamy white skin, but on the inside she was stronger than I'd ever imagined.

She'd worked her way under my skin, and I wanted to be consumed by her. I wanted to spend hours running my hands over every inch of her body, followed by my mouth, then my tongue.

I wanted to be gentle with her—something I'd never been my entire life—and that scared the fuck out of me.

Sitting back on my knees, I pulled her shirt the rest of the way up and off her as she lifted her arms for me. Seeing her bare before me lasted only a fleeting second before she let her arms drop to cover herself. As much as I wanted to pull them away, to work my way under those clutching hands so I could kiss and lick every inch of her, I knew this was hard for her. Whatever assholes had been in her life before now had done a helluva job on her self-esteem. She didn't see herself correctly. She saw her body as something she had too much of.

And all I saw when I looked at her was sensuality wrapped up in heavenly curves made to grip while I was sinking deep inside her.

Instead of doing what I wanted and baring her for myself, I leaned down and placed a kiss on her arm, then I nudged her with my hands on her hips, trying to guide her to the top of the bed. "Scoot up."

She shimmied her way up, still trying desperately to keep herself covered, and I finally got impatient and gripped her by the waist, moving her up myself in a single lift.

When her head hit the pillow, she gasped, her eyes wide. "Gage!"

"You weren't moving fast enough. Now, are you going to let me take these off?" I ran my finger along the waistband of the shorts she was borrowing from me. She was commando under these, and the thought that only the flimsy nylon of these basketball shorts was what was between me and her pussy was driving me insane.

"You first?"

I stood immediately and shucked my pants, my boxer briefs sliding down with them. Once I was naked, I crawled back on the bed, my dick pointing straight at her. Her eyes were wide, her gaze transfixed on nothing but it as I came closer. I watched her swallow, then her eyes flitted to mine before they dropped once again to my cock. The way she was staring at it—part in awe, part in nervous apprehension—I had to wonder if she'd ever even seen one before.

Not knowing how much experience she had forced me to take this slow. Which was a good thing, because I was nearly ready to come. I leaned toward her and put my hands on the waistband of her shorts, eyebrows raised. She gave the subtlest of nods, but it was enough for me to grip the elastic and slowly pull the shorts down as she lifted up to help me. As much as I wanted to look, to see her completely naked and spread out for me like a fucking feast, I kept my eyes on hers.

Once the shorts were off, I tossed them to the side, then climbed into bed until I was straddling her legs, my hands braced on either side of her shoulders.

"Still okay?"

The large gust of her exhale brushed against my chest, and she nodded once again, but she didn't move her arms. She was thinking too much, so I leaned down and sucked her bottom lip into my mouth. She let out this sexy little sigh, and my dick twitched against her stomach. Her eyes flew wide open, then she looked down between our bodies, seeing my cock straining toward her.

She lifted the hand that was splayed over her stomach to reach for me, but before she could make contact, she paused and looked to me again. "Can I touch it?"

I huffed out a laugh. "Normally I'd say fuck yeah, but I'm not sure how much touching I can handle right now. Next time you can. Let's focus on you this round."

Chapter Twenty-three

MADISON

This round? Good God, how many rounds was he planning?

I pulled my hand away from him and nodded. My exploration could wait, though I did want to explore. And seeing Gage standing in front of me, heavily muscled, his erection thick and hard and pointing straight for me, made me want to do things I'd never once thought about doing with anyone before.

Made me need him more than I'd ever needed anything.

Gage leaned down to capture my lips again, his tongue immediately slipping into my mouth, and I opened for him. He kissed me soundly, tilting his head to the side so he could deepen the kiss before he pulled back and let his teeth scrape my lips, followed by the fluttering of his tongue against them.

By the time he moved his kisses to my neck and the exposed part of my chest, I was on fire. The need inside me was now a raging inferno, and I wanted more. I wanted to feel his mouth against mine, feel his body pressed against every inch of me. Without thought, I reached up and gripped his face, pulling him to me, and he groaned as our lips met. He lowered his body, enough so the tips of my breasts brushed against his chest and his erection brushed against my stomach.

"Let me touch you, Madison. Can I touch you?" His voice was ragged and rough, breathless, and if I needed proof that this was affecting him as much as it was me, I had the answer right there.

Not sure I could speak, I simply nodded.

I didn't know if he was worried I'd change my mind or if he was as hungry for my body as I was for his, but he immediately lay on his side next to me, propped up on one arm. His fingers made a slow, torturous, wonderful path from my mouth, down my chin and across my shoulders, between the valley of my breasts until he cupped one in his hand. With one swipe of his thumb across my nipple, I was ready to shoot off the bed. He continued his slow torture, though, his fingers mere whispers against my upper body. He traced circles around both my nipples and the curves under my breasts while I tried in vain not to writhe against him. My head turned restlessly against the pillow, my mouth open in silent moans.

"Can I use my mouth?" His lips were right next to my ear, his voice a raspy whisper.

My eyes flew open and I turned my head to look at him, then gave him a subtle nod. Truth be told, I didn't care what he did, so long as I got some relief from the fire spreading bigger and bigger inside me.

He pushed himself up farther so he could lean over me. At first, his lips were just the same fluttering brushes his fingers had been, and I tried not to groan out in frustration. I needed something more than fleeting touches, and then almost as if he could read my thoughts, he licked down in the valley between my breasts, and this time I couldn't hold in my moan.

Gage took it as encouragement, moving to one breast, licking a straight line up the underside until he got to my nipple and gave a sharp, short flick to it with his tongue. I gasped, my hands flying to his head to hold him to me. But he wasn't going anywhere. He traced a thousand circles around my hardened peak before finally engulfing it in his mouth, and I thought I'd cry from the pleasure. And then he moved to the other side and repeated everything all over again.

I couldn't do anything but lay back and take it. His name tumbled from my lips over and over again, and finally he pulled back enough so he could look at me. I didn't know if I looked as crazed as he did, but I felt it. I felt absolutely consumed by this need for him, and I wanted more.

Above all else, I wanted more.

He watched me as his hand went to my knee, his fingers gentle as he gripped me there and pulled my leg up, opening me to him. Before I could freak out or move my leg back, he was there again, kissing me, calming me. Against my lips, he asked, "Have you ever been touched here?" His fingers traced up the length of my thigh, stopping just before my center.

My answer was only a breath. "Just once. A long time ago."

The stiffening of his body was subtle, but I felt it against me. "Was it that asshole tutor?"

Reaching up, I tried to pull him down to me, to feel his lips against mine again. "I don't want to talk about that. Not now. I don't want to ruin this."

He froze, not continuing to come closer to me, his eyes turning hard. "Did he hurt you?"

I scraped my fingernails against the scruff covering his jaw, trying to calm him down. Shaking my head, I said, "Not the way you think."

"Then how." He wasn't budging, his voice as hard as steel, and he wasn't melting into my hands like I'd hoped he would.

I sighed. "Please, Gage."

"Tell me and I promise I won't ask any more questions. I need to know, Madison."

I took a deep breath and let it out. "I was just a naive little girl. I trusted him and he lied to me. That's it."

Gage's jaw ticked as he clenched his teeth. Now he was the one lost in his head, and I needed to bring him back. I reached down and grabbed his wrist, slowly sliding his hand up my inner thigh. I kept my eyes on him, but his focus was on the place I was guiding him to. I stopped just before I got to where I wanted him, then moved my hands back to his shoulders, sliding them down to rest against his biceps. I needed him to do this on his own.

"Please, Gage. Please touch me."

He groaned, his head falling to hang between his shoulders. And then his fingers were there, softly at first, tracing every inch of me, and then he was more insistent, his fingers sliding deeper against me. When he brushed against where I was most sensitive, I nearly shot off the bed, a moan ripped from my throat. But he didn't stop there. He let his fingers slip lower until he easily slid one inside me, pumping slowly, and all I could do was try to catch my breath.

I couldn't concentrate on anything but the feel of him next to me, of him inside me, and I wanted to bottle this feeling and carry it with me all the time. It was euphoric, being on the receiving end of Gage's ministrations, and I needed more.

"More . . ."

"Christ," he groaned. But he did as I asked, slipping another finger inside of me, and then he lowered his head and added his mouth to the mix. His tongue traced my nipple, and then he sucked it into his mouth at the same time the heel of his hand pressed and rubbed against me, and I didn't even see it coming.

I exploded, my eyes closed, my mouth opened in a silent scream as I arched off the bed and pulsed around his fingers still deep inside me.

GHOST

Seeing Madison come had me reaching down and gripping the base of my cock hard enough to hold back my own orgasm. *Jesus fucking Christ.*

This girl was so unknowingly sexy, it was unbelievable. Her tits heaved with her rapid breaths, a flush working its way over her chest and up her neck to pool in her cheeks.

And fucking hell, she was so wet . . . so ready for me. She wanted this. She wanted *me*. That, combined with the tightness of her pussy around my fingers, was nearly enough to have me shooting off right then and there.

When I had myself under control, I relaxed again next to her, slipping my fingers from inside her and rubbing them up her slit, circling her clit but never touching it. She was a boneless puddle in the bed, sweet mewls coming from her throat, and I wanted to grab my sketch pad and draw her like this. Her dark hair all fanned out on the pillow, her head turned to the side, cheeks flushed and eyes closed, a small smile on her lips. While she was relaxed completely, I finally took in the body I'd been fantasizing about. But my fantasies had nothing on the real thing. She was soft . . . everywhere, in the sexiest way. Every inch of her was the perfect contradiction to the hard, unforgiving edges of my body. She was succulent, and I wanted to run my hands over every part of her.

When I lifted my eyes from my perusal of her body, I found her watching me, the flush that was on her face more pronounced now. Her eyes held a shadow of doubt, and if I ever got my hands on the fucker who'd done this to her, who'd made her doubt how sexy she was, I'd kill him without a second thought.

I moved closer to her, so she could feel how hard I was for her.

How hard I *still* was for her. "You're so fucking sexy, Madison. I could spend all night doing nothing but making you come, over and over again." As the words left my mouth, I realized what a scary revelation it was. I *took* gratification; I didn't give it. But with her, I wanted to make sure she found pleasure, especially after all the pain she'd been through in her life, and if it was at my hand or my mouth instead of my dick, so be it.

"Why are you still laying there then?"

Laughing out a breath, I slid off the bed and went over to my bag, which I'd stashed in the corner earlier today. "Because I just about came all over you, watching you like that. I needed a breather." I glanced up at her, eyebrows raised at the look of shock on her face, as I dug through my bag. I finally came across the foil squares I knew were in there. Unfortunately there were only a few—though I was lucky I still had that many stashed in here—and I had way more plans for Madison than only fucking her a few times.

Grabbing one out of the bag, I stood and ripped it open, tossing the foil wrapper on the nightstand before I rolled the condom down my shaft. She was still sprawled out on the bed, exactly how I'd left her. One leg flat against the mattress, the other bent at the knee, leaving her wide open for me to see. And from this vantage point, I could see everything. She had an arm lying limply against her stomach, the other bent and resting next to her head. By the stubborn glint in her eyes, I could see it was taking everything in her not to move, not to close in on herself or cover herself up.

Before I could stop myself, I walked over to the bed, then leaned down, my tongue sweeping once up the line of her pussy. She gasped, just like I knew she would, and I couldn't wait to bury my face between her thighs and feel her come against my mouth.

Later.

I settled on the bed between her legs, bracing myself above her and licking my lips. "You taste good."

Her mouth dropped open, and she moved to cover her face with both her hands. I chuckled, then plucked them both away before I kissed her again.

Being with Madison was so different from anything I'd done before. Even years ago, when I'd been the one who was inexperienced, I'd never witnessed the kind of sweet innocence Madison had. She was fresh and pure and good. Everything I wasn't. I didn't deserve to be here, not cradled between her welcoming thighs, not pressing against the slick warmth of her pussy. I certainly didn't deserve the look she fixed upon me when she lifted her eyes to mine as I reached down and slid the head of my dick up and down the length of her slit.

I might not deserve it, but I was still taking it.

The look she gave me as I rubbed against her was nothing compared to what came across her face when I found her entrance and pushed forward. I was barely an inch in, but the look of bliss on Madison's face was enough to make me feel like I was fucking Superman.

The farther in I pushed, the farther open her mouth dropped until she was staring at me, slack-jawed, her nails biting into my upper arms. I leaned down, kissing her as I continued rocking into her, back and forth, back and forth, wanting nothing more than to thrust forward, bury myself balls deep into her sweet pussy. But she'd said it'd been years, and I wanted to let her get used to this again, get used to me.

Her breath hitched when I was nearly all the way in, and I pulled back to look at her. "You okay?"

She nodded, biting her lip, her eyes closed. "Keep going."

"*Fuck.*" I braced myself on my forearms, my hands cupping her head, my fingers buried in her hair and my thumbs rubbing against her temples as I pushed in farther until I was as deep as I could get. Clenching my eyes closed, I hissed, "Jesus Christ." Being inside Madison was unfuckingbelievable. She was tight and wet and warm, and she fit me like a glove. When I opened my eyes, hers were still wide and locked on me. I couldn't tell if she was terrified or nervous or both, but I needed to make sure she was still in this with me. My voice was strained as I asked, "Okay? Does it hurt?"

I moved a fraction of an inch, and she gasped, her eyes rolling back in her head, and I wanted to do it again. And again. And again until I felt her lose control.

"Madison, does it hurt?"

"No . . . no." She shook her head and licked her lips as she looked up at me. "I just feel . . . full." She loosened her grip on my arms, the bite of her nails stinging and sending a zap of heat straight to my dick. "Can you . . . can you move?"

"Shit," I groaned. It wasn't the dirty talk I was used to . . . just a simple question, but it felt like the filthiest thing ever coming from her sweet mouth. She was so sexy, and yet she had no idea.

I did as she'd asked, pulling out nearly all the way and sliding back inside. Slowly, so slowly, because I wanted to make this good for her.

"Oh, God." Her mouth was open, her eyes wide, and her fingers were gripping me once again.

"Does it feel good?"

She didn't answer, but I didn't need her words. She lifted her legs and wrapped them both around my hips, her heels digging into my ass, and it took everything in me not to pound into her. I kept my pace steady, rocking into her in long, deep strokes, as I kissed her face, her neck. I pulled back enough so I could lean down and lick her nipple, suck it into my mouth. I lifted my eyes to see her reaction as I let my teeth scrape against the hardened peak. She gasped, her pussy clenching and unclenching against my dick, and I groaned around her.

"Will you go faster?" she whispered.

Fuck yeah, I'd go faster. I moved to suck her other nipple

while I pumped into her, grinding my pubic bone against her clit every time I pushed in. I wasn't going to last much longer—I was surprised I'd lasted this long already—so I slipped a hand between us and found her clit with my thumb. Circling it, I thrust a little quicker, a little harder, and Madison's nails dug farther into my skin.

"Gage . . . Gage . . ."

She was close, contracting around me, squeezing me, and I knew the second she came, I'd be right behind her. Her pussy was like a vise grip, and there was no way I'd be able to hold back when I felt her coming.

"Come on, Madison. I want to feel you. Let me feel you, baby." I leaned down and flicked her nipple with my tongue before sucking it into my mouth. I added pressure to her clit, circling it faster as my teeth scraped against her, and then she exploded.

Her body bowed up toward me, her neck exposed, her head pressed harshly into the pillow. She was gorgeous . . . beautiful inside and out, and I didn't deserve this . . . I didn't deserve her, and I was an asshole for taking advantage of her like this.

With those thoughts bombarding me, I let myself feel the pleasure of her body while she pulled me over the edge, all the while knowing this would be the last time I could allow myself to do so.

Chapter Twenty-four

MADISON

Fluttering my eyelids open against the light filtering in through the curtains, I stretched, cringing at the ache I had in a place where I'd never ached before.

Yes, I'd had sex—only once, and once had been plenty—but it was nothing like last night with Gage. It wasn't just his size or strength that was new. From the way he looked at me, to the way he kissed me, to the way he touched me, everything with him was different. All my life, I'd ached for someone to truly know me, to see the real me. And for the first time, I felt like someone did . . . that someone was caring for me unconditionally. It made no sense— none of this did—and yet nothing in my life had ever felt so real.

I smiled, reaching out to the side to feel him, but I came up empty. I lifted my head and turned in the direction of where he'd lain next to me last night. Nothing but cool, white sheets greeted me, and I frowned.

Sitting up, I clutched the blanket to my chest, looking down into the main room through the railing. I didn't see him down there, and when I listened, the only sound I heard was a rhythmic thumping coming from somewhere outside the cabin. I slipped out of bed and looked for the clothes I'd borrowed from Gage, my face heating as I recalled him removing them from me last night. He'd been so careful, so gentle and reverent, and everything I'd needed. He'd been perfect.

So why wasn't he here with me now?

Once I'd slipped my clothes back on, I went to the window, trying to find the source of the noise I heard. Tentatively, I moved the curtains aside to look out. The sun reflected almost blindingly off the snow, and I blinked against the brightness. Once my eyes adjusted, I followed the direction the noise came from and saw Gage in front of a huge tree stump, a smaller log set atop it. He was only in a pair of jeans, a long-sleeved shirt, and a knit cap as he swung an ax, splitting the piece of wood in front of him into two solid pieces. They fell off to the side, and he replaced them with another solid log and then repeated the process.

I stood, mesmerized, watching the way he moved, the way his body arched as he worked. Even though his shirt covered him, I could still see the muscles in his arms and back flexing with each pass of the ax, the hem of his shirt riding up on the backstroke. I didn't know how long I stood there watching him before he stopped and leaned against the handle of the ax, bringing one of his arms up to wipe his forehead. He was breathing heavy, white puffs escaping his mouth, as he stared off into the trees surrounding the cabin.

Wanting to catch him while he was still out there, I hurried downstairs and into the bathroom, grabbing my clothes and coat from the dryer. After changing into them, I headed to the front door, pausing as I reached for the handle. Staring at the new lock Gage had installed, the one that needed a key to be unlocked, a sudden wave of unease swept over me. It was just a lock . . . a piece of metal meant to keep people safe, but *this* lock meant so much more. To me, its sole purpose had been to keep me prisoner. What if he'd locked it now? What if, after everything we'd shared, I was still nothing more than a job to him? I was still just the girl he'd been paid to keep captive?

I wasn't sure I could take that slap in the face after the night we'd had. It would be so much worse than the outcome with Marc, because with Gage, I felt a connection I'd never had with my former tutor. I felt a connection I'd never had with *anyone*.

I'd struggled my entire life to fit in, to be seen as more than the smart girl or the rich girl . . . to be seen as just Madison. With Gage, I'd finally found a kindred spirit, despite our differences. I'd found a connection with him I'd always hoped I'd find, but never really thought would actually happen.

Taking a deep breath and preparing for the worst while hoping for the best, I twisted the knob and pulled. The breath escaped me in a whoosh as my shoulders sagged in relief when the door opened easily. My fears were unfounded—at least in this instance—but it did shed some light on what I'd gotten myself into. Gage was closed off. He kept his cards close to his chest, and based on what he did for a living, I understood the desire to do that. But I needed something different from him. I didn't know what he was thinking . . . what he was feeling. I didn't know if it was even half the emotions that had bubbled up inside me, but that was something we needed to talk about.

I'd learned a lot in the four years since Marc, and while I hadn't yet been able to put any of it into practice, I was going to now.

Stepping outside, I closed the door behind me, then moved to the porch steps and sat down. If Gage had heard me come out, he didn't show it. Instead, he let the ax handle drop to the snow-covered ground, then began gathering up the logs he'd chopped. When his arms were full, he started toward me, his face a closed book, and something hard settled in my stomach.

The smile I'd been wearing slipped away the closer he got to me. Because his expression . . . it wasn't anything like the man who'd been on top of me last night—the man who'd been inside me. No, the straight line of his mouth, the stubborn set of his jaw, his harsh stare showed someone else completely.

This was the face of Ghost, and I hated it.

I hated it because something had happened in the last ten hours to make him go from the man who'd held me in my sleep to the man who couldn't even look me in the eye, who walked right by me without even a nod of acknowledgment.

Four years ago, I would've slunk away. I would've ducked my head and accepted his disinterest. I would've carried it on my shoulders as just another thing I'd done to drive someone away.

But I wasn't sixteen anymore. And I was getting answers.

GHOST

It killed me to look at her and keep a mask of indifference on my face, especially when I saw the confusion and uncertainty reflecting back at me in her eyes.

I'd thought chopping some firewood would burn off some steam, allow me time to think, to process and accept what I needed to do. It made sense. From a practical standpoint, no other option was plausible.

But nothing with Madison was practical, and I liked it that way.

Waking up next to her, curled into my side, had been the best and worst moment of my entire god-awful life. She was trusting and so vulnerable, and I was the fucker who'd kidnapped her for money. I was the fucker who was keeping things from her—important things she had a right to know. And even knowing I was the worst kind of person, I still *took* from her last night. She gave herself to me, she gave me everything, and I didn't even pause. I took.

And that just served to increase the guilt I felt tenfold.

The longer I'd lain there, the harder the regret pressed down against me until I felt like I couldn't fucking breathe. She deserved better than me, better than a thief and a kidnapper and a liar. Madison wasn't the kind of girl who could sleep with someone once and then be done with it. And then just . . . move on. Madison was a forever kind of girl, and I didn't have a forever to give her.

I picked up several logs, then walked toward her, trying to remember the way I'd looked at her in the beginning. Trying to see her through the eyes of the man who'd taken her prisoner, who'd brought her here. The man who'd hated where she'd come from, hated that she'd been afforded things I never would.

Except now when I looked at her, all I saw was Madison. Nothing more, nothing less. Just her.

I averted my eyes, outwardly ignoring her as I walked right past her up the steps and into the cabin. If I was going to go through with this, do a clean break with her, stop this shit before it really got started, I needed to grow some balls.

I was an excellent liar, just one of the many qualities I had that served to make an even wider gap between us, and it was going to come in handy now. Because from the sound of her footsteps behind me, she wasn't going to let this go, and I was going to need every weapon in my arsenal to get her to see my side of things. To get her to understand the two of us just didn't work together.

MADISON

I followed him into the house, letting the door close behind me. I was on his heels all the way to the main room, but I hung back by the couch, my hands fisted by my sides as he dropped the logs next to the woodstove. When he turned around to face me, his expression was the same as it had been outside. He was looking at me like he had on that very first day. Like he hated the very ground I walked on.

I pushed down the uncertainty that clawed at me, because I

wanted to know what was going on. I *deserved* to know. "What is this, Gage?"

"What's what?" His voice was flat, his expression the same.

"This," I said, gesturing to him. "Everything. The way you're acting. Did something happen?" And then a thought came to me, panic unfurling in my stomach. I swallowed, then asked, "Did you get a call? Is . . . is someone else coming here? Are they taking me somewhere?"

"No, no one called. No one's taking you. The plan hasn't changed. You're here with me for a while, then you'll go home, where you can resume your life as if none of this ever happened. That's it."

What should have come as a moment of relief felt like a punch in the gut. *Resume your life as if none of this ever happened.* I swallowed, attempting to control the shaking of my voice, and folded my arms to ward off the pain in my chest. "I didn't know if something had changed. If maybe you got orders to slaughter me at the end of this."

With his eyes narrowed, his voice came out gruff. "You were never going to be hurt, and that's not going to change. Ever. That was the whole reason I took this fucking job—because I knew if I was the one here, you wouldn't be with one of those other assholes like Frankie who wouldn't be so nice."

"Yeah, well." I shook my head and looked out the window. "That would've been wonderful to know at the beginning instead of imagining all the ways I could be murdered or tortured or both."

"Yeah, well," he said, repeating me. "I don't share shit like that with marks."

My head snapped in his direction, my heart stinging at his words. I cataloged every inch of his face, trying to read the expression I saw there. But he was blank . . . no emotion, no nothing. My throat felt like it was closing in on itself, but I still managed to ask, "You still think of me as just another job?"

He didn't say anything, his eyes burning holes right through me, and his silence spoke volumes. Shaking my head, I said, "No, I don't believe you. Because I was there last night. I was present for the entire thing, and there was no way you faked the connection we had. So my question is, why?"

He looked at me for a long moment, then smiled coldly. "What, exactly, do you think is going to happen here, princess? You think I'm gonna come back to your fancy mansion so I can be your boyfriend? You think your daddy would like that? What'll you tell him when he asks how we met?" He laughed, a sharp, cutting sound. "You're out of your mind."

"And you," I said, pointing a finger at him, "are acting like an asshole."

He shrugged, unaffected. "Nothing new there."

I shook my head, huffing out a breath. "I know you and I don't make any sense. But what happened between last night when I fell asleep *naked* next to you and now? Why are you acting like this?"

He stood silently, and I didn't care what I had to do. I needed to get Gage back.

"No," I said sharply, walking up to him and shoving him hard in the chest. It was like trying to move a brick wall. "*No.* You don't get to be the silent, stoic asshole right now. Tell me what changed. *Tell me.* You owe me an explanation."

For a moment, I thought he wasn't going to answer me. He crossed his arms and fixed his icy blue eyes on mine, glaring down at me with his jaw clenched. Just when I was about to spout more demands, he spoke. "We shouldn't have done that last night."

My mouth popped open with my shock, and I took a small step back. Shaking my head, I said, "You don't believe that."

"Yes, I do."

"You're lying. You're *lying.* You know how I know that? Because I was there last night, Gage. You were with me every step of the way."

"That's where you're wrong, because despite what you so desperately want to believe, the entire time I was with you I was telling myself over and over that I shouldn't be. I shouldn't have been with you."

A punch to the stomach would've been less painful than his words were. I felt so foolish—so much more than I ever had, and that was an extensive list. Shame, humiliation, and regret churned inside me, and I felt so *stupid*.

Attempting to control the waver in my voice, I said, "So last night, while you were on top of me, while you were *inside* me, you were trying to find a way to let me down? All you had to say was, 'Madison, you're not my type.' You certainly didn't need to give me a pity fuck."

His jaw clenched as he stared at me. "Jesus Christ, you weren't a goddamn pity fuck."

I turned away, lifting my hand over my shoulder to wave off his lies, then started down the hallway and to the stairwell. I didn't stop until I was in the loft, and I prayed he wouldn't follow me up here. I couldn't look at him, not now.

Not when it was just like before.

And, honestly, how stupid could one girl be? I was brilliant in school, could ace a test without a single second of studying, but put me in social situations and I was as inept as a preschooler.

Even after four years, I hadn't learned my lesson.

And just like before, I had become the source of someone else's amusement, just a game. Except this time, I didn't have the relief of Gage disappearing and never coming back. This time, while I licked my wounds and tried to move on, I didn't have the luxury of doing so in private.

Chapter Twenty-five

Despite praying he would leave me be, I listened as his heavy footsteps sounded up the stairs. Walking as far from him as I could up here, I moved to stand at the far end of the loft against the railing overlooking the main room below, my back to him. I didn't want to see him, didn't want him to see *me*. I already felt pathetic. I didn't need another dose heaped on top of everything else.

"You think you were a pity fuck?" His voice held a hint of bafflement, and did he really think I wouldn't figure that out?

"Just leave, please."

"No, answer me." The bafflement was gone, replaced with the hint of steel I was so familiar with in his tone.

"I'd like to be alone."

"Well too fucking bad. You don't get to be alone in this cabin. And certainly not now. Now *answer me*."

Was this some kind of game for him? Hearing me repeat my humiliation over and over again? Did he get some sick satisfaction from it? From stringing along the naive little rich girl and then having a laugh over it?

Instead of hearing his retreating steps like I'd hoped, I heard him move closer. Worse still, I could *feel* him. And then he was behind me, his arms braced on the railing outside mine, the entire length of his body pressed up against me, and I wasn't sure I could take this. Not when he was large and firm and unrelenting against me. Not when the scent I'd come to associate with him was invading my senses. Not when his breath was right next to my ear.

"Answer me." It was a harsh command, his voice gravel and steel.

I shook my head and looked down at my hands white-knuckling the wood railing. "Why, so you can humiliate me more? I get it. Mission accomplished. Now would you *please leave*."

"You were not a goddamn pity fuck." He pressed against me harder, flexing his hips so he was flush against me, and I gasped. I couldn't help it. Because I felt him. I *felt him*. "Yeah, princess. That's me you're feeling. And in case my dick isn't a clear enough message for you, I want you. All the fucking time. Even when you're stomping around, acting pissy. Even when every instinct in me is yelling at me to back the fuck off. To leave you alone. To run and never look back. Even then."

Everything he was saying contradicted what he'd said downstairs not even five minutes ago, so which was it? Now, he was hard, pressed against me, and I didn't know what he was doing, but I wasn't interested in playing. Because this wasn't just sex. Not to me. It had never been. Whether I liked it or not, whether it made sense or not, my heart was in the mix. Not completely, not all-consuming—not yet—but it was still all tied up in knots with Gage.

I took a deep breath and let it out along with the only words I could, "Stop playing games with me."

He laughed, though there was no humor in the sound. "That's what I'm trying to do."

"You're talking in circles. I don't understand what you're trying to say. Which is the truth, Gage? Because you've changed your story in the last ten minutes. Stop lying about it and just tell me the truth."

"That's what I just did. The truth is I want you. And I shouldn't."

As much as I wanted to focus on his admission that he wanted me, I couldn't. Because for some reason, he didn't think he should be allowed that with me. I turned my head to look at him over my shoulder. "Why?"

"*Why?* Take a look around, Madison. Isn't that answer enough? I'm a terrible fucking person—otherwise you wouldn't be here with me. And you think what we did last night was okay?"

"If we both wanted it, yes, I think it was okay. And you're not a terrible person—you just think you are. But I know there's more to you. I've seen it."

"Of course you'd think that."

I tried to turn around, but he had me pinned to the railing, his unforgiving body like a concrete wall blocking me in. "What's that supposed to mean?" I asked. "I'm not an idiot and I'm not incompetent."

"No, you're not, but you're naive, and you don't always know what's good for you."

Despite how hard I tried to make my voice push against him as harshly as his had against me, it still came out shaky. "Fuck you, Gage."

"You wanted the truth, Madison, and I'm giving it to you. If you weren't in this situation, you wouldn't have spared me a second glance. People like us don't connect, we don't form friendships or relationships or whatever the fuck. You were scared yesterday, and I took advantage of that. And I shouldn't let it happen again. Despite my dick begging me to."

My lips parted, my jaw dropping. "You shouldn't *let* that happen? So, what, yesterday you thought I was so out of my mind I wasn't cognizant? That I wasn't aware enough to make the decision to sleep with you? What about before? What about when we were making out in bed? Did I feel scared to you then?"

I felt his jaw brush against my hair as he shook his head. "You didn't know any better."

Tired of feeling trapped, I snapped my elbow back and connected it with his stomach, the suddenness of it surprising him. He let out a puff of air as he took a small step back, but it was enough to allow me to slip out from between him and the railing. I spun on him, my voice rising with my ire. "I am *not* a child, Gage. I haven't been one in a very, very long time, so stop treating me like one. I knew exactly what I was doing yesterday. That was *my* choice. Don't you dare take that away from me. If you do, you're no better than every other person in my life."

"But I'm *not* better! I never have been, and that's the fucking problem. Look at my life, Madison. Do you think I want you to get wrapped up in this shit more than you already are? Do you think I want to drag you into this?"

"Maybe not, but you don't get to make that decision for me. That's not fair, and you know it. I'm an adult, and I'd appreciate it if you'd treat me like one, whether or not we're sleeping together. You know how much I've been through in my life, and you know how many of my choices have been taken away. Don't treat me like I'm a china doll who's going to break at any second."

"You won't break?" He stepped right up into my space, making me walk backward until I was pressed into the wall. And still he was there, looming over me. He pressed his hands to the wall on either side of my shoulders and brought his face down to mine, so close our noses were nearly touching. So close I could feel every puff of his breath against my lips. "You sure about that? Because I'm rough, Madison. I'm not gentle."

I refused to look away. I met his stare head-on and kept my voice even. "You were last night."

"Last night was the exception, not the rule. I'm not a gentle person. I'm rough and hard and I hurt people. I'm the opposite of everything you should have."

"Stop trying to tell me what I should and shouldn't have. That's *my* decision."

"Then tell me what you want. Right now. Is it me that you want?"

He was dark and imposing, his shoulders eclipsing the light coming in from the windows behind him. He was nothing like what I thought I'd want, no part of him resembling any of the teenage crushes I'd had. When I'd fantasized about being with someone, a man like Gage had never entered the picture.

But now he was all I could see.

"Tell me, Madison. Is this what you want?" He pressed closer to me, his eyes boring into mine. He was trying to scare me, trying to get me to feel what I had in those first two days here, but I couldn't. Not anymore. Not after what we'd been through and what I'd seen in him. Something he didn't even know was there.

"Yes," I whispered.

GHOST

This girl was going to drive me fucking crazy. One minute, she was scared and unsure of herself, and the next she had balls the size of mine, and she wasn't backing down.

As soon as the whispered word left her lips, I was on her, pressing her fully against the wall. I gripped her face, my mouth taking hers harshly, because I hadn't been lying to her. I wasn't gentle. That wasn't my thing. And despite my conscience screaming at me to leave her alone, I wasn't listening. Not anymore.

I wanted her now. Fuck the circumstances and our differences and the secrets I was harboring. Fuck everything else.

I pressed farther into her, bending at the knees so I could kiss her harder. She met each pass of my tongue, groaning into my mouth, and I couldn't get close enough to her. I reached down and gripped her under the ass, lifting her up, startling a yelp from her. Her eyes flew open, her mouth parting as I lifted her and pressed her against the wall.

"Wrap your legs around me." Jesus Christ, was that my voice?

It sounded too low, too desperate. What the hell was this girl doing to me?

"What? No, not like this." She shook her head, a mixture of panic and arousal swimming in her eyes.

"Yes, just like this. Come on, do it."

"You can't hold me up like this! Let's just—"

"Does it look like I'm having any fucking problem holding you up? Now, wrap your legs around me." I pushed my hips against hers, steadying her against the wall as I reached one hand back and guided her leg around me. "Good, now the other."

She stared at me, her eyes darting between my arms and my face, but she did as I asked. Satisfied, I moved both hands back to her ass and thrust into her jean-covered pussy. A moan tore from her throat, her head falling back to the wall, and I smiled.

"See, that wasn't so bad." I licked up her neck, bit at her jaw, sucked hard enough at the space just below her ear to leave a mark, and the thought that I was leaving something of myself on her got me even harder than I already was. I throbbed behind the too-tight zipper of my jeans.

"Gage, oh, God . . ."

"That's it. I want to hear you. Do you like this? Do you feel how much I want you?"

I pressed hard against her mouth, slipping my tongue inside just to taste her again. I snaked a hand between us and slipped it under her shirt, moving it up until I could peel the cup of her bra down to get at what I wanted. Her nipple was already hard against my thumb as I rubbed it back and forth. She gasped and arched against me, and Christ, I might actually come in my fucking jeans if she kept this up.

Slipping my hand out from under her shirt, I lowered it straight to her pussy, rubbing the seam of her jeans against her. They were bulky, though, the material too thick, and I had no idea if I was hitting the right spot. I wanted to get her off, and I wanted it right now.

As much as it killed me to do so, I reached back and un-hooked her legs from around me, then lowered her to the floor. Her eyelids fluttered open. "What—"

She didn't get any more words out before I was tugging at the button of her jeans, then yanking the zipper down. I leaned next to her against the wall as I slid my hand inside her pants, bypassing her panties, until I got to the warm wetness of her. We both groaned at the first contact, our mouths seeking each other as soon as I brushed a fingertip against her clit.

"Spread your legs a little more, baby."

Uncertainty swam in her eyes, but she did as I asked, then moaned into my mouth when I moved my hand down and slipped a finger inside her. And Christ, she was wet. I wanted to feel it against my dick. I wanted to feel it against my mouth.

Impatient and frenzied, I pumped first one finger, then two into her while I tried to shove her jeans and panties down with my other hand. Finally they were down far enough that she could kick them off and to the side, and I couldn't wait. Despite her panting against my ear, despite the way her pussy was clenching around my fingers—how close I knew she was if I just kept this up a little lon-ger—I needed to feel her against my mouth, so I dropped to my knees right there.

"Gage?" She was breathless, her eyes heavy-lidded, her voice ringing with apprehension, and I didn't want her questioning any-thing. This was, no doubt, another thing she'd never experienced, and it made me ache in a way I didn't want to examine right now to know I'd be the first one to do this for her. I'd be the only one to know the taste of her.

I gripped one of her legs behind her knee and lifted it over my shoulder. She gave out a startled little squeak and grappled for pur-chase, one hand sprawled against the wall behind her and the other on my head, but I didn't stop. I spread her open then leaned forward and licked a long line straight up her pussy, flicking my tongue against her clit.

"Oh my God." It was only a breath, an exhalation, and that was still too much talking. I wanted her incoherent. I wanted her babbling and blissed out of her fucking mind.

I wanted her as lost with me as I always seemed to be with her.

Chapter Twenty-six

MADISON

I didn't know whether to be embarrassed or turned on, and it seemed my body didn't, either. I wanted to yank my leg down from his shoulder; I wanted to open myself up to him further. I wanted to lower my hands and cover myself from his piercing eyes; I wanted to reach down and grip his head, pulling him closer to me.

I wanted, and yet I was nervous to actually have. To take. Just like everything with Gage.

It didn't matter to him, though. As if he knew the internal struggle I was going through, he reached up and took both my hands, intertwining our fingers and pressing them back against the wall at my sides while his tongue did unspeakable things to me.

Last night had been amazing, but this . . . This was something unbelievably different. This was a concentrated effort, strictly for my pleasure. And the look in Gage's eyes as he stared up at me from between my legs showed he was enjoying it as much as I was, even though he got nothing from it.

Letting my head fall back against the wall, I closed my eyes and just *felt*. I gave myself permission to let go and just feel. I didn't need to overthink it, didn't need to analyze the whole exchange. I just needed to concentrate on the heat of Gage's rough hands against my own, squeezing like he didn't want to let go. The brush of his scruff against my inner thighs and then the place between where I was aching for him. The juxtaposition of that roughness followed by the smoothness of his lips, the gentle glide of his tongue.

And then there was the answer to one of my moans, his response vibrating against me, and that combined with his focused efforts exactly where I wanted him most shoved me right over the cliff I hadn't even known I was at the edge of.

Through the ebbs and flows of my orgasm, I managed to stay upright, though I wasn't sure how. I was still breathing heavy, my world spinning, and I wanted to crawl over to the bed and feel him on top of me again.

Despite what I wanted, Gage had other plans. He stood, wiping his hand over his mouth as he looked me up and down, his eyes as hungry as I'd ever seen them. "Don't move."

"Wha—" On weak knees, I pushed away from the wall, and he fixed me with a hard stare.

"I said don't move. I want you right there."

Here? He couldn't possibly mean . . .

But as he came back from across the room, pulling his shirt over his head and unbuttoning the fly of his jeans before he pulled himself out and rolled the condom down his length, I knew that, yes, he did mean. Right here.

He didn't stop until he was on me again, his rough hands gripping my face as he stole another kiss. And then his hands were everywhere, one moment soft and gentle, the next harsh and demanding. He caressed my neck, my arms, yanked my shirt over my head and nearly tore my bra off in his haste. His teeth were rough against the sensitive skin of my breasts, and I wanted this. I wanted it all. Because this felt more like Gage than anything else had so far.

When his hands were below my butt, lifting me, he said, "Again. Like before."

I tried not to think about how much I weighed, how *exposed* I felt like this. Instead I focused on Gage, on the hungry look in his eyes, on the hardness pressing into my inner thigh that clearly showed how much he wanted this. How much he wanted me.

And for once in my life, I was going to enjoy that.

He held me up like I was nothing more taxing than a backpack, and as much as his bulk had been intimidating initially, I loved that it meant he could do this with me. I thought back to yesterday when that other man had been here, how I'd felt utterly safe with Gage in front of me, how his size had been *comforting* to me. Such a disparity from what I'd felt at the beginning, and I didn't know when I'd turned down that path. When had I started looking to him as a source of comfort instead of fear?

"Look at me."

My eyes, which I'd closed at some point, snapped open at his request. He was staring right at me, his breathing rough and ragged, his lips parted, his cheeks flushed.

"Rough, remember?"

I nodded, cupped his face in my hands, and felt as he brushed the tip of his length over me. Top to bottom and back again, until I was lifting my hips, needing him inside me.

And then he was. And despite what he'd said, despite his promise of being rough, despite his denial that he was ever gentle, he slid into me slowly, watching me carefully for any hint of discomfort. It was only after I exhaled and relaxed in his arms that he moved out and back in again, and then he started the frenzied rhythm he'd tried to warn me against.

He had me open completely to him, my legs hooked over his elbows as he held me up easily. His hands rested on my lower back, gripping me and pulling me down on him. And he wasn't lying. This wasn't the gentle encounter we'd had last night. This was want and frustration and desire all culminating in one explosive point. This was Gage, pure and raw and real, and I loved every second of it.

I pulled his face to mine, trying to capture his lips, but it was too awkward, our bodies moving too roughly against one another. Instead, he stayed close, his open mouth resting against mine, our breaths mingling between us, and even though this was rougher than it had been last night, it felt different.

What was happening between us now was real and raw, empty of pretenses, and I welcomed everything he gave me. I cherished it, because this was Gage, undiluted.

His eyes never strayed from mine, even when my name left his lips in a whispered groan. When he pushed all the way inside me and stilled, he finally crashed his mouth down on mine, his tongue licking against the seam of my lips. He was everywhere, all around me, inside me, infiltrating my thoughts and stealing my emotions.

And I didn't want him to leave.

GHOST

I took her like a goddamn animal against the wall. But that was the thing—when I was around her, I couldn't control myself. She brought out something in me I hadn't even known was there— something I didn't *want* there.

Well so fucking much for that, because despite my efforts to stop it, this was happening. And I wasn't going to fight it anymore.

And worse yet? I didn't care if that made me a selfish asshole of the worst kind.

I needed this woman. To hell with everything else.

After cleaning up in the bathroom, I ascended the stairs to the loft and found Madison exactly where I'd left her. She was sprawled out on the bed, her dark hair a mess against the white pillowcase, her lips full and pink, her cheeks flushed, completely relaxed. The picture-perfect example of freshly fucked.

And her body? Jesus Christ. Even with the sheet covering her, the arch of her hips was pronounced under the thin cotton, and I remembered exactly what those tits looked like when they'd been in my face less than five minutes ago.

My dick twitched, and I didn't know how she did it.

In all my twenty-four years, I'd never felt like this. Not once. And it was some kind of fucked-up destiny bullshit that it would happen with the girl I'd been paid an obscene amount to hold captive. The one girl I should keep my hands off.

The one girl I wasn't *able* to keep my hands away from.

She lifted her eyelids when I slipped into bed next to her. I lay on my back, one arm propped behind my head while I looked over at her. I didn't know where we were now, what this had changed—if it had changed anything, though I knew deep down it probably changed *everything*. Once could be passed off as a fluke, something we did in the heat of the moment, but twice? I knew she wasn't the kind of girl to fuck just for the sake of it, but I had no idea what her feelings were beyond that.

And the truth of it was, I was scared shitless about what all this meant. Because ever since Madison had come into my life, things weren't how I was used to them being. I'd never—not once—had to worry about compromising myself with a job before. That wasn't who I was, and it sure as fuck wasn't my reputation. I did what I was paid to do, and I did it well. I did it with efficiency and skill and very little, if any, emotion. That was how I'd been so good at it for so long.

But with her? I'd do just about anything so I could keep her safe, despite what my job was. Despite the money or my boss. Right now, that meant I was questioning everything—everything I knew about the job, and everything I didn't. Was it best to stay here and wait for word for this to be over? Even doing that, I didn't know if she'd be safe being delivered back home, which was the original plan. I didn't know if I could trust the asshole who'd hired me in the first place not to do anymore harm to her, whether by his hand or another hired one.

From the beginning, little details had been eating at me, things that didn't seem right, and my instincts, which had been loud throughout this entire job, were now screaming at me. Part of me thought it was just my mind playing tricks because of my desire to make sure Madison was taken care of, to make sure nothing happened to her. The other, bigger part was certain something was off about this whole thing, and my gut was telling me I needed to get her out, that I needed to move her somewhere else to keep her safe and just call this whole fucking thing off.

"What are you thinking about?" Her voice was quiet, but it snapped me out of my thoughts just the same as if she'd shouted.

I snorted despite where my mind had just been. I couldn't help it. It was just such a clichéd question, and Madison was anything but a cliché. She was staring up at me, her eyes open and so trusting, despite the secrets I was still keeping from her. And didn't that make me feel like an even bigger asshole?

"Honestly, I'm thinking about how fucked I am."

She scooted a little closer to me, her bare leg brushing up against mine, and I had to stop myself from pulling it over a little farther until she was straddling my lap and I was inside her again.

"How so?"

If only it was that easy. To just tell her all the ways this was going to blow up in my face, ways that didn't have anything to do with our differences or social standings. Those had nothing on the kind of shit I was going to have to navigate after this was all over. And if the big boss man ever found out I'd fucked Madison while she was under my supervision? *I'd* be the job, and you could fucking well bet it wouldn't be for a simple capture.

And worse than all that was this heavy cloak of guilt I felt at keeping the details of the job from her. She deserved to know, even though doing so might royally fuck the rest of her life, she deserved the chance to make the choice herself. Like she'd said, she didn't need any more choices taken away from her. I just didn't know how the fuck I was going to tell her what I needed to.

"I'm in over my head here, Madison."

"This isn't exactly chartered territory for me, either, you know."

"I'm not talking just about our current situation. I'm talking about everything with you. I don't do this. Ever."

"When you say, 'this,' what exactly are you talking about?"

"All of it between you and me. Simple shit like just talking or showing you my drawings. But then other stuff that isn't me, like getting territorial yesterday when Frankie showed up. I don't do jealous or protective because I don't do relationships. But you took a fucking two-by-four to my whole goddamn outlook. I don't know what's up and what's down anymore."

She tentatively reached out to touch me, and even after everything we'd done in the last two days, she was still apprehensive to instigate anything. I knew that was my fault, though, especially after this morning. I was a fucking idiot.

When her hand rested against my bare stomach, I covered it with my own. She was looking at them when she said, "It's the same for me."

And that was what I was worried about. Because if we were both knocked on our asses, who was going to make sure we were standing at the end of this?

Chapter Twenty-seven

GAGE

We spent the rest of the morning and part of the afternoon in bed. Madison had fallen asleep a while ago, her head resting on my chest as I ran my fingers up and down her back. And though I should've been relaxed, should've been enjoying every second of it, I was jittery. Nervous. And I wasn't ever either of those things.

I couldn't ignore it anymore. Something was off. I didn't know what, and I had absolutely no solid evidence, but little things kept pinging around in my head . . . details that didn't quite add up. I wanted to call this whole fucking thing off, but I didn't know how the hell I was going to do that without putting Madison in jeopardy or a hit on my ass.

But something wasn't right, that much I was sure of. My instincts never led me astray, and right now, warning bells were going off like crazy. I just didn't know why.

I grabbed the phone from the nightstand and navigated to the call screen, my thumb hovering over my brother's name. If I made this call, if I breathed even an ounce of uncertainty to him, that was it. He'd know something was up, and even though he was my brother, I didn't know how he'd react. He was counting on this payday just as much as I was.

"Fuck it," I mumbled and pressed the button to call.

"Ghost, thank Christ. I was just going to call." The sharp, hurried tone of his voice had me tensing, all senses suddenly on alert.

"What's going on?"

"Fucking hell, man, everything's gone to shit. Something isn't right, and I'm getting twitchy as fuck about it."

Hearing Riley voice everything I'd been feeling only solidified my gut reaction. "Has something happened there?"

"No . . . not like you think. But shit's getting shady as hell around here. Guys aren't getting paid, things aren't happening on the original timeline, and asshole numero uno isn't answering my calls anymore. Is he returning yours?"

"I haven't tried calling him in a few days. He told me not to bother unless something was off." In fact, the last time I'd spoken to him was the night Madison had run.

"It's been eating at me for a couple days—that things just don't seem right. It could mean nothing, but . . ."

I blew out a breath and scrubbed a hand over my hair. "No, I think you're right. I've felt the same."

"Jesus," he bit out. His words were coming faster now. "Okay, I don't care if we're overreacting. Both of us feeling this way means something. Move to the fallout plan. You need to get out. Now. Leave the girl and go. I don't know if he's planning to bring the fucking cops down on the place or if he's getting shit in place to, but this screams setup to me."

"Fuck."

"Call me when you're clear." And then the line went dead.

"Fuck!"

"Gage?" Madison pushed off me, sitting up as she clutched the sheet to her chest. Her eyes were sleepy, but panicked, and that hit me like a wrecking ball. Despite what Riley had told me to do, there was no fucking way I was leaving her here. I wasn't going to run off to avoid the cops and leave her to fend for herself. Not when there were so many questions left unanswered. Not when I wanted her by my side so I could make sure she was safe.

This could all be an overreaction on my part, and if it happened to be, a shitstorm was going to rain down on me. But I didn't think it was. And I wasn't willing to leave her behind to find out for herself. Not when I knew the depths people had gone to to make sure she was captured in the first place.

When I did this, though . . . it meant I'd never again be able to do another job. I'd be blacklisted from every contact I'd ever made. I was sealing this life closed once and for all, and instead of panic at the uncertainty of what I'd do in the future that I was sure would come when I finally reached this point, instead of being unsure about my choice, all I felt was anxiety and urgency at making sure I got Madison out. Making sure I got her somewhere safe. And once that happened, once I was satisfied we hadn't been followed, I could concentrate on finding out exactly what the fuck was going on.

"I need you to get up now, okay? Get your shit, as fast as you can, Madison, do you understand?"

She followed my movements as I got out of the bed, her eyes wide and worried. "What? Why? What's going on—"

"As fast as you can, baby, please. I'll explain in the car."

Her brows lifted at the mention of the car, and I didn't know if it was seeing me scramble around the room to get dressed or the tone of my voice, but something scared her enough to snap her out of it and then she was moving.

I grabbed my bag from the corner, then hurried down the stairs to the main room and kitchen, doing a quick sweep to make sure I didn't leave anything behind. Coming here, I'd packed light, made sure to keep my stuff contained to my bag, but I didn't want to make a rookie mistake and leave something behind that would bring the fucking cops right to my doorstep.

Madison's footfalls echoed above me in the loft as I opened the safe and pulled everything from inside. I stuffed Madison's laptop and her phone into her messenger bag before I slipped into my coat. When she came down the stairs, I tossed her jacket to her, then shouldered both our bags before walking past her to the door.

"I've got your laptop in here." I patted the leather bag at my side. "Did you leave anything else around?"

She shook her head as she pushed her arms into her coat, then zipped it up.

Nodding, I pulled the key from my pocket and unlocked the door, scanning the surroundings. Once I was satisfied it was clear, I gestured her out in front of me before I locked up. There was no fucking way I was making this easy on anyone. I pocketed the only key as I walked down the front porch steps. Madison was standing by the passenger side door, her face pale and eyes worried, arms wrapped around herself as she watched me walk toward her.

In all this, I hadn't stopped to think about what her reaction would be. What she'd think about me dragging her off, especially knowing what the supposed outcome was to be—that at the end of this capture, she was to be delivered back at home, unharmed. But something wasn't right. I felt it straight to my bones.

I didn't know if this was the right reaction, if I was making the right choice. And when Riley found out I'd taken her with me, he was going to flip. But none of that mattered.

The only thing that mattered to me right now—the only thing I could see—was getting Madison out and keeping her safe.

MADISON

Silence engulfed us like a shroud. Gage's entire body was tense, his eyes darting to the side and rearview mirrors every couple of minutes, his knuckles white as he gripped the steering wheel. He would speed up, then realize how fast he was going and slow down with a muttered curse. Getting pulled over for speeding wouldn't be the best thing right now.

I didn't know what was going on, and he hadn't offered any information yet. Whatever we were fleeing from—and I had no doubt we were . . . the way we left made that clear—he wanted to get us as far away from it or them as possible. We were only about twenty minutes away from the cabin, and from his body language, from the rigid set of his shoulders, it looked like we weren't far enough.

And while his reaction had me nervous, had me contemplating every bad outcome possible, the thing of it was . . . I wasn't scared. I trusted Gage to keep me safe. And wasn't that the biggest surprise of all? Trusting the guy who'd been hired to kidnap me to keep me from getting hurt. But I did. Unwaveringly. He'd shown me the lengths he'd go to in order to do so, and I tried to focus on that instead of the tension radiating off him.

I fidgeted in my seat as I stared out my window at the scenery whipping past us. It was a quiet afternoon, hardly any other cars on the road with us, and I couldn't help but think of how different this ride was from the one that had brought me up here. It wasn't just the circumstances, though those were the most obvious. It was also who I was, the person I'd become—or had allowed to finally emerge—in the short days we'd been there.

But it wasn't only me who'd changed. Gage had, without question. I glanced over at him once more, his eyes focused in front of us. I tried to remember when I'd first noticed the differences in him, but I couldn't. It had been a gradual thing, like the leaves changing in the fall. One minute they were green, and in the next breath, they were a kaleidoscope of colors. I'd watched him go from someone who was cold and harsh to someone who was protective and fierce and, yes, gentle, even though he'd deny it.

I moved my attention once more out my window. Had anything else changed while I'd been gone? It'd only been five days—a blink of an eye, really—but it felt like so much longer to me. It felt like a lifetime had passed. This had been life-altering for me, in more ways than one. Had it been a wake-up call to my parents? Was my mother finally fighting the struggles of sobriety? Was my father an active member of our family once again, consoling my mother while they searched for me instead of submerging himself in his work?

I wanted to call them—if for no other reason than to tell them I was okay. Sylvia was worrying herself sick, that much I knew for certain, and I wanted to set her mind at ease. Now wasn't the time to approach Gage with that, though. I had no idea where we were even going or how long we'd be there. For all I knew, he was driving me straight home to drop me off. And for some reason, that twisted a knot in my stomach, because once I was home . . . once I was back to the real world, what did that mean for us?

And I knew what a ridiculous thing that was to contemplate at a time like this, but I couldn't help it. I was invested in this—in us—despite logic. Despite the outside world.

When I couldn't take it anymore, I finally broke the silence. "Gage?"

He slid his eyes to me, then checked the mirrors once again before staring out the windshield as the SUV ate up the asphalt in front of us.

That was as much of an acknowledgment to continue as I was going to get. "What's going on?"

He didn't answer for a moment, and just when I thought he wasn't going to say anything at all, he said, "I wish I knew." His uncertainty wasn't something I was used to. He did everything with purpose and focused direction. For him not to have solid answers but to make us leave anyway . . .

"Well, something made us flee." I thought back to the tail end of the phone call I'd heard when I'd woken up from my nap. "Did your brother say something?"

"Nothing concrete, no. And you're going to think I'm crazy for doing this based on nothing more than my gut, but it's never failed me before. I just . . ." He shook his head and glanced at me again, tightening his grip on the steering wheel. "I couldn't take a chance. Not with you."

Chapter Twenty-eight

GAGE

I drove us straight into the heart of downtown, wanting the anonymity the heavily populated location provided us. We could get lost in the crowds here much easier than we could if we were at a boutique hotel in her posh northern suburb. And I didn't want her anywhere near there, anyway. Not yet. Not ever. There was no telling the lengths to which the man responsible for orchestrating this entire, elaborate kidnapping would go.

Madison didn't speak as I checked us in under fake names and then led her up to the room. I'd asked for a room near the stairs, just in case we needed to make a fast exit. Coming this far, I wasn't going to start taking chances now.

Holding the door to the room open, I gestured for her to walk in ahead of me. She slipped inside and took her jacket off before moving to sit on the foot of the bed. After the door was double locked, I dropped our bags on the side of the bed then shed my coat. Spinning the chair from the desk around to face Madison, I dropped into it with a sigh. I leaned forward, elbows braced on my knees, and looked at her.

She was staring at me, a crease between her brows, but her body wasn't vibrating with the tension I felt coming from mine. I knew her lack of anxiety was only because she didn't know all the details of her kidnapping. There were things I hadn't told her—facts she wouldn't like—and as much as I wished I could keep it that way, as much as I wished she could forever remain in the dark, that just wasn't going to happen. It couldn't. I needed to figure out a way to tell her the one detail I knew would hurt her the most, but first I had to take care of this situation before whatever had my gut going haywire came to fruition.

I needed time to think, time to figure out how I could make this right—and if not *right*, at least end it—because I couldn't see it right now. The only thing I knew for sure was that I wasn't letting the asshole who thought he was running the show pin this whole fucking thing on me. I was going to strike before he could even think about it. And to do so, I needed to talk to my brother. He'd be ready with the information I'd need for our fallout plan, because of course we'd had one. Working for a first-timer, especially one as shady as this one, that was a no-brainer. We covered our asses, always.

More than that, though, I needed to ensure nothing was going to happen to Madison. Because my ending this whole thing didn't mean Frankie wouldn't get a call to do it all over again. I couldn't live with myself if something happened to her.

"Gage?" Her voice pulled me from my thoughts, and I glanced up at her. She'd moved to the corner of the bed so she was sitting directly in front of me. "Can you tell me what the plan is?"

The plan, as it was playing out in my mind, was something she definitely didn't need to know. Not now. Not yet. I didn't want to pile that on her and then leave to take care of this. I'd let her know once it was over and done with, and then I could help her figure out what she was going to do since she'd be free to do as she pleased. Something that preferably had her leaving that prison she called a home.

Instead of giving her nothing to go on, I told her what I could. "I need to call my brother and have him get me some things."

"What kind of things?"

"Voice recordings. Paper trail. Photographs."

Her eyes grew wide. "For what?"

"So I can make sure the guy who hired me doesn't turn right back around and hire someone else to finish the job. I need to make sure you're safe."

Her eyes darted between mine, worry and uncertainty reflected in them. "What about you?"

I nodded, though my safety wasn't at the forefront of my mind right now. "Yeah, that, too. All that information will make it so he doesn't get any ideas about bringing the cops to my front door."

"Do you think he's already got the cops involved?"

"I wouldn't put it past him. The thing is, I don't know what he's done—not for certain—but I'm not willing to take the chance to find out."

"But what if you go there and it's a setup? What if he's already got the cops waiting for you?" She reached out and took one of my hands, her fingers restless against my palm.

I brought my other hand to hers, cocooning it between both of mine and brought it to my mouth. Placing a kiss on the side of her pinky, I said, "I'll be careful. I'm not going to walk into anything that looks like a trap."

She shook her head. "I don't like it."

"Yeah, well, I'm not willing to risk the alternative."

Her eyes searched mine. "Because of me."

I stared at her, cataloged every one of her features. Over the last forty-eight hours I'd become intimately acquainted with them. When I met her eyes again, saw the vulnerable hope and trust reflecting back at me, I realized I'd walk to hell and back if it meant she'd get out of this unscathed. If it meant I could keep her safe, even if it caused my demise.

MADISON

The look of determination in his eyes had me scared to death, because there was nothing I could say that would change his mind. He didn't reply, didn't answer my question, but he didn't have to. I knew he was doing this for me as much as he was doing it for himself—more so. And that thought killed me. If something happened to him, if he got caught or hurt because he was trying to make this right for me, I didn't know what I'd do.

I didn't know if he was doing this as redemption for taking the job to capture me in the first place or not. I wanted to tell him redemption wasn't needed—not in my eyes. Because I knew if it hadn't been him, it would've been someone else. Someone who'd been in prison for rape or domestic violence or murder. Someone with a black heart and no soul. It would've been Frankie, who'd threatened to beat me and cut off one of my fingers, or someone just like him.

Before I could voice a thousand reasons why I didn't want him to go through with this plan, he reached one hand out and gripped my neck, pulling me to him and pressing his lips to mine. Despite wanting to remain impassive so I could talk more about this, I melted into him. Into his lips and his tongue, letting him guide me, take what he wanted. Resting my hands against his chest, I felt his heartbeat against my palm as I forgot everything else but the feel of him against me. He moved his hand higher, his fingers threading through my hair as the other rested on my shoulder, his thumb brushing down over the ridge of my collarbone and up the length of my neck over and over again.

When I was with him like this, when I was surrounded by Gage, it was like everything else fell away. Like nothing else mattered. Like nothing else existed.

And if I needed that escape at any time, it was now.

I didn't resist when he stood, pulling me up with him. Nor when he walked me backward until I was at the side of the bed. I didn't utter a sound of protest when he slowly stripped us of our clothes, or when he lowered us to the bed. I barely let myself dwell on the fact that I was naked and the lights from the side tables were on and shining brightly against my skin. Instead, I focused on the path his hands took. Down my neck, over my chest, sweeping across a nipple, playing in the valley between my breasts. Up and down, again and again, over the flare of my hips, the dip of my waist.

Gage reached around and tugged me closer to him. I gasped into his mouth at the feel of his erection against my stomach. And then I was gasping for another reason entirely when he pulled my leg up and over his hip, then reached around and pressed his fingers right where I was aching for him.

I broke away from the kiss, gasping for air, a moan spilling from my lips. He continued to rub circles around me as he kissed along my jaw, his tongue licking a path down my neck. Pulling back far enough so he could reach, he flicked his tongue against my nipple, nearly making me shoot off the bed.

"Gage," I breathed, my fingers going to his hair. I wanted to touch him, to make him feel as good as he made me feel, but I had no idea what I was doing.

When he kissed his way back up to my mouth, I met his tongue with my own as I brushed my hand down the front of him, passing over his chest, the ridges in his abdomen, until I came to exactly what I was searching for. Tentatively, I ran a finger down the length of him, eliciting a groan from Gage. He kissed me harder, deeper, his reaction making me braver as I wrapped my hand around him and gave a light squeeze.

This time it was Gage who pulled back enough so he could look between us. *"Jesus Christ."*

His attention was held by what I was doing with my hand, moving it slowly up and down his erection, and I wanted to watch, too. I wanted to see what had him so captivated. With my forehead resting against his neck, I watched my hand move over him, watched him slip through my fist, my breathing picking up. I loved seeing him, hard and flushed in my hand, knowing I was the one who'd done this to him. It was exhilarating.

"You like watching, baby?" His voice was quiet and gravelly, his breath warm against my ear.

A shudder racked my body as heat bloomed in my cheeks, but I couldn't stop. I *did* like watching us together. I loved it. The softness of my hand against the hardness of him . . .

Suddenly, Gage's hand was gripping mine, pausing my movements and squeezing him harder than I ever would have on my own. "*Shit,* wait."

I looked up at him, eyes wide, afraid I'd done something wrong. Before I could even question it, his lips landed on mine and then he was pulling away, twisting around to grab something off the floor. A moment later, he was back, a small square packet in his hand. He ripped open the package and rolled the condom on, and then he pressed himself right up against me, moving my leg up and over his hip once again. He reached around and circled his fingers over me again, sliding them up and down, dipping a finger inside me.

Without conscious thought, I started rocking my hips against him, yearning for something more. As soon as I realized what I was doing, I stopped, nervous and embarrassed about my forwardness.

He gripped my upper thigh, right below my butt, and mimicked the motions I was just making. "No, don't stop. Show me what you want."

I let him guide me into the rhythm again, and eventually I was doing it all on my own, rubbing myself against the length of him. It didn't take long before I needed even more. I needed to feel him inside me.

Placing a kiss just below my ear, Gage said, "Good girl. So good. Now tell me."

It was one thing doing the act, letting my body speak for me. It was another thing altogether actually voicing what I wanted.

"Come on, baby. Tell me what you want."

"I want you," I breathed, my eyes closing against my embarrassment.

"How?"

I paused, swallowed down the lump of nerves in my throat. On a whispered breath, I said, "Inside me."

With a groan, he reached around and guided himself into me, and then I felt that delicious fullness I'd felt every time we were together like this. He didn't stop pushing until he was all the way inside and he was as close to me as he could get.

"Jesus, that's good. You feel so fucking *good*."

Before I could answer, before I could tell him it felt amazing for me, too, he captured my mouth with his, and then he was moving. I tried not to think about what I knew was coming when we were outside this cocoon we'd made for ourselves, once this distraction was complete. He was going to leave, going to do something to try and keep me safe, when I wanted to do the same for him.

"Stay with me, Madison. Stop thinking."

I opened my eyes to find him staring at me, his hips still moving against mine, and then he tilted a different way, and I couldn't think anymore.

"*Oh.*"

"Yeah." His reply was a satisfied rumble against my lips as he slipped a hand between us and rubbed his thumb against me. "I'm so close. Come on, baby, get there."

Mouth agape, I nodded, clenching my eyes closed as every muscle in my body tightened, climbing climbing climbing, until I was in free fall, Gage right behind me.

Chapter Twenty-nine

GAGE

Madison was quiet as I talked to Riley, making the arrangements to have him bring me what I needed. She watched me with worried eyes, and I knew how much she didn't want me to do this. But not doing it wasn't an option. If I didn't take care of this now, there was no telling what kind of shit I'd run into in a week or two. Worse than that, there was no telling how long he'd wait until he tried to have Madison taken again. I would not let that happen.

"How long will you be gone?"

I glanced up at her. "I'm not sure. I need to meet Riley, then take care of this."

She fidgeted with the blanket on the bed, her concerned eyes locked on me. "What happens when you get back?"

I walked over to where she was sitting on the side of the bed and squatted in front of her. I didn't know how I was going to do it, how I was going to find words to tell her what she deserved to know, but I would. "Then I tell you the whole story. And after you know everything, you can tell me what you want to do."

She swallowed and nodded as I pushed myself up to stand. I

slipped my phone and switchblade into my jeans, then reached for my coat.

"Do not answer the phone, do you understand? And do not, under any circumstances, use your phone. That's very important, Madison. I don't want anyone knowing where we are. Not yet." She gave me another nod, so I continued, "In case I need to call, I'll call the room, let it ring twice, hang up, and call back right away, got it?"

"Yes."

"Stay in the hotel room. Don't even go to the fucking ice machine, okay?"

She stood up and walked toward me, and I pulled her in for a hug, kissing her on the forehead. "I'll be back soon. Lock this up behind me."

And then I was gone, slipping down the stairwell next to our door. Riley was meeting me in thirty minutes with everything I'd need to bring with me. I knew Madison was worried, but the truth was there wasn't anything to be worried about. There were two types of people I dealt with: men who'd kill if given a reason, and everyone else. My employer was firmly in the latter. He might be an asshole, a liar, and a bully, but he wasn't a killer. And I wasn't even sure he had it in him to make the call so he didn't have to do the dirty work himself.

I walked through the lobby and straight out the front doors into the brisk early evening air. The sun was setting, still bathing everything in pale light, and I headed to meet Riley, ready to put an end to this once and for all.

MADISON

I tried to occupy myself with TV, with a movie on my laptop, but I kept watching the minutes tick by on the clock. I wondered what Gage was doing at this very moment, hoping he was fine, that everything was going to be fine. It didn't work, though, my brain conjuring up a thousand different ways this night could end—all of them ending in devastation for him. I was scared to death he was going to get hurt or caught or arrested.

He was still keeping the major details of this to himself, and I feared the secrets he was protecting had to do with who, exactly, he was meeting with tonight, who had hired him. Was it because of the danger the man posed? Was Gage worried for my safety if I knew the answer? If that was the case, I didn't want to contemplate what that'd mean for him.

After everything that had happened, after spending the last several days with him, I'd grown to care for him—truly care for him. And it wasn't just some reaction to a traumatic life event. What I felt for him was real and powerful, and I wouldn't ever be able to forgive myself if he went to jail because he was trying to protect me.

I got up from the bed, walked the length of the hotel room, wearing a path in the patterned carpet. Anxiety held me in a choke hold, every worry I had bearing down on me. My thoughts kept coming back to Gage, to what he was doing now, who he was speaking to . . . If something bad was happening to him.

Because I'd only get myself more worked up if I continued down that path, I forced myself to think of something else, and my home—my parents and Sylvia were the first things that came to mind. What were they doing? Were they scared? Had they assumed the worst after I'd been gone for so long? Had my dad involved the police or had that been too public for his image? The weight that settled in my chest at the thought of his image being more important than my safety was unwelcome but not unfamiliar.

Glancing over, I saw my messenger bag sitting on the floor next to the bed, and I bit my thumbnail as I stared. Gage had stuffed my phone inside the front pocket before we'd left the cabin. It would be so easy to call, to pull up my contacts and hold down the button designating *home* and then hear Sylvia's voice, calm her fears . . .

Almost as if I didn't have control of my actions, I walked over to my bag and picked it up, setting it on the bed. Rummaging through the front pocket, I pulled out a few papers and finally came across my phone. Setting them all on the mattress, I stood over them, my eyes fixated on the tiny electronic object. Even though Gage had told me not to call anyone, I wanted to tell Sylvia I was okay. Five days was so long, and I wanted to ease her fears. Tell her that I wasn't sure what was going on now, but that Gage had rescued me, had taken me somewhere safe, and we were trying to find a way to get me home again.

Just as I was reaching for the phone, the straight, block letters of my father's handwriting caught my eye. Interspersed with other notes of no consequence was a folded sheet of paper, my name on the front, and I remembered with a pang in my chest that he'd left it for me the morning I'd been taken. The morning I'd found my mother bloody and bruised in the bathroom because he always left early enough so he was able to ignore things like that.

I picked up the paper and turned around, lowering myself to the bed as I opened the note and read.

Let's talk soon about your mother. I've found a few options for where we can admit her. It's not fair to you to keep taking care of her like this. I'll make it right, Madison. Just give me a little more time.

~Dad

The note sparked something in my chest I hadn't felt in so long: hope. My father always ignored my mother's addiction, ignored any plea I'd uttered, saying she didn't have a problem, so I'd eventually stopped trying. Sylvia was the only one who knew how taxing it was to take care of my mom, but I wondered now . . . Did my dad know? Did he finally realize what a sacrifice it had been for me?

The hope that had sparked in my chest grew until it filled my whole being. Maybe everything was already different at home. Maybe he'd started working less, keeping an eye on her. Maybe he'd already made the call to get her checked into rehab, so things could finally get better. So this crushing weight on my shoulders could finally be lifted. So I could finally live the life I wanted now more than ever.

Despite knowing that Gage would be absolutely livid for what I was about to do, I had to. An urgency had erupted in my veins, and I couldn't stop my curiosity, my need to know.

Instead of calling from my cell, I went to the hotel phone and dialed the number I knew by heart, holding my breath as it rang.

"Frost residence."

A choked laugh fell from my lips, and suddenly my eyes were watering, tears spilling over.

"Maddie?" Sylvia gasped. "Oh, God, *Maddie?*"

I nodded my head, a smile on my lips. "It's me."

"Good heavens." The words were merely a breath, and I could hear the relief pouring out of her. I imagined her in the kitchen, her entire body sagging against the kitchen counter, hand to her heart. "Oh, Maddie. My dear, sweet Maddie. Are you okay? Are you safe? Where are you?"

"I . . . I can't tell you that."

"Wha—"

"But I'm safe. I'm safe now, okay?"

"You won't be safe until you're here. Until you're *home*."

I twisted the cord of the phone around my finger. "I know, but I can't come home just yet, but I . . . I wanted to tell you that I'm okay."

"I've been so worried . . . I can't believe it's really you. What happened? Where have you been? Are you hurt?" Her questions came rapid fire, one right after the other, and I knew she must have so many for me. I wanted to answer them all, to offer her even more relief, but I couldn't. Not yet.

"I'll tell you everything when I get home, okay? I can't talk long. Are . . . are my parents there?"

From the time I asked and then the few seconds of silence coming from her end, my hopes soared and then came crashing to the ground. I knew everything I needed to without her uttering a word. And everything I'd felt, those brief moments of wonder at what my life might be like when I went back home, all of it was crushed. "So nothing's changed, then? Me being gone . . . it did nothing?"

"I . . . I'm sorry, Maddie."

Closing my eyes, I sunk to the bed, sitting at the edge, and shook my head. I should've known . . . I should've realized. Nothing was ever going to change. Not unless I took the step to make the change myself. And after this? I just might be ready to.

I cleared my throat and said, "Nothing for you to be sorry about, Sylvia. Listen, I have to go. I wasn't supposed to call anyway. Promise me you won't say anything to anyone. Don't tell my parents . . . no one. *Please.*"

She was silent for a moment, two, and just when I thought she was going to tell me it was too late, my parents were standing there, and the cops were tracing the call and bringing a whole squad down on my location, she whispered, her voice shaky, "Okay. But you come home to me, Maddie. Soon."

I swallowed against the tears clogging my throat at the affection I heard in her voice. "I will. I promise."

And then I hung up the phone, tears blurring my vision as I stared at it. Sadness bloomed in my chest, grief for a life I'd only lived in my mind for short minutes. The longer I sat staring, though, the more that sadness gave way to anger. It overwhelmed me, bubbling up and over until it was all I could feel. Even after everything that had happened, an event that had changed my life irrevocably, it had absolutely no bearing on them. They were still the same people

I'd left five days ago. Still the same people who would let me down, day in and day out. Still the same selfish people who cared more about their addictions than they did their own daughter.

Meanwhile, the person I'd known less than a week was out there risking his neck—possibly his *life*—to make sure I was safe, that my future was mine and mine alone. Who knew what his employer was doing, if he had the cops at the ready—or worse. And my parents were oblivious in their worlds of luxury, my mom numbed by alcohol, my father wining and dining the most important people in Chicago while his daughter was in the middle of the scariest event of her life . . .

I froze, a gasp leaving me as a sudden realization came. For the little my mother and father were worth as parents, they were good for something. My father was widely known in the city, well connected and well regarded. He had friends everywhere, and even if he couldn't help with the legal aspects, there wasn't a doubt in my mind that he could come up with a plan to help get Gage and me out of this mess unscathed. All it would take was a twist of the truth—that Gage had found me, rescued me, and was now being framed as the person responsible for orchestrating everything. And I had no qualms at all about lying to my father about that. Not if it kept Gage safe.

Without any second-guessing and before I could talk myself out of it, I picked up the hotel phone and dialed the direct line to his office. It was after seven, his secretary long gone, and pleas left my lips as the ringing droned on and on. When his voicemail picked up, I swore under my breath, hung up, and dialed again immediately.

After three more times with no answer, I slammed the receiver down and stood. I didn't stop to think as I put my shoes on, then my coat, as I shoved my phone and those loose papers back in my bag, tucking the plastic room key into the front pocket.

I didn't think about my safety at all when I unlocked the door and slipped out into the long, empty hallway. I couldn't think about myself at all when all I felt was anxiety and bone-deep fear for Gage.

And for once, I had the power to do something. I had the power to help.

Chapter Thirty

The ride to my father's office building both took too long and didn't last nearly enough time. Anxiety and nerves swarmed in my stomach, a flurry of butterflies ready to erupt. I paid the cab driver with the emergency credit card I always carried in my bag. Gage would have a fit if he knew, but at this point I didn't think it much mattered. I was about to ask my father for help and that would out us completely—or as completely as I safely could while still making sure Gage got help—so it wasn't like my location was going to be secretive for much longer.

With the strap to my bag slung over a shoulder, I ran up to the front of the building, nearly out of breath as I raced inside. The lobby was empty, save for a doorman I'd seen once or twice in the handful of times I'd come here to visit my father.

"Ms. Frost! Well, this is a pleasant surprise. I wasn't expecting to see you. I thought you and your mother weren't due back until next week," he said, smiling broadly at me.

The words halted my movement, and I looked at him quizzically. "Me and my mother? Due back from where?"

His brow creased as he watched me. "The spa? In Arizona? Mr. Frost said it was a mother-daughter bonding vacation."

It was just another piece of information that served to knock me down a little further. My father hadn't told anyone about my abduction, probably too concerned with his image, with the impending buyout he'd been coaxing to fruition for months. Instead of doing what was best for me, instead of actually looking for me, he'd made up a story to explain my absence.

I swallowed past a lump in my throat as I realized that if I hadn't been with Gage, if it had been Frankie who'd taken me, I'd still be there. I'd still be there, hoping and praying for someone, anyone, to find me while it remained business as usual around here. While I'd been at the cabin, I'd assumed my family was doing everything they possibly could to see to my safe return. In actuality, they'd done nothing.

The doorman was watching me, the concern in his eyes growing with each passing second of silence. I offered what I hoped passed for a smile. "Oh. We, um, we cut the spa trip a little short. Is my father in, by any chance?"

He nodded. "I believe he's still up there. You remember the floor?"

"Yes, thank you." Without looking back, I hurried over to the elevator and pushed the button for the seventeenth floor. I pressed my back against the wall, holding my breath as I waited for it to ascend.

GAGE

Riley had been early, waiting for me to pick up the envelope full of evidence. We'd picked a location close to the office building I needed to get to so Riley could be close, just in case. He was fearful the cops were already involved, but I wasn't so sure. The more time I had to think about it, the more I was certain that the chicken-shit who'd hired me wouldn't do that. For one thing, it would bring unwanted attention to his name. For another, he talked a big talk, but I wasn't sure he could walk the walk.

The high-rise office building wasn't far, and I managed to get by the single on-duty doorman as easily as I'd done the other times I'd come here. While there were stragglers around here and there, hardcore workaholics still at it, the building was mostly quiet. No one met me as I ascended the steps to the floor I needed. Darkness greeted me as I quietly slipped through the metal door leading to the stairwell. The only light I could see was peeking from an open door at the far end of the hall, and I knew exactly whose office that was.

I crept down the hallway, senses on high alert for any noise, any movement, but I found none. Standing frozen outside the open office door, I listened for signs of life—shuffling of papers, the creak of his leather office chair—but heard none. Confident he'd gone out for a minute, I strode into his office and looked around. It was obnoxious in its size, two walls of floor to ceiling windows doing nothing to bring warmth into the space. It was stale, almost medicinal. There were no personal artifacts. No pictures of his wife or his daughter. Nothing that would suggest he was anything other than the professional persona he gave off.

I walked around to the other side of his desk, tossing the envelope I'd brought onto his desk as I plopped into his chair. Relaxing back, I clasped my hands over my stomach and propped my feet up on his desk. I couldn't wait for him to show up, to see the look on his face when he realized who was sitting here waiting for him. I was anxious to see how this was all going to play out, because I wanted to get back to Madison as soon as possible. The look in her eyes when I'd left had nearly gutted me. She was worried about me. *Me.*

I couldn't remember the last time I had someone who did that besides my brother, and even he knew I could take care of myself so he didn't waste a lot of energy on it. But the fact that

Madison did had something settling deep in my chest. I wanted so damn bad to be the kind of man worthy of her concern. But I wasn't. Not yet.

Steps sounded down the hallway, and I fixed my gaze on the open doorway. He barely made it a step inside the room before he froze. He composed himself almost immediately but not before I saw the widening of his eyes, the stiffness of his shoulders. I smiled internally, knowing how I'd gotten to him even as he tried to play it off, standing a little taller and narrowing his eyes at me.

"Ghost. How'd you get in here?"

I let the smile I'd kept hidden creep over my face as I watched him squirm. I uncrossed my legs and dropped my feet to the ground, placing my folded hands on his desk and leaning toward him. "Did you forget who you hired, Frost?"

Madison's father cleared his throat and smoothed down his tie. "No, no, of course not. I'm just surprised to see you, since you're supposed to be at a cabin, holding my daughter."

"Cut the bullshit. Unlike you, this isn't my first time, and I can smell a rat a mile away."

His acting skills were stellar, a look of shock going across his face, but I wasn't buying it. "A rat? You think I ratted you out?"

I nodded, leaning back in his chair. "I do. In fact, I'd bet this entire payday on the fact that hours after I left that cabin, you had people coming in. Police?" I shook my head. "Nah . . . you wouldn't want the publicity. Unless you have a few of them in your pocket, which I wouldn't doubt."

The mask slipped from his face briefly, and that was all I needed to know.

"You're the scum of the fucking earth, you know that? You sent people out there, and even knowing the cabin was empty, that your *daughter* was gone, you're here in your fucking office. All the while, you were thinking your daughter was, what? Dead? You really don't give a shit about her, do you?"

He narrowed his eyes at me. "Where is she?"

"None of your fucking concern."

"Bullshit, that's my daughter!"

"The daughter you paid someone to kidnap? That daughter?"

He clenched his jaw, his steely gaze focused on me, but I didn't move, didn't show any kind of reaction. Even though he was towering over me in my sitting position, he knew exactly who was in control here, and that was how I wanted it.

"No answers, huh? You know, I've done some shady shit in my life—a lot of which I've done for you in the years we've worked together—but this tops the fucking cake. Paying someone an obscene amount to snatch your daughter right from campus? You never did tell me the reasoning behind it, and I haven't figured it out yet. Course, after the obnoxious payday you offered me, I didn't really need to know."

"And you do now?"

"Yeah, I fucking need to know. Because your daughter doesn't deserve to go through this again because you botched shit up."

He laughed, a cold, heartless sound, and shook his head at me. "I didn't botch anything up, Ghost. Everything went according to plan."

"Whose plan? Certainly not mine."

"*My* plan." He pointed a finger at himself, a smirk curving one side of his mouth. "Once you came to me and told me White had contacted you to kidnap Madison, I knew I could use it to my advantage." He shrugged, as if he were talking about losing a bet instead of arranging an abduction of his daughter. "White and I were both after the same thing—his company. He thought that by having Madison held captive he could blackmail me into leaving it alone, not going through with a buyout." He laughed then. "That idiot certainly didn't count on me being one step ahead of him. And he certainly didn't count on the guy he hired for the kidnapping to already be working for me, feeding me information."

He stepped closer, his eyes narrowing on me. "You got a healthy paycheck for this, Ghost, working both sides. It worked perfectly for everyone involved. Having you go through with the kidnapping, White thinking he was the one in charge when in reality it was me. And then the blackmail—" He barked out a laugh. "You should've seen his face when I showed him pictures of the two of you meeting, exchanging money, and told him about the voice recordings. It truly was priceless. After that, he couldn't sign his company away fast enough. And the best part was I never had to breathe a word of it to the police. Sure I could've had him locked up right away based on the info you gave me, but where would that leave me? I wanted his business, and I was getting it, whatever the cost."

That cost being the safety of his daughter. Even knowing what kind of man he was, I was still disgusted at the lengths he went to for his business. "That still doesn't explain the bullshit you tried to pull on me at the cabin."

He shook his head, a sinister smile on his face. "I thought you were smarter than that, Ghost. I had people coming in to do cleanup. None of those other guys on your team knew me by name, so you were the only loose end. Couldn't have that, now could I?"

I clenched my jaw, wanting nothing more than to pound this fucker into the ground. If I hadn't trusted my gut . . . if I hadn't gotten Madison out when I did, what would the guys her father sent have done to her? I couldn't think about it, or I'd forget the whole reason I came here. I grabbed the envelope off his desk before tossing it at his feet. "Looks like we've got one thing in common."

With narrowed eyes, he bent to retrieve it, then opened the flap. He looked through everything, glancing up at me occasionally. When he was done, he put everything back and sealed it once again.

"What do you want, Ghost."

"I want you to forget about me. No retaliation of any kind—

against me or my brother. And even though it seems you already got exactly what you wanted from having Madison abducted in the first place, let me be perfectly fucking clear." I stood up, hands braced on the desk as I leaned toward him. "If I ever find out you did anything to endanger her again, it would bring me the greatest fucking pleasure in the world for Chicago's finest to receive copies of everything in that envelope. Do we understand each other?"

MADISON

The elevator doors opened on my father's floor. Most everyone was gone now, the desk chairs abandoned, all the lights turned out save for the small bit of illumination spilling out from the doorway to my dad's office. Taking a deep breath, I walked down the long corridor toward it, and as I got closer, I could make out the faint murmuring of voices. One deeper, calmer than the other, and I prayed whatever meeting he was holding, it could wait. Because my problem couldn't. And at this point, I wasn't willing to put my needs on hold until my father deemed it appropriate for me to see him.

The closer I got to the office, the louder the voices grew until I could make them out perfectly. I froze midstep, not just from the voice I'd recognize anywhere, but from the words that came out of his mouth, shattering what tiny bit of faith I'd had left in my father.

"The daughter you paid someone to kidnap? That daughter?" Gage's voice was harsh, biting, and I couldn't breathe. I sagged against the wall just outside the open office door as he continued talking. And every word felt like a punch to the stomach, a stab to the chest, each one leaving me more broken than the last. I couldn't move, couldn't speak, could do nothing but stand and listen as my father detailed my abduction and everything he'd gained from it.

My entire body felt flushed, hot, a wave of nausea washing over me, and I clamped my hand over my mouth, willing myself to swallow down the bile creeping up my throat. Long enough so I could hear everything. I *needed* to hear everything. The two men in my life—one who'd never been there for me, but who was supposed to love me unconditionally, and the other who didn't love me at all, but who'd fooled me into thinking he actually cared for me . . . that he connected with me in a way no one else had ever done before—were in this together. Against me.

Tears pooled in my eyes until they spilled over and trailed down my cheeks. I thought about the first day after I was abducted, how I'd hoped and prayed my parents were doing whatever they could to find me . . . that once they knew where I was, they'd do everything in their power to come get me. In reality, my father had known all along. And he'd left me there on my own.

That simple fact was crushing, and as hard as I tried to keep silent, a muffled sob left me at the realization that I was still truly alone, more so than I'd ever felt before.

Everything in the office went silent, and then Gage murmured, "You expecting company?"

I knew I had seconds before I was going to be discovered. Only a week ago, I would've run, I would've escaped and hidden away, kept my head down and my mouth shut.

Except I wasn't the same Madison I was a week ago.

Wiping my face as best I could, I pushed off the wall and stepped into the doorway. Even though I wanted to fight it, my eyes were immediately drawn to Gage's. His were wide as they met mine, first showing surprise, then sadness, and what the hell did he have to be sad about? This was *my* life he'd screwed up. Him and my father.

"No, I think it's safe to say he wasn't expecting me." I turned my eyes on my father—now truly in name only—and searched for an ounce of remorse, of regret. Anything to show me he hadn't meant what he'd done, that it had all been a mistake. His face was a blank slate, showing absolutely no emotion.

"Madison, it's not what you think."

I huffed out a disbelieving laugh, shaking my head. "I don't know, your explanation was pretty clear."

"You don't understand. White was always going to kidnap you. At least this way, it was in my hands. I could make sure you were safe."

"Make sure I was *safe*?" I snapped. "Like when the guy who would've taken the job if he"—I gestured to Gage—"hadn't showed up at the cabin and threatened to beat me until I was bloody and bruised? Or maybe safe like when he threatened to cut off one of my fingers? Is that what you meant by making sure I was *safe*? You know how else you could make sure I was safe? By going to the fucking *police* in the first place. Oh, but that wouldn't work, would it? Because with the police, you wouldn't stand to gain, what was it this time? Ten million? Fifteen? I'd like to know a specific number, so I know exactly how much your only daughter is worth to you."

"I was doing it for *us*, Maddie. For all of us. So we could get your mother the very best treatment. You want that for her, don't you?"

I stared at him, unable to believe I'd never before seen his manipulation for what it was, but I realized now it had always been there. "You are unbelievable."

I turned my attention back to Gage. If my own father could do this to me, why should I have been surprised that he was willing to, as well? "And you." I wanted to ask him about the days we'd spent together, all the times he'd had the chance to tell me the truth. I wanted to ask him if he kept his mouth shut just so he could get in my pants. *God,* I slept with him, with another asshole who didn't really care about me at all. How many times was it going to happen to me before I learned my lesson? Despite trying to keep my voice level, it cracked as I said, "I *trusted* you."

He opened his mouth to respond, but I didn't want to hear it. I held up my hand to stop him, shaking my head. "You can't say anything to make this right. You can't say anything to make it okay."

I'd had enough with lying men in my life, and I was *done*. This life was never mine in the first place, and it was about time I took over and owned it.

Chapter Thirty-one

GAGE

I watched her turn on her heel and flee the office. For a moment, all I could do was stare at the space where she'd been standing. And then I was moving. I didn't think about anything else as I took off after her. Madison was my only concern now; her father could go fuck himself. I'd done what I'd come here to do, and I was sure she would be safe from any future plans from Frost. But Madison . . . *Fuck.* She wasn't supposed to have heard that way. I wanted to be able to sit down and tell her, explain to her why I waited to talk to her about it, how I knew it'd topple her whole world upside down.

Now, though, all I wanted was a chance to explain. I ran out of Frost's office, seeing Madison at the end of the hall, just getting into the elevator. "Madison, wait!"

She turned around and stared at me, her face impassive even as I was running full speed toward her. And then the doors were closing between us, and she made no move to stop them. Just before I got to her, the doors slid shut in my face. "*Fuck!*"

I turned and took off toward the stairs, shoving through the door, the loud echo of it banging against the wall following me as I descended the steps two at a time. There was no way I was going to catch her. I was seventeen floors up, and the rest of the office building was nearly deserted, so it wasn't likely she'd be stopped on the way down.

Pushing myself harder, faster, I finally got to the bottom and ran into the lobby, past the doorman who'd had no idea I'd been there in the first place. He tried feebly to get me to stop, yelling after me, but all I could focus on was the long, dark hair I saw flying out behind the girl on the cement steps in front of the building. At this time of the day, in this part of downtown, cabs were going to be lined up and ready. She'd be able to get in one in a second, and I needed to catch her before she did.

I flew through the front door and down the steps, seeing Madison at the sidewalk, already opening the door of a cab.

"Madison!" I ran toward her, the distance between us getting smaller every second.

She turned around and stared right at me, her hair blowing around her face, and the look in her eyes stopped me cold. Even when she was having it out with her dad, she didn't have that look in her eyes—that look of pure, utter devastation. If I'd been unsure of what she thought of her father before, I wasn't anymore. She wasn't surprised by this . . . she might've even *expected* something like this from him. But me? I could see it written all over her face that she hadn't ever counted on that from me. Ten feet from her, I looked at her face, cataloged every detail as I watched her heart breaking right in front of me.

She'd been gracious enough to forgive me for the kidnapping, for following the orders I'd been given, but I knew now she'd never forgive this. And why should she? I'd known all along I wasn't right for her, that she deserved so much better than me, and I'd just proved that point a thousand times over. The best thing I could do for her, the thing I should've done five days ago, was leave her alone.

When I made no further movement toward her, she turned away, slipping into the cab, and I did the only thing I could.

I watched her go.

MADISON

I wiped the tears from my cheeks as I stared out the window of the cab, watching as the congested streets of downtown gave way to the interstate. The crushing devastation that had settled in my chest when I'd first heard Gage's voice in my father's office had only grown, planting roots and spreading until I felt weighted down by it. Until I felt *consumed* by it. My stomach was twisted in knots, confusion and anger . . . betrayal all swirling around inside me.

The sad part of it was, I wasn't even surprised at my father's involvement. Though it'd hurt that he would betray me like that, would put a price on the safety of his daughter just so he could acquire another company, make fistfuls of money this year, on some level, I'd expected nothing more from him. He'd shown me time and time again how little I meant to him, and this was no different.

The one person I had expected more from? Gage.

The way he'd looked when he'd run after me . . . the way he sounded . . . If I was trusting my gut, I'd have said he looked contrite, regret ringing heavily in the tone of his voice. But I'd learned my gut wasn't something I could trust. It'd only ever led me to devastation . . . to heartbreak, and I'd had enough of that to last a lifetime.

After a lengthy ride, the cab driver rolled to a stop in front of the house. Once I'd paid him, I got out and just stood there, staring up at the stately home in front of me. Just a few short days ago, I would've been ecstatic to see this sight. To have the chance to walk back into my home without anything standing in my way. To have the freedom to do so.

But now? After the days I'd spent away, after speaking to Sylvia and learning nothing had changed for my family . . . that it was business as usual while their only daughter was missing, after hearing my father's betrayal, I didn't even want to go inside. I didn't want to spend one more night there, let alone *years*. And for what? More expectations? More duties and responsibilities I no longer had the patience or the desire to follow through on?

It'd taken me a long time to get here—years of being taken for granted, of putting my life on hold for my parents, followed by a crash course in the frailty of life, but I was finally here. Sometime over the last five days, this place went from being my home to being nothing more than a shelter with fancy trimmings.

And it was time I started weathering the storm on my own.

With my bag slung over my shoulder, I followed the path that led to the back door of the house. I froze with my fingers on the knob, realizing this was probably going to be the last time I walked through this door. The pain I'd expected to feel, the regret I'd always thought would be present was blissfully absent, and in its place was an urgency I was finally ready to listen to.

Taking a deep breath, I turned the unlocked knob and slipped inside. A faint light came from around the corner telling me Sylvia was in the kitchen, no doubt waiting for me, hoping I hadn't been lying when we'd talked on the phone.

The door had just shut behind me when I heard a gasp, and then there she was, engulfing me in her arms, rocking me back and forth, her hand brushing down the length of my hair just like she'd done when I was a child. I let myself melt into her embrace, let myself feel comforted by the one person in my life who I'd always been able to count on.

Closing my eyes, I tried to commit everything to memory—the soft murmur of her voice, the sugar cookie scent that was pure Sylvia, the gentleness of her arms surrounding me—because I knew memories of her would be all I'd have to go on after tonight.

"Maddie. My dear, sweet Maddie. I can't believe you're home. You're here." Her voice was shaky with tears. She pulled back, checking over every inch of my body as she ran her hands down my arms. "You're not hurt, are you? I was so worried. I don't understand what happened. After you'd called here and sent Ronald the text, and then never showed up . . . we knew something was wrong. Ronald came back here in a frenzy because you hadn't been there, demanding we call the police. Your father wouldn't let us—said he had a private investigator he was hiring to work the case."

Despite trying to hold back the tears, at the mention of my father and what he'd done here at home to cover up his involvement with the abduction, they came unbidden, flooding my eyes and running down my cheeks.

"Oh, dear. Come here, sweetheart. Come in here and sit. What can I get for you? Are you hungry?" Sylvia hooked my arm through hers and guided us to the breakfast nook, pushing me to sit in a chair and taking my bag from me.

Shaking my head, I said, "No, I'm not hungry." With the way my stomach was churning, I wasn't sure I'd ever be hungry again.

"I know what you need." Without saying anything more, she dashed around in the kitchen, pulling a mug down from a cupboard, then the ginger ale and honey, and my throat got tight when I realized what she was making—what she'd dubbed a hot teddy, the childhood version of a hot toddy. It was my favorite drink from when I was little—the one thing that could make any day better. And that she remembered something like that, something I'd long forgotten, proved to me that I wasn't as alone as I'd thought.

When she set the mug in front of me, I wrapped my hands around it, letting it warm me, but nothing was helping this chill I still felt deep in my bones. I looked up at Sylvia, her worried eyes settled on me, and everything poured out of me.

"It was my father. All along."

She froze, her arm partially extended toward me. "What do you mean it was your father?"

I took a drink of the sweet liquid and closed my eyes, steeling myself to tell her what had really happened. Taking a deep breath, I said, "He was the one who set the whole thing up—the abduction, the holding, all of it. He paid someone to do this to me so he could acquire a company—the one he's been trying to buy out for months. He did this to me for money." My voice was shaking, and I could barely look at her as I admitted just exactly how screwed up my family was. How little I meant to him.

Sylvia gasped, her hand flying to her mouth, her face draining of its color. "No, Maddie. No. He wouldn't do that. I know he's not the best father, but he wouldn't do that . . ."

Nodding, I said, "He did. I swear it. I went to his office for help. He didn't know I was listening, but I heard the whole exchange between him and Ga—and the man who took me."

"H-how? I just cannot understand this. I always knew your father was a jackass—pardon me, honey—but this? I never guessed he'd do something like this. Oh, Lord." She reached for one of my hands, holding it between her own. Her caresses were gentle, probably to soothe herself as much as me. "What do you want to do, sweetheart? What are you going to do?"

I stared at the mug cradled in one of my hands, keeping my eyes focused on it as I whispered, "I don't know, but I can't stay here, Sylvia, not tonight. Not after that."

"It's okay, it's okay. You can stay in the guesthouse with me as long as you need, however lo—"

"No," I said adamantly, shaking my head. "Not just tonight. *Ever.* I have to leave. This isn't the life I want to live anymore."

She was quiet for so long I finally looked up at her. Tears were pooling in her eyes, but her face was content, a small smile on her lips. She squeezed my hand, then gave a decisive nod before she stood. "Well, then, let's go get you packed."

Chapter Thirty-two

It didn't take long. My entire life had been confined to this house, to this room, and all it took was twenty-five minutes. Twenty-five minutes, and everything of consequence I had, everything that meant anything to me, was packed in a rolling suitcase, the rest stuffed in my messenger bag. Sylvia sat on my bed, wringing her hands together, her eyes worried, but underneath the worry, I could see pride shining back at me.

That was what kept me going, pushed me forward, because while I knew she'd be worried for me, anxious about how I was going to make it on my own, this was what she'd wanted for me for so long. And it felt good to finally be doing it.

I flipped open my messenger bag and double-checked that I had my wallet, my debit card to my personal checking account tucked inside, plus the account information for the trust my grandparents had left me when they'd passed away when I was small. I'd always thought it'd be years before I'd use it. Maybe to buy a house once I got married, or to travel the world after graduating college, since any need I'd have before then my father would have foot the bill for. Now, though, I was grateful for it. It meant

I had the power to leave this place, to leave this life behind without looking back. And I'd be able to do so without the assistance of my father.

The freedom of it was as exhilarating as it was terrifying.

After closing my bag, I hefted it over my shoulder and looked to Sylvia. "I think that's it."

She gave a nod of confirmation and pushed off the bed to stand. Without so much as a fleeting backward glance, I pulled the suitcase behind me and walked out of my room, Sylvia following.

The rest of the house was silent as we descended the steps, no other signs of life anywhere. This house was too big, but more than that, it was *empty*.

Once we were in the foyer, she grabbed my hand and squeezed. "Do you want to say good-bye to your mother?"

I turned to face her, the guilt I'd been doing so well with threatening to make its presence known. My mother . . . the whole reason I'd stayed as long as I had. The whole reason I'd put my life on hold, choosing her well-being over my own. I used to think my love for her held me captive, but I realized now that wasn't love. It was obligation. Love came from two people connecting, from mutual affection, commitment, and concern, and I couldn't remember the last time I'd felt something even close to love. Not from my parents. It had taken this life-altering event to realize what Sylvia had been telling me for years was actually true. My mother left me behind a long time ago. Right now, she was locked in her bedroom, numb to any and everything thanks to her nightly cocktail of vodka and Percocet, unconcerned or uncaring about her missing daughter. She'd left me so long ago, and finally—*finally*—I didn't feel the overwhelming guilt at doing the same to her. For the first time in my life, I was doing what was best for me, thinking of myself first, and I wouldn't apologize for it.

"She said good-bye to me a long time ago, right?"

The corners of her mouth pulled down in a frown as she gave me a nod, then pulled me close, squeezing me as tightly as she could. I hugged her back, soaking up as much of her as possible, my heart aching that I wouldn't be seeing her every day.

"What are you going to do?" I asked, my throat scratchy from withheld tears.

"Oh, don't you worry about me, honey. I'll get along just fine. You worry about *you* for a change, okay?" I nodded as she rubbed her hand up and down my back. Against my ear, she whispered, "Where will you go?"

I thought about the endless possibilities. I had no one holding me back anymore. Whatever I dreamed of, whatever path I wanted my life to take was no longer just a fantasy, no longer something out of reach. I had the power to do anything at all. And I was going to.

I closed my eyes and squeezed her back. "Anywhere."

GAGE

Riley was quiet as we took the 'L' back to the shithole neighborhood we both lived in. We left the SUV behind, knowing one of the other guys would pick it up and flip the plates on it before putting it back into rotation.

Pulling my knit cap farther down on my head, I leaned back in the seat and crossed my arms, hoping for a moment's reprieve from the images that kept flipping over and over in my mind. Madison's face in Frost's office, the confusion and realization, then later, when she'd stared at me over the opened door of the cab, devastation in her eyes.

But despite attempting to block them out, they came to me unbidden. No matter what I did, I saw her. And every time I did, I relived that moment of gut-crushing certainty that I'd fucked up. I broke every ounce of trust she'd had in me, crushed it in my hand and proved to her exactly what kind of asshole I was.

Even worse was that I'd always known I would. From the beginning, I'd always known I couldn't keep what I had with her.

Riley shifted next to me, exhaling a long breath as he bounced his knee hard enough to shake my seat. I kicked the foot that was closest to me, but that didn't deter him. "Jesus Christ, Ry, knock that shit off," I mumbled.

"Oh, good, are we talking now? Because I have a shitload of questions. Like why you look like someone who's getting sent to fucking *prison*. Except I can't imagine we're on the run from the cops while riding the train, so what the fuck happened?"

"Fuck, man, can you keep your voice down? Jesus."

"There are, like, four people on the train. Calm your tits. Now what happened?"

"Nothing."

"Bullshit, nothing."

I blew out an aggravated breath and scrubbed my hand over my face. "I got into Frost's office, and the bastard wasn't anticipating a visit from me. Told him what I expected, tossed the envelope to him, and told him to back off. Easy as that."

He was silent, and I opened my eyes just far enough to peer at him. His were narrowed as he stared me down, and if this was any other day, I might've laughed at him trying to turn my interrogation tactics around on me. "You think that's going to work on your big brother?"

"If this doesn't, maybe my right hook will. Cut the shit, Ghost."

I looked at him—really looked at him. He was like me in so many ways. Same hair color, same eyes, same mannerisms. His hair was longer, though, his eyes not as haunted as mine, and our personalities were the complete opposite. He was less intense, light where I was dark. He was supposed to be everything I couldn't be, and yet here he was, right fucking next to me, in this life I never wanted for either of us. "You know how long it's been since you've called me Gage?"

"I—" His forehead creased, and he scratched the side of his head. "What?"

Shaking my head, I said, "Nothing, never mind." I had no idea why I'd even said that. No one called me Gage. Not now. Not anymore. I'd been Ghost since I was sixteen years old, and that was all I knew.

He let it drop and didn't say another word the rest of the ride, nor when we got off the 'L' and walked the short distance to my apartment. The dingy walls and piss-stained carpets of the hallways welcomed me home. This place had always been adequate. Not the nicest or the cleanest—not even fucking close—but it served its purpose. But now? It just reminded me of everything I wasn't . . . everything I'd never be.

Riley threw his coat on the arm of the couch, then relaxed back on the cushions while I went to the fridge and grabbed us both beers. I tossed one to him and went to crack mine open before thinking better of it. That wouldn't put much of a dent in me, and getting good and fucking plastered tonight sounded like a stellar idea. After I popped the beer back in the fridge, I pulled down a bottle of Jack and poured myself a glass. Facing Riley again, I leaned against the wall and took a deep pull, cringing slightly against the burn at the back of my throat.

He lifted his brows as he regarded me. "What're we drinking to tonight, big brother?"

I stared down at the amber liquid in my glass, swirled it around. Thought about the path I'd taken to get here, the choices I'd made—both when I'd been backed up to a wall, and when I'd just been good and greedy. Thought about how I'd never really fought to keep Riley out, to send him to college, push him in any other direction but this, and now he was stuck in it as sure as if I'd put him there with my own two hands.

I thought about everything I'd had at my fingertips, if only for the last few days, everything I'd let slip through my grasp. I had someone good and pure and fucking amazing, someone who I didn't deserve, but who'd seen past that, past all the shit and wanted me anyway. And I'd gone and fucked that up by just being me.

Raising my glass in a mock toast, I said, "Our shitty-ass lives."

Chapter Thirty-three

MADISON

A bitter March had given way to a much milder April, the sun shining brightly in a cerulean sky dotted with perfect clouds. It was a picturesque day, the kind always present in romantic comedies, but for the nerves churning in my stomach, it might as well have been overcast, gray and rainy.

I glanced at the address I'd written on a scrap of paper, then back up at the sprawling brick building in front of me. It was the right place, the numbers in my handwriting matching those next to the glass front door, yet I couldn't make myself move. I couldn't take that first step. Somehow in doing so, it was like I was admitting defeat, admitting that everything had truly happened. I was admitting how screwed up my family was, how screwed up *I* was, and that it wasn't just all in my head.

" 'Scuse me." A woman brushed past me on the sidewalk and walked right up to the door I'd been staring at for the last five minutes. She pulled it open, then twisted around to me. Her face was round and full, too much blush dotting her cheeks, but her eyes were bright and open as she looked at me expectantly. "Comin', hon?"

I swallowed, attempting to impart some moisture to my bone-dry mouth, then gave a subtle nod. If I didn't tell her I was coming, who knew how long I'd stay out here for, just staring at the space I was too scared to enter.

I took one step, then another and another, until I was able to catch the open door she held for me. She offered a knowing smile, the gentleness of it combined with the laugh lines around her mouth comforting in a way I hadn't expected. "It gets easier. First time is always the hardest." She patted my hand, then turned around and walked toward the receptionist.

I stood there, letting the door shut behind me, hoping she was right. Because if it didn't get easier, if it was this hard every time, I was afraid this would not only be my first time, but also my last.

The hallway seemed to be endless, dark wood doors leading to unknown places shut tight to my inquiring eyes. The receptionist stopped in front of the second to the last one on the right and gave two quick knocks. After receiving verbal confirmation from the other side, she pushed down the lever handle and opened the door.

"Here you go," she said with a smile, gesturing for me to enter. Tentatively, I walked into the space and then I heard the snick of the door closing behind me as the receptionist took her leave.

The office was cozy, the butter-colored walls making it feel warm and inviting. A plush, gray couch sat against a far wall, bracketed on each side by tall, mahogany bookcases. Two reading chairs sat parallel to the couch, a coffee table with a box of tissues atop it placed in the middle. On my right, in front of the large window that looked out to what would probably be a very pretty garden in a few weeks, was a small desk that matched the bookcases.

A woman stood from behind it and walked around the other side toward me. She was older, maybe late-forties, and petite, at least a head shorter than me. Her hair was dark blonde streaked with gray and pulled back into a low ponytail. Warm eyes and a warmer smile greeted me as she extended her hand. "Hello, Madison, I'm Dr. Ford."

"Hi, it's nice to meet you." Despite the circumstances, despite my nerves threatening to stage a revolt the second I opened my mouth, my manners were still as impeccable as ever. Old habits die hard.

Her smile grew and she gestured to the rest of her office. "Why don't you take a seat where you'd be most comfortable, and we can get started."

I didn't think I'd be comfortable in any of my options, but chose the corner of the soft couch. Dr. Ford grabbed a clipboard and a pen from her desk, then took a seat in the reading chair across from me.

"Is this your first time seeing a therapist?"

I nodded, smoothing my sweaty palms down my jeans and trying to get a handle on my anxiety.

She glanced down to my hands running up and down the length of my thighs, then offered me another smile. "Okay, nothing to be nervous about. I want you to feel comfortable discussing anything at all with me. This is a safe place, and whatever you share with me while you're here will remain confidential unless I'm concerned for your safety or the safety of others."

"Okay."

"Let's get started, shall we?" She settled back in the chair, the clipboard resting on her crossed legs. "Can you tell me what brings you in today?"

With an open-ended question like that, I didn't even know where to begin. Did I start with the last decade of my life, caring for my mother, depending on our housekeeper to act as my parental figure? Or did I go right for the big guns and dive into the kidnapping my father had orchestrated?

Figuring honesty was my best bet if I hoped to accomplish anything during this, I said, "I don't really know where to start."

She nodded her head. "That's okay. It can be a little overwhelming at first. How about telling me how you're feeling today?"

"Nervous, I guess. A little anxious. And unsure."

"Just about the appointment or is something else bothering you?"

"The appointment, but that's not the only thing. I'm, um, I'm on my own for the first time in my life. I mean that literally, because I suppose I've been figuratively on my own for a lot of years."

"And which of those scare you more? The literal on your own or figurative?"

"I guess . . . probably the figurative."

She nodded, scribbling notes on her paper. "What made that scarier for you?"

I swallowed, finding it easier to answer her than I thought it'd be, especially when she guided the direction of the talk. "Because . . . because with this, at least it was my choice."

She paused writing and looked at me. "You didn't feel like you had a choice before?"

"No, not really."

"What happened to make you feel that way?"

"My parents . . . well, I guess I felt responsible for them. Or my mother, anyway. My father worked long hours, all the time really, so he was never around. And my mom, she . . . she was an alcoholic." God, the relief I felt at saying it aloud. The only other person I'd ever told had been Gage, and the situation had been so different, it hadn't allowed me this . . . this freedom. "And in the last few years, she's started mixing in prescription pills."

Dr. Ford made another note, then lifted her eyes to meet mine. "How do you feel her behavior as an alcoholic affected you?"

I tucked my legs under me on the couch and leaned against

the arm, my nerves melting away the more we talked. "It affected me completely. Socially, emotionally, all of it. Her addiction kept me tied to her for so long. I picked a college just a few miles from home—it was the only one I applied to, actually—because I didn't want to move out. I was afraid no one would look after her anymore."

"Are your parents still married?"

"Yes."

"And you didn't feel your father could or would look after your mother for you, should you decide to go to school across the country?"

I shook my head. "No, I knew he wouldn't."

She scribbled on the clipboard for longer than she had before, then she asked, "You mentioned that you're living on your own now. What caused that growth?"

For a moment, I was taken aback by her choice of words, because for so long—for every day, every hour I'd been gone—it had never felt like growth. It'd felt like running.

"Something happened about a month ago that made me realize a few things."

"And what was it that happened?"

"My—my father, he . . ." I dropped my eyes from her everwatchful gaze, swallowed down the lump of shame in my throat. I didn't know why *I* felt shameful about this. It wasn't like I'd been the driving force behind it, but even so, I couldn't help but feel like it all reflected back on me somehow. Dr. Ford was silent as I worked up the courage to tell someone what I'd only told Sylvia weeks prior. Looking up and meeting her eyes again, I said, "He paid someone to kidnap me."

"Okay, Madison, our time's up for this week, but you did great. I'm going to look over my notes and come up with a short- and long-term therapy goal that we'll discuss during your next session. To start out, I'd like it if you could come see me twice a week. Does that work with your schedule?"

I nodded, my body slumped against the couch, feeling drained and exhausted, the emotional equivalent of running a marathon.

"Good. You can get your next appointment set up with Janelle out front. Between now and then, I'd like you to keep a journal of sorts. It can be in any form you'd like—a notebook, your phone, a voice recorder, whatever is easiest and most comfortable for you. I want you to record your thoughts, emotions, anxieties, anything at all you'd like, and then bring it to your next appointment."

"Okay."

She moved to stand, clipboard hanging from her left hand, and I followed behind her on shaky legs, my purse clutched against my side. Reaching out, she opened the door, then offered her hand to me with a warm smile on her lips. "It was a pleasure to meet you, Madison. I'll see you later in the week."

"You, too. Thank you, Dr. Ford."

I did as she'd suggested, setting up my next appointment for Thursday of this week, then I walked out into the bright April day and headed home. Or not home, exactly, but to my apartment. Even though I'd been settled there for weeks already, it didn't feel like home yet. I wasn't sure when it would . . . *if* it ever would. But it was mine and mine alone, a tiny square of a place close to campus, close to Dr. Ford's office, within walking distance of half a dozen restaurants as well as the grocery store. Getting around would be more difficult in the winter, the season even harsher here than it had been in Kenilworth, but I'd cross that bridge when I came to it.

My motto since I'd left the house I'd grown up in, since I'd said good-bye to Sylvia and walked blindly toward the unknown, was that I'd take things one day at a time.

That was all I had the emotional stability to do.

Chapter Thirty-four

GAGE

I slipped the key in the dead bolt and twisted, then pushed open the door to my apartment, kicking it shut behind me. No matter how many times I'd come and gone, the overwhelming feeling I got when I stepped foot in here never changed. I hated this place, hated coming home to it. Dark, dingy walls, leftover furniture from who knew how long ago, stained with more things than I cared to examine, the constant sounds of fighting or drug deals seeping through the thin drywall . . . It was the same place I'd lived in for the past two years, and in all that time, it had never bothered me before. I'd made do with what it was. It'd been fine to get by.

At one point, I thought that was enough. I thought just getting by was enough. I'd always had dreams that maybe someday I'd be able to get out of this life and take Riley with me, but I never really thought it'd be an actual possibility. I never believed I belonged anywhere but on the streets, living the rest of my life in run-down apartment buildings, the only things of importance in my life my brother and the next paycheck.

And then I took a job that changed me. *Madison* changed me. And now nothing was the same.

I tossed my keys on the faded mustard yellow counter in the kitchen and walked toward the living room, flipping on a light as I went. Movement out of the corner of my eye caught my attention, and I reached for the knife in my back pocket as I spun around.

My brother was sprawled out in my chair, completely uncaring that he'd come close to getting a blade to the throat. I blew out a frustrated breath as I relaxed my stance and dropped my arms. "Fucking hell, Riley, do you have a death wish? Jesus Christ, don't ever do that again. I could've stabbed you, you idiot."

"Aw, I love you, too, bro."

"Goddamn moron," I mumbled as I sat down on the couch perpendicular to him. "How the hell did you get in here?"

He grinned at me. "You forgetting who my big brother is?"

I shook my head, dropping it back to the top of the couch cushion. "What are you doing sitting in the dark and waiting for me like a serial killer?"

He was quiet, and I looked over at him, seeing his normally carefree face creased with worry. He was leaning forward, his elbows resting on his knees, hands hanging between them as he regarded me carefully.

I bolted upright, my senses suddenly on alert. "What's going on? You been staying low like I told you to? Jesus, Ry, you didn't get cornered, did you?"

He waved off my concern. "Nah, you know I'm better than that. I've kept my nose clean like you asked."

I sank back into the couch, my heart racing—I was getting too old for this shit. I was only twenty-four, but I felt like I was middle-aged. I couldn't do this anymore. Ever since the night I'd confronted Frost, the night I'd let Madison walk out of my life, I'd flown under the radar, making sure Riley did the same. Even with the insurance I'd tossed at Frost's feet, I still wasn't sure we could trust him. And in this business, word of mouth was everything. One bad deal could mean the difference between being top dog and being on someone's list. I wouldn't put it past him to make sure we were at the very bottom.

Riley cleared his throat, yanking me out of my thoughts. "But that's kind of the problem."

"What is?"

He took a deep breath and met my eyes. "It's been two months, man. When's this gonna end? My fingers are itching."

"Itching for what?"

"Something, *anything*. I'd take a goddamn petty theft right now, just to fucking *do* something."

It killed me to hear him talk like that, like he craved this life, craved the kind of work we did. The kind of work that paid the bills but sometimes made it hard to sleep at night. The kind of work he was never supposed to be involved in to begin with.

"You weren't ever supposed to be wrapped up in this, you know that? I only started doing it to keep a roof over our heads so you could finish school. So I could keep you safe after Mom died."

"I did finish school."

"*College*, not high school."

He snorted. "You think college is for me? You think I'd last a minute sitting in classes all fucking day long? I barely made it through high school." He shook his head. "No way. And you don't need to keep me safe anymore. I can do that fine on my own."

"Yeah, well, tough luck, man. You're stuck with me."

He smiled, his cheeks creasing, but it didn't reach his eyes. Something was still bothering him.

"Just fucking spill it already."

He ran a hand over his jaw, rubbing it up and down as he stared at me. "Ronnie called. He's got a job for me."

I clenched my jaw, thoughts of what this could entail . . . what could be waiting at the end for Riley—a trap just to get back at me somehow, or a setup like the last one. "No."

Riley's eyebrows flew up to his hairline. "No?" He huffed out a disbelieving laugh. "You think you can tell me no and I'll just swallow that and follow your orders like a three-year-old?"

"Yeah. I do."

"Ghost, listen to me. We're talking serious bank. Fifty grand if I pull this off. The job's not for a while . . . six weeks prep time."

"*If* being the key word. What if it's a trap, Ry? What if you get stuck in something you can't get out of?"

"Ronnie's straight, you know that. This job'll be easy. Fast cash."

"I said you're not doing it!"

His eyes flashed and he leaned forward, matching the raised tone of my voice. "Last time I checked, you weren't my goddamn boss, so lay off!" We stared at each other for a moment, both of us pissed off and on edge, primed for a fight. Finally, Riley pulled back, exhaling and pushing a hand through his hair as he sank back into the chair. "He already gave me the details on it. It's standard. An easy payday. And a lucrative one at that."

"Do you remember where our last easy, lucrative payday landed us?"

Images of Madison flooded my mind, and I didn't even try to stop them. She haunted my thoughts and my dreams, like a ghost I couldn't exorcise. I'd taken to drawing her every chance I got—full-face shots, profiles, images of the body I dreamed about, snippets of her . . . her mouth, her eyes, the curve of her shoulder. I had sketchbooks filled with her. The girl who changed me. The girl who I let walk away.

"That situation was a fluke, and you know it. How long have we been doing this? How many times have we *ever* had to implement a fallout plan? Once."

"Doesn't matter, the next job could easily be twice. If it

sounds too good to be true, in our world? It is. You need to leave it the fuck alone."

"Look, man, I don't know what that job did to you. I know something went down there, and I've got enough sense in my head to realize it probably had something to do with the girl. But what are we supposed to do? Put our whole lives on hold? Not take any more jobs? Get out completely?"

"Yeah," I said, meeting his eyes, "that's exactly what I want."

He stared at me for a moment, disbelieving. "You're serious."

"Dead fucking serious."

"Jesus, Ghost, I don't understand you anymore."

"What's to understand? I want something different for us, something better."

"What's so bad about what we're doing?"

"What's so bad? Living in shitholes, always having to watch our backs, being on the run from the cops . . . Is this the life you want, then? You want to be running like this for the next fifteen . . . twenty years?"

He shrugged. "It's what I'm good at."

I hated that he viewed himself like that, but the truth of it was, I knew exactly where he was coming from, because I'd felt the same way not too long ago. It took a girl I'd never counted on to make me see something different. To make me see something more. I just wished I could make Riley see the same thing.

"You're more than this."

He shook his head. "This is all I know, man."

I didn't plan on springing this on him like this. While I'd done little more over the last two months than try to figure out a way I could get Riley on board with cutting our ties, I wanted to slip it in, plant a seed and let it grow. Blindsiding him with it wasn't the way to do it, especially because he was so fucking stubborn. Tonight wasn't going to be the night I was going to get through to him about quitting free and clear, so I changed tactics.

"Just don't take this job, all right? Not when we still don't know where we stand in the grand scheme of things. I don't want you taking something if we have targets on our backs."

He shook his head, blowing out a defeated breath. "I'll tell Ronnie I need more time to decide, but I'm not saying no. Not unless you can give me a good goddamn reason. You need to figure your shit out, because I'm not going to play this for much longer. I'm tired of laying low. I'm bored out of my mind. And the money I have stashed isn't gonna last forever."

"The last thing you need to worry about is money. I got enough for both of us to do whatever we want. Why do you think I've always lived in shitholes like this?"

"I'm not going to take your money when I can make plenty on my own."

"Yeah, doing shit I don't want you doing."

"It's not your choice," he bit out.

I clenched my jaw, biting my tongue because nothing I could say was going to get through to him tonight.

We were both quiet for a few minutes, stewing in our anger, when Riley's low voice broke through the silence. "What happened in that cabin?"

It was the first time he'd come straight out and asked. After the night when everything went down, he'd let me be, taking my unspoken request to leave it alone. I knew it wouldn't last forever, though, and it seemed he was collecting tonight.

I blew out a breath, scrubbing my hand over my face. If it was so easily defined, maybe my head wouldn't be the jumbled mess it was. "I don't know."

"Bullshit. Something happened to you in that cabin. You haven't been the same since you came back. It was the girl, wasn't it? You fall for her or something?" His voice was light, disbelieving, and all I could do was stare at him.

Because that was exactly what had happened. Somehow over

the course of five days—a tiny blip in my life—I fell hard and fast for Madison Frost. And then I'd let her walk away.

"No way. No fucking way." He shook his head, his eyes going wide.

"Doesn't matter anyway."

"Well, hell, Ghost, I never knew you to be a masochist. Or a pussy. What's holding you back?"

What was holding me back was the desire for Madison to have the kind of life she was meant to live . . . one without a criminal and a thief and a kidnapper by her side.

I never realized how hard it would be, though. How *painful* it'd be to just let her go. I'd tried to put her out of my thoughts, force her out until I had no memories of her, but that did nothing but manifest itself in my sketches. There wasn't a page in my book that wasn't filled with some part of her. I'd found myself thinking about what she'd said that day in the cabin, about my drawings, when I'd brushed off her suggestions with a snide comment. One afternoon I'd actually looked into art programs in the area, under the ridiculous idea I'd be able to go through with something like that. That I was the kind of guy who went to fucking college.

But I wanted to be. I wanted to be the kind of guy who strove for something better.

Because, in the end, I wanted to be the kind of man Madison deserved, whether or not I had her.

My phone buzzed in my pocket before I could reply to Riley, and I answered it without looking at caller ID. "Yeah."

"Ghost. Hey, man."

I recognized the voice immediately as one of the guys who'd been with me for the last eight years . . . one of the ones I knew, without a doubt, I could trust. "Aaron, what's up?"

"You know that chick you had me tracking?"

I stiffened, all thoughts of the discussion with my brother gone. "What'd you find?"

"Nothing serious, but I wanted to let you know about a change."

"What kind of change?"

"I did my weekly search on her, and it looks like she's no longer registered as a student at Northwestern. It was complete about a month ago, but they must've just updated the records."

That didn't make sense. There was no way Madison would drop out of school . . . not in her junior year, and not so close to the end of the semester.

"Did you find anything else? Is she still living at the same residence?" I flicked my eyes to Riley and saw him watching me intently. It didn't matter, though. He already knew something was going on, and right now, I needed to find out all I could about Madison.

"I can't tell if she's still living there, since none of the records are in her name, but I did find a hit on her name and birth date. They were listed on a lease for a studio apartment in Minnesota. Google tells me it's a college town, so she may have transferred."

"Where." I scrambled for a piece of paper as he gave me the details. "All right. You call me if anything else changes."

"You got it."

"And Aaron?"

"You don't even have to say it, man. Just between us."

"Thanks."

"After all the times you had my back, it's the least I can do. Later."

I hung up and stared at the information I'd written down, a warm sensation spreading in my chest. She did it. She got out. She finally escaped that prison she once called home, got away from the people who were supposed to love her but who only used her. She'd moved on with her life, despite the hand she was dealt, despite the shitty things she'd had to go through, exactly like I wanted her to.

So why did it hurt so goddamn bad to know she was gone?

"That about her, then?"

"Yeah."

Riley sighed. "Look, man, I'm probably the last person in the world who should give you advice on this, but I'm going to anyway. You either need to go after her . . ."

"Or?"

"Or you need to move on." He pushed up from the chair and clapped a hand over my shoulder on his way to the front door. With eyebrows raised in challenge, Riley opened the door and left, leaving me to think over the phone call and everything I'd learned.

And if I was going to do anything about it.

Chapter Thirty-five

MADISON

The woman who'd held open the door for me on my very first session had been right: it did get easier. Little by little, appointment by appointment, it got easier until only the barest hint of butterflies were present when I walked up to that glass door that had held me frozen the first time I'd seen it.

Curled into the corner of the couch—the same spot I'd taken that very first day—I fanned the corner of my journal, flipping the pages as Dr. Ford settled in the chair across from me. She wrote something on her clipboard, then looked up at me with a smile. "How are you feeling today, Madison?"

"Good," I answered automatically, the knee-jerk reaction so ingrained it was rare I replied with anything other than that immediately. Closing my eyes, I forced myself to really think about how I was, what I was feeling, and replied honestly, "I'm okay. A little nervous."

She scribbled a note and nodded her head at me. "What's making you feel that way today?"

"I signed up for a few summer session classes and everything was finalized yesterday. I start next week."

"And you're nervous about the classes?"

"No, not exactly. I'm actually excited about them. I'm anxious about being around my peers. I have a hard time fitting in with them. Making friends."

"Have you tried making any friends since you've been living here?"

I shifted in my seat, fidgeting with the material of my jeans. In the six or so weeks since I'd been here, I hadn't ever once made the effort. At first because I hadn't been in a place to do so. I'd wanted to focus on healing, on getting better. For once in my life, I'd wanted to focus on *me*. But now? I had no excuse except fear. Shaking my head, I said, "No."

Her pen glided across the paper again before she lifted her eyes to mine. "Why do you think that is?"

I lifted one shoulder in a shrug. "Because I'm afraid it'll be the same as it always has been."

"How has it always been?"

"Isolating."

"How so?"

"I guess I just have a hard time connecting with people."

Crossing her legs, she settled her clipboard in her lap. "Do you think you not being able to connect is a reflection of your personality or you trying to protect yourself from letting people get close because of your mother's addiction?"

I opened my mouth to respond, then snapped it shut and really thought about what she was asking. The two people in my life with whom I'd been able to connect, Sylvia and Gage—God, just thinking his name had my chest aching—had both been aware of my mother's addiction. It was never something I had to hide, and while I was ashamed of it, it wasn't something I'd let define me with either of those people. "I guess maybe a little of both?"

"You don't sound too sure."

I cracked a smile. "I'm not."

Her lips lifted at the corners. "Let's try another approach, then. Other than your family, has there been anyone in your life you've been able to feel a connection with?"

I swallowed, knowing where this was going. In the month I'd been coming to see Dr. Ford, I'd talked about Sylvia, of course. Plenty. And while I'd mentioned Gage before, we hadn't yet discussed him at length. I didn't know if I was ready. "Yes."

"Can you tell me about them?"

"One is Sylvia."

"Your family's housekeeper."

"Yes."

"Why do you think it was easier for you to build a connection with her?"

"Maybe because she'd been in my life for so long."

"In a previous session, you mentioned she was aware of your mother's addiction." I nodded. "Okay. Was there anyone else you've been able to form as strong of a connection with?"

"Yes, one other." I looked up at her, finding her expectant eyes on me, and I didn't know if I was ready or not, but I wanted to be. I wanted to grow and move forward, and keeping everything inside wasn't going to help me do that. "Gage."

"You've mentioned him before." She flipped back in her notes, then her pen was moving on the page again. After she'd written what she needed, she settled her gaze on me. "Was he aware of your mother's addiction?"

My memories immediately drifted to that day in the cabin, sitting at the dining room table and sharing with him something I'd never shared with anyone before. I'd never before had to come right out and say the words. Sylvia had been *there*, right by my side, living it along with me. It had always been unspoken between us, but with Gage . . . I'd taken the step. I'd opened up to him about it, and he'd done the same with me. Fanning the pages in my journal again, I said, "Yes, he was."

"Do you think it's a coincidence that the two people with whom you've been able to feel a connection both know about your mother?"

"No."

"I understand it's hard for you to open up to people about this, and I'm certainly not suggesting you do it with everyone, but I'd like you to try to be open to the possibility. Your mother's addiction is not a reflection on you, Madison. It wasn't something you could control. I think once you feel comfortable with that, you'll find it easier to let go and open up to your peers. One of the things I'd like you to do this week is befriend one person—as just Madison, not the daughter of anyone. Just Madison, okay?"

I dipped my chin in a subtle nod. "Okay."

She gave me a warm smile and glanced up at the clock. "We've still got a bit of time left. I'd like to go back and talk about Gage. Are you ready for that?"

I swallowed, the nearly dormant butterflies in my stomach erupting into a swirling vortex. "Okay."

She flipped back in her notes and settled on a page, reading something she'd written before looking back up at me. "He was your captor."

It was such a simplified definition for him. In the beginning, yes, but he was so much more than that. He'd gone from being my captor, to being my protector, to being my betrayer. "Yes."

"And yet you feel like you connected with him."

"Yes."

"Do you think that was a result of the highly stressful conditions you were under?"

I was shaking my head before she'd even finished the question. "No."

"You seem sure about that."

"I am."

"Why do you feel you had such a strong connection with him?"

"I think a lot of it is what you mentioned—because he knew about my mother. We came from such different places, but we'd both been through similar situations with our families. I think that was the foundation, and everything else grew from that. But there were other things, too. He was so . . . aware of me, you know? It felt like for the first time in my life, someone really *saw* me."

"Do you think that could've happened with anyone?"

"I'm not sure what you mean."

"If someone other than Gage had taken you, been with you at the cabin, and had also had a childhood similar to his, do you think you'd have felt as strong of a connection with that person?"

I tried to picture someone else in Gage's place, revealing the same childhood Gage had told me about. Then I tried to imagine someone else standing by my side, protecting me, taking care of me . . . Tried to imagine a connection forming with them the same way it had with Gage, but no matter what scenario I came up with, I couldn't. All I saw was Gage.

"No, I don't think so. It was Gage, specifically."

"Do you think that's why his betrayal at the end had such a devastating impact on you?"

The memories of that night came to me unbidden. Starting with the walk down the hall toward my father's office, and ending with the ache I'd felt watching Gage over the door of the cab, wanting so much to ask him *why*. To ask him if everything we'd had had just been a joke to him, or if any of it had been real.

The ache that had been present in my chest every day since then told me it had been. What we'd had, or what I'd felt, anyway, was very real.

When my eyes refocused, I saw Dr. Ford sliding the tissue box closer to me, and I realized with a start that I was crying. In all that we'd talked about, through everything we'd discussed—my mother's addiction, my father's abandonment and subsequent betrayal—I'd never once shed a tear.

I plucked a tissue from the box and wiped my face, taking a few deep breaths so my voice wouldn't quaver when I finally answered. "I think it had such a devastating impact because I was falling in love with him."

Chapter Thirty-six

I stood outside the classroom, just staring, my nerves a tsunami in my stomach, trying to talk myself into walking inside. All I had to do was open the door. Just twist the handle and pull, take a few steps, and there I'd be. I'd sit down and listen to the lecture, and everything would be fine. *I* would be fine.

Despite knowing this logically, I still came up with a dozen reasons why I was going to fail at this. How I was going to become an outcast in my new college, just like I'd been in my last one. Just like I'd been my whole life. How people were going to look at me with thinly veiled looks of disdain, how I'd be the source of barely whispered jokes.

I didn't know if I could take it, not after my last two months. Not after everything else that had been dumped on my shoulders.

Dr. Ford's words were in my head, reminding me that my parents didn't define me, that I needed to look at the situation differently. Approach it as just Madison, not Madison, daughter of Sharon and Steven Frost.

"Hello?" A voice came from behind me, and I startled, clutching my bag to my side as I spun around. The girl who'd spoken was shorter than me, her thin face bright and open . . . friendly. Her blonde hair was pulled back in a messy bun, her eyes wide and sparkling, lips lifted in an amused smirk. "Yeah, hi. You, uh, you wanna come in?" She gestured with her head toward the classroom.

"What? Oh. Yeah. Yeah, I should." I darted my eyes to the closed door and then back at her.

Her smile grew as she watched me fidget. "You a new transfer?"

My breath left me in a whoosh, my shoulders slumping. "Is it that obvious?"

"Nah, not to most people. I kind of have a sixth sense about finding the ones who need a little guidance." She slipped her arm through mine, then reached for the handle with her other hand. "Come on, you can sit by me. If you're new here, I need to fill you in on super important things. Like where to get the best coffee on campus. I'm Sierra, by the way."

"Oh, I'm Madison. Maddie."

"All right, Maddie. Now that we're friends, I hope you don't have plans after class, because I'm already starving. I barely had time to brush my teeth this morning, let alone grab something to eat. I'm definitely going to need to get some lunch, and you're going with me."

"I am?"

"Yeah, friends remember? Friends don't let friends eat shitty vending machine food when they can accompany them to a semi-decent food establishment instead."

I stared at the back of this small powerhouse as she tugged me along, disbelieving. Could it really be this easy? In all the years I'd been holding back, telling myself that I didn't make friends easily, had I actually been sabotaging myself? Had it been a self-fulfilling prophecy? Because while therapy had helped me grow, helped me develop into the kind of person I wanted to be, deep down I was still just Madison. And maybe that was the key all along. I wasn't worried about bringing Sierra home to see the embarrassment of my private life. I wasn't worried about her learning my last name and immediately connecting it with my father. I wasn't worried about any of it.

I was just being me.

After I hadn't said anything, she stopped abruptly, twisting around and looking at me over her shoulder. "Oh, man. Don't tell me you already have plans?"

"What? Oh, no." I shook my head as I took a seat next to her. "No plans." I smiled at her, the first new friend I'd made in so long, and took my first step. "I'd love to go to lunch."

Sierra said there were a few restaurants around campus that were deemed appropriate to eat at. We were at a small Mexican place that didn't seem to be too popular, but apparently their burritos were to die for. We'd settled into a booth, and Sierra had only stopped talking long enough to shovel chips and salsa in her mouth. I didn't mind, though. It relaxed me, actually, being around someone obviously so comfortable in their own skin.

"So where'd you transfer from?"

I took a sip of my water, then said, "Northwestern."

She stopped with a chip halfway to her mouth, her eyebrows lifting. "No shit. Wow. That's quite a change in schools. What's up with that?"

I shifted in my seat, unsure of what to tell her, how much to tell her . . . My life story wasn't exactly suitable lunch conversation. Or anytime conversation, really.

"Sorry, I can be a little"—she waved her hand and shook her head—"whatever. I tend to forget other people have boundaries."

"No, it's okay."

Without waiting for me to answer, she moved straight into another topic. "How long have you been here for then?"

"Um, about six weeks, I think." That was a lie. I knew exactly how long I'd been here. Six weeks and two days, to be specific.

"What do you think of it so far? Tiny town compared to Chicago, huh?"

"It's not so bad. I actually really like it."

"Yeah, it's grown on me. I didn't feel that way when I came here as a freshman, though. I hated it. Thought about transferring to U of M, but stuck it out. Hey, what's your major?"

"Social Work with a minor in Child Advocacy Studies."

"That sounds a lot fancier than my *undeclared*." She grinned.

A laugh flew out of me, and I couldn't remember the last time I'd felt this sort of comfort with a girlfriend. I'd *never* felt this with a girlfriend—or anyone, for that matter. With Sylvia, it was a parental relationship more than anything. I looked to her for guidance more than camaraderie. And with Gage . . . with Gage it had always been intense and all-consuming. I loved Sierra's ability to make me feel so completely at ease. Even when she was asking questions I wasn't comfortable with, I didn't get that pit in my stomach, that uneasy feeling that used to overwhelm me.

"So what made you pick that? You love kids?"

At Northwestern, my major had been Economics. Something practical, something that made sense with the rest of my lifestyle. But I didn't have that lifestyle anymore, and it had never truly been a part of me. I'd never felt excited about it—it was just another thing I did to fulfill the expectations of my parents. And when I'd been looking through the information for the possible undergraduate degrees and the minors here, this had stood out in stark relief to everything else. But how could I tell her the reason I'd picked it? That my heart hurt for all the other children like me who were trudging their way through something similar right now, and I wanted to do something—anything—to help.

She must've read something on my face, because she said, "Ah . . . Well, that'll be a topic for another time, then."

That simple sentence—something she'd probably said a hundred different times to a dozen different friends—made me feel lighter, made my heart happy.

Because the thing of it was, I knew there actually would be another time with her.

Dr. Ford settled in the chair across from me, her clipboard perched on her lap. "How did your first day of classes go?"

I thought back to my first day—and my second, and my third—and couldn't stop a smile from spreading across my face. "They went better than I thought they would."

She returned my smile. "Good. Did you do what we talked about last time?"

"Yes."

"Tell me about that."

"Well," I laughed, "I feel like I kind of cheated, actually."

"How so?"

"The girl—the friend I made? She sort of did all the work. I was standing outside the room, psyching myself up to go in. Then Sierra—that's her name—she came up and just sort of . . . I don't know . . . plowed her way right in."

"Interesting choice of words. Did that make you uncomfortable?"

"No, not at all. It actually made me *more* comfortable. I feel like . . . like I could get to be really good friends with her."

"That's wonderful, Madison." She smiled and nodded to the book in my lap. "What did you write about in your journal this week?"

I flipped to my most recent entry, though I didn't need to. I knew what I'd written. What had consumed my thoughts since last time. "Gage."

"Do you think our discussion last time prompted that?"

"Yes, but that's not the only thing. I've been thinking about him a lot." I took a deep breath and let the truth come out. "I haven't stopped thinking about him since I left."

"What do you feel when you think about him?"

"Anger. Hurt. Betrayal. Confusion." I swallowed, glancing up from my journal so I could meet her eyes. "Longing."

She scribbled notes on the clipboard, then asked, "Can you tell me a bit about each of those? What makes you feel angry with him?"

"That he lied to me. It was a lie of omission, but it was still a lie."

"Why do you think he lied to you?"

I thought about what he'd kept from me, that my father was the one who'd hired him, and tried to put myself in his shoes. "To protect me, maybe. From the truth of what my father was."

She made another note, longer this time, then returned her attention to me. "And what about the others? Hurt, betrayal, confusion?"

"I just . . . I have a hard time reconciling the things we . . . did . . . with how it all ended."

"Meaning when you slept with him?"

My cheeks warmed, but I didn't look away from her. "Yes."

"Do you think that had been just one-sided?"

I thought back to each of the times we'd been together, remembering the look in his eyes, the words he'd whispered to me, the way he'd held me, almost reverently. "I don't think so."

"If he lied to you about your father's involvement for the reason you speculated, would that be something you could forgive?"

"I don't know."

"Okay, that's a fair answer. It's hard to give forgiveness, especially to people we care about, especially if it's similar to a previous situation that didn't turn out well. But I want you to really think about if this is something you want to carry around with you the rest of your life. Sometimes, while it may not be the easiest, it can be the healthiest thing to let it go."

And that was exactly it. Letting it go, letting go of the anger and the pain that I felt meant letting go of him. And I didn't know if I was ready for that. I didn't know if I was ready to truly say good-bye.

Chapter Thirty-seven

"God, that was like the never-ending class." Sierra groaned as she shouldered her bag, leading me out into the fresh air. "I swear, it's like listening to a monotone accountant. I mean, can we get a *little* inflection? Some enthusiasm? Jesus. Thank God that class is almost over."

I laughed, following alongside her as we walked through the courtyard. It'd been nearly a month since our first class together, and I still couldn't believe how well we'd clicked. I couldn't believe how comfortable I felt around her, how easily things seemed to fall into place for us.

"You wanna grab something to eat before your afternoon class?" she asked.

"Yeah, we can. I just need to run by my place quick. I forgot my notes for class."

"Cool. Thai sound good?"

I glanced at her out of the corner of my eye, grinning. "You're lucky I don't get sick of having the same thing over and over . . . and *over* again."

"What?" She feigned innocence, even going as far as to bat

her eyelashes at me. Dropping the act, she said, "It's not my fault the guy who works there is freakin' hot. Like, seriously *hot*. I don't understand how you can't think so. I would climb him like a tree."

"It's not that I don't think so, it's just that . . ." He was blond with dark eyes. And lean and wiry in a cute gamer sort of way. The kind of guy Sierra went for nine times out of ten. And the exact opposite of what I found attractive anymore. With a shrug, I said, "He's just not my type."

She snorted as we turned down the sidewalk leading toward my building. "I haven't seen you get excited over a guy once since you've been here, so for all I know, your type is some overweight grizzly dude with a foot-long beard and bifocals."

My head fell back as a full laugh bubbled from my lips. Through my giggles, I said, "Yes, that's exactly the type I go—why are you stopping?" I glanced back at her, frozen on the sidewalk a few steps behind me. Her eyebrows were lifted nearly to her hairline, her mouth agape as she stared past me at the front of my building. I turned back around to see what held her attention rapt. "What are you look—"

All the breath left my lungs, my chest constricting as I stared at the front steps. He sat off to the side, a wall of a man, still as big as I remembered, his elbows resting on his knees, his eyes glued to me. Those eyes pinned me into place as he pushed off the concrete step and stood, walking a couple steps toward us.

"Gage."

Sierra whipped her head to stare at me, a gasp leaving her. "*Gage?* You *know* him?" She leaned toward me, lowering her voice and hissing, "You have a lot of explaining to do, Missy." Bright smile back on her face, she turned to Gage with a wave. "I'm Sierra, and I'm leaving." She spun around, narrowing her eyes and pointing her finger at me. "You'd better call me."

I nodded, then looked back at Gage . . . at the man who'd

held my heart in his hand and then crushed it. Swallowing past the nerves that were threatening to jump right out of me, I asked, "What are you doing here?"

"Sorry." God, I'd missed his voice, all low and deep and rough. "I didn't know if you'd be more comfortable if I came here, or if I ran into you at school . . . I thought you'd maybe prefer the privacy."

"No, I mean what are you doing *here*? Why aren't you in Chicago?"

I hadn't moved from the spot I'd stopped at on the sidewalk, so Gage walked toward me with tentative steps until he was right in front of me. So close all I had to do was lift my hand and I'd be touching him. He looked at me, his icy blue eyes roving over every part of my face, lingering on my mouth, and I felt it like a caress.

He licked his lips, lifted his gaze to meet mine, and said, "Because you're not in Chicago."

My breath caught and I froze, my heart freezing along with me before it stuttered, then burst into a gallop. "I . . . I . . ." Shaking my head, I closed my eyes, still not able to articulate anything. I couldn't make sense of this, of him—*here*—standing in front of me and saying things that just didn't make any *sense*.

The longer I stood there, the more I thought about it—about how he'd let things end, about the last time I'd seen him—the more my heart flutters settled, my ire igniting instead. When I looked back up at him, I found my voice. "You let me go. Without an explanation. Without anything, you let me go."

He nodded, not trying to deny it. "And it was the hardest thing I've ever done."

"Then why did you do it? Not just that, but all of it, Gage. *Why?*" My voice broke on the last word, and I hated myself for not holding my composure.

He lifted his hand like he wanted to reach out to me, to comfort me, but he stopped before he came in contact with me and let his arm drop back to his side, his fist clenched. "I'm sorry, Madison. I'm so fucking sorry, and if I had to do it over again, I'd do it differently. I know there's nothing I can say to make it okay, and there's no excuse for me keeping your father's involvement from you. But, at the time, I didn't know how to tell you. I *knew* it would crush you—that it'd change your whole life. And up until that last day, I didn't know anything was off. I was never worried about your safety because you were with me. But then everything went to hell and my only concern was keeping you safe, making sure you got away from him because I didn't trust what he might do. I didn't trust that he wouldn't hire Frankie the second I was out of the picture to do the job all over again, and I needed to keep you safe. That trumped everything else. It was all I could think about."

I shook my head, not wanting to fall victim to his pretty words, wanting to hold on to my anger longer, because it had been the only thing keeping me from falling apart. "But all the times before that. You could've told me. A hundred different times. You could've told me . . . Do you know what it felt like to know you *slept* with me but were keeping this huge secret?" I bit the inside of my cheek, willing the tears I felt clogging my throat to stay at bay. "Did any of it mean anything to you?"

"It meant *everything* to me." This time when he reached out, he didn't stop. He brushed my hair back from my face, his calloused fingertips sliding along my cheek to my neck, and a shiver racked my body. "*You* mean everything to me." His fingers curled around the nape of my neck, his thumb brushing against my cheek, and he stepped closer, forcing me to tilt my head back to look at him. "I let you walk away because I wanted better for you. You deserve someone so much more than who I am, than who I *was*. But I'm trying. I'm trying to be better for you. I got my GED. And I started taking a class here at the Art Center. I applied to art school. I know it's probably a pipe dream, but I figure it doesn't hurt to try. And I know it's not a lot, not compared to the kind of person you are, but it's a start. It's something."

With every word that left his lips, I felt my indignation melting away, little by little, until I might as well have been a puddle at his feet. His face was open, his eyes sincere and hopeful. But, still, I didn't know if I could trust it. If I could trust him. He'd broken it in the worst way.

Quietly, he said, "If I could, I'd go back and do it differently. I'd still take the job—I can't regret that because it brought me you—but I wouldn't keep anything from you."

"I wish you hadn't."

"Me, too. I wish we could start all over again."

And while I wouldn't want that, because despite the pain it'd caused me, those five days with him had given me so much—they'd given me clarity, strength to move on with my life, and the knowledge that I had a right to do so—I wondered what would happen if we were just meeting now. If we'd just seen each other in passing. If maybe he worked at a restaurant and I was the girl dragging her friend along twice a week to admire him from afar. "If we could start over, if you were just meeting me, what would you say?"

His eyes brightened and darted between mine, and he caressed my cheek one more time before dropping his hand and taking a step back. A noise of protest left my lips, and my hand twitched at my side, wanting nothing more than to reach for him.

"Hi. I'm Gage Everett." He held out his hand toward me, and I was so stunned it took me a minute to extend mine. His engulfed it, the heat from him seeping into my skin. "I'm taking a class in pencil drawings at the Art Center and need a model. I think you're beautiful and I'd love to draw you."

Epilogue

"I can't believe I'm letting you do this. I feel like Rose in *Titanic*."
It was a testament to how much I'd grown, how far my confidence
had come that I was letting him do this at all. I could feel the blush
all over my body, trailing from my cheeks to my neck, down to my
breasts from the way Gage's eyes ran over me like a caress, how
they paused on the parts of me only he got to see. Until now.

"No one else better see this," I grumbled.

He snorted, flicking his gaze up to me, then back to the
sketch pad in front of him. "You think I'd let anyone see you like
this? I'd gouge their eyes out if they did."

We were at my apartment, and while it was a perfect fall day to
be outside, the leaves golden and crisp, I was lying in bed. The
rumpled sheets pooled around me, not doing anything to hide any
part of me at all, but they helped with the illusion, he'd said. He'd
roped me into doing this, saying he needed to practice his shading
for class. Why that involved sketching me naked, I didn't know. But
with the way he looked at me, with the heated, heavy weight of his
stare, I wasn't complaining. I also wasn't complaining about the
stipulation I'd put into place: if I had to be naked, so did he.

I looked at the sculpted lines of his body, the curve of his broad shoulders as he leaned forward over his sketch pad. With an imaginary finger, I traced the edges of his tattoos, across his abdomen and up to his chest, circling the newly inked design there. Two antique keys tied together with a ribbon—one for him, and one for me, he'd said, symbolizing how far we'd each come in breaking free from our own personal captivity. I'd cried when he'd shown me. Cried, and fell a little more in love with him.

He interrupted my thoughts. "Now stop talking so I can get this done. I have other things to do."

Lifting my eyebrows, I asked, "Like what?"

"Like you."

My blush intensified, and from the way his lips lifted at the corners while his head was dipped toward his paper, he could see it. We slipped into a comfortable silence, the only sound in the room the scratching of his charcoal on the paper. I stared at him, watching as he worked. His eyes were so intense, so focused, and I didn't have words to describe what it felt like when that gaze was directed at me. It warmed me from the inside, filled me with so much love it felt like I'd burst.

Our path hadn't been easy. The first few weeks after Gage had shown up, we'd stumbled through, trying to find our footing again. When we'd been in the cabin, we'd been so isolated, our situation high-stress, nothing compared to the tedious ins and outs of daily life. But we'd managed. Dr. Ford had helped—Gage had even gone to a few appointments with me—and I think having her guidance, having her encourage me to trust my gut, even when it'd failed me in the past, made all the difference.

The bed dipped next to me, and then Gage's lips were at my ear. "What are you thinking so hard about? Probably how to implement world peace or something, and all I can think about is when I get to be inside you."

I gripped his shoulders and laughed, the sound cutting off

when he rolled me to my back and settled between my legs so I could feel exactly how much he wanted me. He brushed his lips down my neck, across my collarbone, and up the other side until he nipped at my other ear. "Did I bore you?"

I could barely answer as he pressed his hips to mine, the hard length of him gliding between my legs. "No," I whispered.

"What were you thinking about?"

I didn't know how he expected me to answer when he was rubbing against me, his lips driving me crazy, but I managed a breathy, "Us."

He pulled back, resting his weight on his forearms as he hovered above me, my head cradled in his hands. Raising his eyebrows in silent question, he stopped moving his hips and waited for me to elaborate.

With a groan, I clutched his ass, digging my fingers into the flesh, hoping he'd start moving again.

"Tell me," he said as he dipped down to nip at my mouth.

"Just about how it's been. Since you've been here."

His face fell, his eyes going worried as they darted between mine. "It's been good, hasn't it?"

Reaching up, I ran my palm over the scratchy whiskers of the several days' worth of scruff there. "So good. Why are you worried I'd think something else?"

"I'm always worried you'll think something else. That one day you'll wake up and realize what a mistake you made, how much better you could do, and leave."

It hurt my heart to know the worries that had plagued me for so long were settled deep in his heart, because I knew what a struggle it was. I could only work to show him, like he'd done for me, that I was in this with him. "That's not going to happen." I lifted up, curling toward him and kissing him, eyes still locked with his. "Because I love you."

His fingers threaded through my hair, massaging my scalp in

small circles while he regarded me. "After everything I've done, all the shit I've done in my life, I don't know how I got lucky enough to have you with me. I don't know what I did to deserve you."

I thought about what my life had been like before he'd come into it. Isolating, depressing, overwhelming. I thought about what it would've been like if anyone but Gage had been the one to take me, how much worse everything could've been. Thought about how he made me feel, loved and cherished for the first time in my twenty years. How him coming into my world, and then all the events that followed, had led me to the exact spot I was in now, the place I'd ached to be for so very long—a carefree college student whose only worry was passing her next exam.

I looked at him, ran my thumb over his lower lip, my heart so full with happiness and contentment. For the first time in my life. And it was all thanks to him.

"You helped me save myself."

Don't miss Riley's story

EXPOSED

Summer 2015